Unnatural

Captain Iain Sinclair has looks, charm, military honours—even the favour of the king himself. He has everything—everything, that is, except the friendship of the one man whose good opinion he has ever cared for, scientist, James Hart.

James has loved Iain all his life, but after the last disastrous encounter between them, he vowed to accept no more crumbs from Iain's table. If Iain cannot be the lover James wants, then James will have no more to do with him.

Disenchanted with his career, and miserable without James in his life, Iain decides to leave military service and embark upon a new career in India. Before he leaves England behind, though, he is determined to try one last time to reconcile with his dearest friend.

An invitation to a country house party from James's sister provides the perfect opportunity to pin James down and force him to finally listen to Iain's apology. But when Iain discovers that an apology is not enough—that James is not willing settle for less than a lover—he is forced to reconsider everything: his life, his future career, and most of all, his feelings for James.

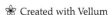

UNNATURAL

AN ENLIGHTENMENT NOVEL

JOANNA CHAMBERS

JOANNA CHAMBERS
AUTHOR

THEN: 1808

21st July, 1808

Wylde Manor, Derbyshire

James Hart lay on his belly in the grass, cupping his chin in his hands as he stared at the pond skater balancing on the surface of the lake. He was fascinated by its long, splayed legs —they looked like the bendy stalks from the cherries he'd gorged on in the orchard earlier. He couldn't wait to tell Papa about that observation.

He marvelled at the little creature, how it just sat there, never sinking down into the water. Those cherry-stalk legs made tiny dimples on the surface of the lake but never broke through. The water bulged around the pond skater's feet, looking oddly solid, like the jellies that Cook sometimes made for pudding. Experimentally, James crawled forwards and stretched till he was hanging out over the edge of the bank. Moving slowly, he lowered one finger towards the water.

Could he make a dimple like that? He was just about to touch the lake's surface when a voice behind him made him jump.

"James, what on *earth* are you up to?"

Startled, he twisted round, only to yell out as he unbalanced and toppled into the lake, catching a glimpse of Iain Sinclair's shocked expression before the water closed over his head, filling his mouth as he gasped. Luckily, it wasn't awfully deep this close to the edge, and when his feet touched the mud, he was able to launch himself upwards. Just as he was surfacing again—ready to swim the few strokes that would take him back to the bank—there was an almighty splash beside him, and a moment later, Iain Sinclair's head appeared.

"Hold on!" Iain cried and reached out. He grabbed hold of James's sleeve, causing another wash of water to swamp him. "I'll tow you back."

"Get off!" James spluttered, struggling to free himself. "I'm fine. I can swim back myself."

"Stop fighting," Iain scolded him, beginning to swim. "I'm trying to help you!"

"I don't need your help!" James shouted, lashing out. His fist struck something hard, and Iain yelled, his grip loosening. Abruptly free, James sank and had to claw his way back to the surface, gasping and kicking and pawing at the water in a messy dog paddle of a swim that shamed him.

When he finally reached the side, he clambered out, then stood there, scowling and dripping on the bank as the older boy climbed out after him, his face like thunder.

"I was trying to save you, you ungrateful brat!"

A thin trickle of blood ran from Iain's left nostril, and James stared at it, feeling appalled and amazed at the same time. Had he—nine-year-old James Hart—just bloodied the nose of this thirteen-year-old god?

James had only met Iain for the first time two days before. Their older sisters went to the same ladies' seminary, and their mothers knew each other somehow. Having renewed her acquaintance with her old friend, James's mother had decided to invite the Sinclair family to visit Wylde Manor for three weeks over the summer, a fact that James hadn't been the least bit interested in until the Sinclairs actually arrived and he discovered that as well as four daughters, they had brought a son: Iain, a tall, well-made boy with dark chestnut-brown hair and the whitest smile James had ever seen.

Iain was fascinating. Amazing. For the first two days, James had followed him around like a lamb, hanging on his every word and admiring his swiftness and strength and cleverness. Till last night, when his sister Marianne had teased him about it and made him feel like a baby.

That was why he'd gone off on his own this morning.

"I didn't need you to save me," James said now. "I'm not a baby. I can swim."

"It's nothing to do with how old you are or whether you know how to swim," Iain snapped. "Lots of people who can swim end up drowning. It happens all the time."

James was about to argue with that when he noticed that Iain's eyes were glittering, his cheeks flushed. He didn't look angry so much as upset. As though he might cry or something awful like that. Wary now, James bit back the retort that had been hovering on his tongue and said instead, quietly, "I'm sorry about your nose. I didn't mean to bloody it."

Iain frowned at that. He touched his hand to his face, groaning when he saw the blood on his fingertips. "Oh, damnation," he groaned and began to grope in his pocket, finally pulling out a sodden handkerchief.

He held it up, and lake water dripped out of it. "Sodden," he said ruefully. "Just like the rest of me." He squeezed most of the water out, then used the damp square to wipe up the blood. "Mama will be furious," he added when he'd dealt with his nose. "This is my new coat."

The coat was a proper grown-up one. Iain dressed like a

man in pantaloons and coat and waistcoat, not like James, who was wearing one of his skeleton suits today. He hadn't even thought to argue when Rose had buttoned him into this one, with its silly frilled collar, this morning. He never thought much about what he wore. But now, looking at thirteen-year-old Iain, he felt like an infant.

"Will you be punished for it?" he asked. He tried to sound unconcerned, but in truth, he felt guilty. Iain had got wet because of James, and he didn't like to think of the older boy getting a thrashing over it.

"Only if Papa finds out," Iain said with a rueful grin. "If I can sneak in, our maid, Lydia, will help me. It'll be easier to do that if I dry the worst off just now."

James watched while Iain pulled off his coat and waistcoat and shirt, laying them out to dry in the sun. Though lean, Iain had broad shoulders and wiry, muscular arms. To James's eyes, he looked much bigger and stronger than the two stable boys who were similar in age.

"Aren't you going to take your clothes off to dry?" Iain asked as he spread out his shirt on the grass.

James wrapped his arms around his thin, skinny frame and hurriedly shook his head. "No," he said. "They can dry on me."

If Iain had been one of James's sisters, he'd likely have started nagging him about getting a chill or some such thing, but Iain just shrugged and continued with his task, so James returned to the edge of the lake to look in the water again.

A minute later, Iain lay down beside him. "What are you looking at?" he asked.

"I was watching a pond skater before I fell in," James said, eyes still on the water. "I'm looking for another one now. Or something else good."

"I'd like to see that," Iain said, which sent a sudden rush of pleasure through James. The thought of showing something to Iain that might interest him was heady indeed.

4

They stared at the water together for what felt like ages. Other than the drone of insects and the occasional distant lowing of a cow, there was perfect silence. The sun shone warmly down on them, drying their damp backs, but the ground beneath them was cooler, the grass still damp from the unrelenting rain of the week before.

"Look," James whispered at last. He pointed carefully at the water.

"What? I don't see anything."

"It's not a pond skater, it's a water boatman." James moved his finger closer, cautious not to startle the creature away. "Look, it's *under* the water, lying on its back looking up at us."

Iain was silent for a bit, staring, then he hissed, "Yes, I see it!" He sounded excited, and James wanted to grin at having caused that excitement. He found that he didn't want to give his pleasure away, though, so instead he peered at the water boatman even more closely, admiring the perfect oval of its little body and the symmetry of the long legs it used to propel itself around.

"*Noto-necta glau-ca*," he said haltingly into the silence.

"What?"

In his peripheral vision, James saw that Iain had turned his head to look at him, but James kept his gaze on the water boatman. He wasn't just "looking at" the insect, he reminded himself—he was *observing* it. That was what Papa always said. James might still be wearing a lacy collar, but he *wasn't* a baby playing in the mud. He was a naturalist, like Papa, and one day, when he'd studied all the species in Papa's books, he'd find new species that no one had ever named before.

"*Notonecta glauca*," he repeated more firmly, even though he wasn't entirely sure he was pronouncing the words properly. He added, carefully, "That's its Latin name. It comes from the *hemiptera* order."

"The hema-*what*?" Iain asked. He was laughing again, but it didn't sound like unkind laughter.

"*Hemiptera*—it's an order of the insect class. Pond skaters are in the same order as water boatmen, actually."

When Iain stayed silent, James finally turned to look at him, finding the older boy staring at him with what looked like amazement.

"How old are you?" Iain asked.

James flushed hard. He wasn't particularly tall for his age, and with his frilly collar, he wondered how young Iain imagined he was.

"Nine," he replied in small voice. "Ten in January." Too old for skeleton suits.

"Bloody hell!" Iain exclaimed. "You know Latin better than me, and I'm thirteen!"

Again, that rush of pleasure ran through him. Iain hadn't been about to sneer—he was impressed.

"I don't know *much* Latin," James replied modestly. "Mr. Brownhill hasn't hardly taught me any yet. But I know *lots* of plant and animal names. I learned them from my papa." He paused, then added proudly, "He's a naturalist. I'm going to be one too, when I'm grown up."

Iain looked gratifyingly impressed at that. "My father doesn't do anything," he said. "Not anymore. He has the estate, of course, but Mr. Merton looks after that."

"What does he do all day?" James asked, genuinely puzzled. "My papa has an estate too, and he always seems busy with books and things to do with it. But he also collects specimens and looks at them through his microscope—he lets me do that with him. And he writes notes and letters to other naturalists."

Iain shrugged. "Mama says Papa's a gentleman," he said, as though that explained everything. "I don't see him much anymore—he spends most of his time in London now. He only comes up to Northumbria now and then, and when he does, he just sits in his study and drinks."

"Is that what you're going to do, when you're grown up?" James asked, eyeing the older boy and thinking privately that it looked as though that would be very soon. Then he realised what he'd just said and blushed. "Not drink, I mean," he said. "Be a gentleman."

Iain shook his head. "No, my brother Alasdair will inherit the estate."

"Why?" James asked. "Is he the oldest?" James was the youngest in his family, but Papa said he would inherit Wylde Manor because he was the only boy.

"Yes," Iain said, staring down at the lake.

"Oh," James said. "I didn't realise you had a brother."

"I had two brothers," Iain replied. "Till Tom died."

James glanced at the other boy. Iain was staring at the surface of the lake, though James had the feeling he didn't really see it.

"What happened to him?" he asked.

Iain turned his head to meet James's gaze. He looked calm.

"He drowned."

James felt a horrible pang of guilt, remembering his words from before.

I'm not a baby. I can swim.

He stared at the older boy in horror, not sure what to say.

Iain didn't seem to expect him to say anything. He turned his head back to gaze at the water again. "I was with him," he said softly. "I didn't realise. He wasn't thrashing around or calling out. He was just sort of *bobbing* there, with his mouth open." He paused, his throat working as he swallowed hard. "Then he slipped under. It was only when he didn't come up that I knew something was wrong. I swam down under the water to try to find him, but I couldn't. There were lots of weeds, so it was difficult to see. I had to get out and find someone to come and help." He paused, then added, "But of course, he was already dead by then anyway."

James felt like crying. He didn't know what to say, and he worried that if he opened his mouth, he'd sob like a baby. So, he just stared at Iain with stinging eyes and waited.

Eventually, Iain glanced at him again. "Tom could swim," he said. "I don't know why it happened. I was playing in the shallows, and he was playing on the rope swing, jumping off into the deep bit of the river, over and over. I only looked over because he'd stopped making any noise, and when I turned round—" He broke off and shook his head. "Well, I already told you." He gave a soft kind of laugh, but it didn't sound even a bit funny. More like a sad sound.

"Sorry for being a brat before," James whispered. "When you tried to rescue me."

Iain gave him a sad sort of smile. "That's all right," he said. Then he sighed and said, "Why don't you tell me about this water boatman."

Relieved by the change of subject, James did as Iain asked. He pointed out how much the hind legs of the insect looked like oars—hence the name—then explained about the boatman's predilection for eating tadpoles, and its tendency to bite when attempts were made to pick it up. After a while, the insect skimmed away, and James looked at Iain again, picking up the thread of their earlier conversation.

"So, if you're not going to be a gentleman like your papa, what will you do?"

Iain turned on his back and looked up at the very blue sky. It was the same colour as his eyes, James thought.

"Papa intended me for the Church. Tom was going to join the army, as the second son. Now that Tom's gone, I'll probably join the army instead."

"Is that what you want to do?"

Iain gave a small smile. "More than the Church," he said. "Besides, I love horses. So I'll probably join the cavalry."

8

James could see Iain as a cavalry officer. Could see this tall, handsome boy in a uniform, on a fine horse, with a sabre in his hand. Smiling that dazzling smile. The thought made his chest ache in a way he wasn't sure he understood.

"The only trouble with the army," he pointed out practically, "is you have to fight in wars. You could die in battle."

Iain just shrugged. "There are worse things," he said. "At least if you die in the army, everyone says you're a hero." He paused, adding, "And your family can be proud of you that way."

James wasn't sure that having his family being proud of him would make up for being dead, but he wanted Iain to stop looking so sad, so he nodded in agreement.

He found he didn't like seeing that sad look on Iain's face at all. He wanted to see excitement there again, like when he'd first pointed out the water boatman. After a brief hesitation, he said, shyly, "I know where there's some dragonflies. Do you want to see?"

Iain glanced at him, grinning. "Definitely. Where are they?" Something about his grin hit James right in his stomach. James felt winded by it, though in a good sort of way. Breathless and like he wanted to laugh at the same time.

"At the back of the boathouse," he said, clambering to his feet. "Come on, I'll race you there."

He turned on his heel and began to run as fast as he could, laughing out loud when Iain gave a whoop and followed him.

2

Now: 1824

22ⁿᵈ May, 1824

London

Iain sat and stared at the deed in front of him. Once he'd signed this paper, his career in the military was over.

He'd be *Captain* Iain Sinclair no longer.

It was silly to think of it in those terms, of course. To think that this signature was all. In truth, his career was already over. It had been over from the moment he set this in motion, approaching his commanding officer four months ago to tell him he would be resigning his commission.

Still.

On the other side of the desk, Major Bradley gave a short laugh.

"Not having second thoughts, are you, Sinclair?"

Iain's head snapped up, and he met the older man's gaze. The hint of sympathy in the major's pale, slightly bulbous eyes surprised him.

"No," he lied. "No second thoughts." He reached for the pen in the inkpot, smoothing the nib over the lip of the pot to get rid of the excess ink before appending his signature to the end of the deed with a slashing flourish. Then he held the pen out to the major and pushed the paper towards him.

The major dipped the pen again. "How long was your period of service in all?" he asked as he put pen to paper, tutting at a little blot his pen made as he began to scratch his name.

"Twelve years," Iain answered. "First as cornet, then lieutenant, then captain."

"Ah, you're a mere pup, then," the major said, reaching into the box next to him for a handful of sand to cast over the wet ink. "Plenty of time to set yourself up as a country squire, what? Get yourself some land—some tenants too, if you don't fancy the life of a gentleman farmer and just want an income."

The major briskly shook the sand off the paper and laid the deed down, reaching for a stick of sealing wax and lighting its wick from the candle that burned beside him. Iain watched as the wax dripped, the fat red drops looking like nothing so much as blood.

"I bought my commission over twenty years ago," the major said, rolling the stick of wax between his fingers to encourage some to melt from the other side. "And I daresay I'll remain in service for another twenty or so before I'm done, even if it's only to push bits of paper around." He sighed heavily.

"The army is a very different beast in peace than in war," Iain murmured.

"It is that," the major agreed, laying the stick of wax down and reaching for his brass seal. He did not stamp the seal down, as some men did, but pushed it gently into the already cooling wax, holding it there patiently till the wax had hardened round the brass. Only then did he ease it away.

Placing his seal neatly to one side—a fastidious man, the major—he lifted the deed to the light, examining his work before nodding with satisfaction.

"All done," he said and smiled at Iain. "My secretary will have a bank draft ready for you next door."

All done.

Iain forced himself to smile, even as his gut cramped and the oddest feeling of grief swamped him. So this was it. His army career—his very life these last twelve years—was over.

He stood up, offering his hand to the major. "Thank you for your time today, Major."

The major stood too, taking Iain's hand in a firm grip. "You're welcome," he said, then he smiled and added, "*Mr.* Sinclair."

Mister.

Hell. That was going to take some getting used to.

They walked to the door together, the major stretching forwards to open the door for Iain.

"And what will you do with your capital, do you think?" he asked conversationally. "It's a goodly sum you've got for your commission. As I said, enough to buy some land. Or are you the sort that prefers to gamble your money on the 'Change?"

"I don't know," Iain lied. "I haven't thought much beyond today."

The major laughed, jovial. "Then what do you plan for today?"

"I'd like to go to the nearest tavern and get drunk"—that part was an honest answer anyway—"but I've got a dinner engagement this evening, so I daresay I'll go home and spruce myself up for that."

The major gave another bark of laughter and slapped Iain on the shoulder. "Ah well," he said. "You can decide the rest of it on the morrow, I daresay."

The major's secretary, a dry, elderly fellow, was not as friendly as his master. He bade Iain sit on a hard, uncomfortable chair while he located Iain's bank draft. Took his time about it too. The task seemed to require an absurd amount of checking and crosschecking. One by one, he fetched three separate ledgers down from the shelves behind him, making an entry in each one before painstakingly reshelving it and fetching the next. At last, though, he reached for a key ring fastened at his waist, using one of the keys dangling from it to unlock his desk drawer. The sealed envelope he withdrew bore Iain's name, or rather his old name, *Captain Sinclair*. The secretary handed it over with all the reluctance of a man parting with his own worldly goods, his only response to Iain's pleasant farewell a chilly nod.

In some ways it was a fitting end to his army life, Iain thought as he made his way down the four flights of stairs to the front door—an indifferent farewell from a dead-eyed pen pusher. Iain had joined the army with a young man's naïve fervour, dreaming of doing heroic deeds. The thought of his dying had not particularly worried him then, at least not in the abstract. In truth, he'd imagined from the first that he'd leave the army—his very life—in some sort of heroic blaze.

He'd learned, of course, that real-life battles were very different from his boyish imaginings; learned that courage was something much more difficult, and far less glorious, than he'd once thought. He'd lost half his comrades at Waterloo. Good men. It had been his first real experience of combat, and he'd come out the other side changed forever, having discovered that the easy glory he'd dreamed of as a boy was an illusion. The true worth he'd found in the army had been the brotherhood he'd shared with the men he'd served beside, both on and off the battlefield.

That sense of worth had been sadly lacking these last few

13

years. Returning to England in peacetime had led to postings in industrial towns where civil dissent was rife, where factory workers were demanding better conditions and the masses were calling for universal suffrage. After quelling several skirmishes with protestors—Iain and his men on horseback with bayonets against men and women armed with sticks and stones—he'd been ready to resign his commission there and then. But, as fate would have it, unexpected orders to assist at the visit of a minor European royal had led to Iain being chosen to guard the royal personage. Before long, he'd become one of the King's favourites, and that had made him a favourite of his own masters too, for they liked to know what happened in the King's circle, no matter how trivial.

Perhaps someone had suggested to the King that Iain could stay on as part of his personal entourage, or perhaps the King had made the request himself. However it had happened, that had been the result. And somehow, three years had passed.

But life in the King's service was not what he'd imagined when he'd joined the army. The trivialities of court politics bored him, and the constant need to cater to the King's quixotic moods and petty demands was tedious.

And then, a few months ago, he'd been invited to a nondescript building in Whitehall and offered a new position by a nondescript-looking official, one Leonard Burton. A position that was not unlike being in the army, although without the scarlet regimentals and the military title. A position that was steeped in secrets and intrigue and danger.

It hadn't been a difficult choice. In his present life, Iain was bored and miserable. Burton was offering something new and exciting and filled with adventure.

Of course, he'd agreed.

Yet now, today, after signing that paper, it suddenly felt very real and very final. He really was going to India. The thought made him feel faintly sick.

As he reached the bottom of the stairs, Iain realised he was still holding the bank draft envelope in his hand. Folding it carefully, he tucked it inside his coat before approaching the soldier manning the vestibule. The man stood to attention, then opened the door for him, and Iain nodded at him as he walked out. His first steps in the world as plain Mr. Sinclair again.

Soon he'd have another name. He'd have an invented history too, one that he'd have to learn inside out, that he'd have to live as if it were his own.

The sound of the door closing behind him sounded oddly, painfully, final, and Iain found himself swallowing against a sudden obstruction in his throat. It was an effort to make his leaden feet move, to descend the steps from the front door to the street below and start walking away, back to his rooms.

The first thing Iain saw when he returned to his rooms was the invitation to Holmewell that he'd received from the Porters a whole month before. It lay in the middle of his desk, staring at him accusingly. He walked over and picked it up, weighing it absently in his hand. The heavy parchment was dry against his fingertips, the edges of the opened wax seal crumbling a little

Lady Kate Porter was James Hart's second oldest sister. She invited Iain to visit Holmewell every year, but it had been several years since he'd accepted an invitation from her. Usually he dashed off a polite refusal within a few days of receiving the invitation, but this year, he'd held off. Every night he came home and looked at the invitation, and every night he put off replying for another day.

James would almost certainly be there.

Iain stared at the invitation, but he wasn't seeing the parchment, ink and wax he held in his hand. He was seeing serious grey eyes, fine features. A hesitant smile that made his chest ache with longing.

At last he sighed, tossed the invitation back onto the desk and strode to the sideboard, reaching for the whisky decanter and pouring himself a generous measure that he downed in two throat-searing gulps. He rarely drank like that—it reminded him too viscerally of his father—but after today's events, he needed it.

He was out of the army now, for good and all. His immediate future consisted of seven weeks during which he had nothing to do, followed by an unspeakably long sea journey to Madras, where his new life would begin. Once he was in India, England would be behind him, as would everything and everyone England held.

Everyone.

Iain turned his head back to the desk and stared at the invitation.

He wanted to see James Hart. There was no point denying that to himself. It was hardly surprising, was it? James was his dearest friend, and it had been two full years, after all. True, he'd made no attempt to see James since that last disastrous encounter at Kit Redford's, but as of today, things were different. As of today, Iain knew for certain he was going to India and that there was no telling when he'd be back in England.

If he ever returned.

Sighing again, Iain turned on his heel, bypassing the whisky and making for his wardrobe, from the bottom shelf of which he dragged a heavy metal box. Dropping it on the counterpane of his bed, he drew out his keys, then sat down beside it to fiddle with the lock. Carefully, he lifted the lid off and drew out a sheaf of loosely bound letters he'd not looked at for months.

James's letters.

He loosened the ribbon, cast it aside, then picked up the

first letter. James's handwriting was small and neat. Economical. The precise formation of the words on the page belied the sprawling emotions in those lines.

Iain began to read them, one by one, starting with the ones from when they were boys, before anything else happened between them. Things had been so much easier then.

Eventually, though, he reached the more recent, more painful ones.

Let me come to see you, Iain. Let me talk to you...

If nothing else, can't we at least try to salvage some part of our friendship? I give you my word I will not press you for more...

I miss you so much. Write to me. Let me know how you are...

He hadn't answered any of those pleas—oh, he'd sent some brief missives in response, a few dashed-off lines about what he was doing at the time—but no reply to any of those difficult questions James had asked him. No acknowledgement, even.

Iain gazed at the letters, at the unanswered questions that lay scattered over his bedcovers. The last time he'd seen James, weeks after the last letter James had written to him, they'd argued. Bitterly argued. And since then—nothing. A silence that had come to feel impossible to breach.

But now, the thought of sailing to India, with all that anger and resentment still between them...

No.

In that moment, a sudden, swift certainty pulsed through him: he couldn't board that ship till he'd seen James Hart one last time. He couldn't go to India leaving matters as they presently stood. If he never saw James again... A distinct wrenching pain knotted his gut, and his throat ached at that thought.

He stood abruptly, leaving James's letters where they lay, and strode to his desk. He dropped into his chair and yanked open the drawer, snatching up a sheet of notepaper, which he slapped down on the blotter. He dipped his pen in the inkpot and, careless of his handwriting, scratched out a note to Sir Edward and Lady Kate, accepting their kind invitation. Then he sanded it and sealed it, ready to be delivered.

It was done.

He was going to Holmewell.

He would see James Hart one last time before he set sail.

3

THEN: 1811

14th October 1811

Herdstone House, Northumbria

The final blow, the twentieth by Iain's reckoning, was the worst one. He could tell the difference in the instant before the cane fell, in the swiftness and volume of that whistling *thwiiip*. And then it slammed into him, striking him above his buttocks this time, at the lowest part of his back.

He hadn't wanted to make a single sound, shed a single tear. But he couldn't stop a grunt of pain at that final, agonising impact, and when he squeezed his eyes even harder closed, he felt a betraying leak at the corner of his left eye. His nose was running from the effort of keeping his tears back, and he kept his lips pressed tightly shut, scared that if he opened them, all the grief and shame that was clogging his chest would pour out.

"Pull your breeches up and make yourself presentable,"

his father snapped. "I expect to see you in my study in exactly five minutes."

Iain heard his father stalk out of the library, his boots clicking over the parquet floor. The door opened; slammed shut. Finally, Iain was alone.

Slowly, he raised himself up off the desk. With a shaking hand, he explored his damaged flesh, his fingertips meeting raised welts. He could already feel the more profound ache of deep bruising.

His arms felt almost too weak to hitch up his smallclothes and breeches, his fingers trembling as he did up the buttons. The brush of the fabric against his skin made him wince. Eventually, he was decent again, and he reached for the coat he'd hung over the back of a chair before his thrashing began.

As he fastened his coat, he wondered what had happened to Sid. Had he already been turned off and sent away? The thought caused him a pang of guilt, even though it was Sid who had initiated their encounter.

Caught with the second footman by the butler—how could he have been so stupid? He supposed he should be grateful that Prosser had been with the Sinclair family for over thirty years and was almost fanatically devoted to them. Having marched sixteen-year-old Iain to his father's study and haltingly explained what he'd witnessed, he'd seemed relieved when Iain's father had informed him that her lady-ship needn't be troubled with this unpleasantness, that he would deal with the matter personally.

Well, at least the thrashing was over. There was only the interview to get through now, though Iain dreaded this part more. He didn't see a great deal of his father these days, but when he did, he found him difficult and unpredictable. Although his father was occasionally affectionate, more often he was angry, and sometimes he was downright mean-tempered. It depended how deep in his cups he was, and Iain had learned—they had all learned—to stay out of his sight for the most part. Today, though, Iain had spectacularly failed to follow that simple rule.

He walked slowly to his father's study, wishing it was further away, wishing he could delay the inevitable. All too soon, though, he was staring at the closed door. He paused briefly to collect himself before lifting his hand to knock.

"Enter."

His father sat behind his desk, the cane he'd just used resting on the polished walnut surface in front of him, as though he wasn't quite done with it yet. Iain felt sick just looking at it.

Iain stopped in front of the desk and put his hands behind his back, waiting. He didn't attempt to take a seat, and his father didn't invite him to do so. Despite his shaky legs, it was a relief—sitting would have been too painful in his present condition.

For several minutes, his father just stared at him.

They looked really quite alike, Iain and his father. Both tall and broad shouldered, with the same dark brown hair and blue eyes. His father's hair was greying now, though, and his once bright blue eyes were red-rimmed and rheumy from too much brandy and too little sleep.

Right now, his eyes looked blazingly angry.

His first and only question after Prosser had left them earlier, had been short and to the point: "Just tell me this: did Prosser see what he thinks he saw?"

Iain wouldn't have dreamed of telling a lie in response to that. "Yes," he'd said shortly. That was when he'd been ordered to fetch the cane and go to the library to await his thrashing.

Now, though, it seemed, his father had more to say, and Iain waited, dreading what was to come.

"I've asked myself many times," his father began in a voice that shook with suppressed rage, "why it had to be Tom who died that day. If I had to lose one son, why him?"

Iain stared at the man miserably for several long beats, then dropped his gaze to the floor, sick and ashamed, unable to answer a question he'd already asked himself a hundred times over.

"Have I not lost enough?" his father continued, his voice rising. "My favourite child is gone, but now you have to— have to *shame* me like this?" He brought his fist down on the desk, making the cane, and Iain, jump.

"I'm sorry," he whispered.

"Sorry!" His father shook his head, disbelieving. For a long minute, he said nothing more, just sat there, brooding, brow furrowed, jaw set hard. His throat bobbed as he swallowed against some emotion, then he said, "Do you understand what this family expects of you, Iain? What *I* expect of you?"

"Do you mean about my joining the army, sir?" Iain asked warily.

"No," his father bit out. "Obviously, I expect that, but beyond that, I have expectations about how you conduct yourself. I expect you to behave in a manner that places you beyond the reproach of your peers. I expect you to behave in a manner that your mother and I can take *pride* in."

A small, disloyal voice in Iain's head reminded him of how often his regularly drunk father had conducted himself with shocking disregard for his wife's feelings, but he held back the words and waited for his father to finish.

The man fixed his gaze on Iain. Deliberately and quite slowly, he continued, "Let me be absolutely clear on this. If I *ever* hear the Sinclair name being smeared by any suggestion —even indirectly—of this sort of conduct from you again, you may be sure you will be disowned, and without a second's hesitation. I will not have the Sinclair name besmirched by this sort of filth. I will not allow you to humiliate your mother and sisters with a scandal of this nature."

Iain swallowed and nodded slowly. He didn't feel as

though he'd be able to get words out past his dry throat, but he tried anyway. "I promise I'll never—"

"Don't insult me with promises you'll never keep," his father snapped. "I'm under no illusions about you, my boy. Once a sod, always a sod. But be in no doubt, you'll learn discretion or lose your place in this family. Do you understand?"

Iain nodded unhappily and went back to staring at the floor.

"Thank God, we're not relying on you to produce heirs," his father added flatly. "Alasdair might be a milksop, but at least he's capable of tupping a woman and getting her with child." At the tender age of two-and-twenty, Iain's oldest brother was already married and had a son, with a second child on the way. "I can only hope that the army will make more of a man of you than I've managed to do."

Iain heard the sound of his father unstoppering a decanter, the glug of liquid being poured, but he didn't look up.

"If your mother asks what happened today," his father said, "you will tell her that it's a matter between you and me, and that it's been dealt with. I don't want you upsetting her with this."

"Yes, sir," Iain told the floor.

"For God's sake, *look* at me when I'm talking to you!"

Iain obeyed. His father seemed more like his usual self now, with a near-empty glass of spirit clutched in his hand. His expression was set in hard, angry lines as he regarded Iain. Giving a disgusted grunt, he threw back the remaining contents of his glass and reached for the decanter again. His hand shook.

"Get out," he said flatly. "I can't even stand to look at you."

And Iain could only be relieved to leave him to his brandy.

4

Now: 1824

22nd May, 1824
  London
  Iain's dinner engagement, on the night he resigned his commission, was with Murdo Balfour, a good friend he'd not seen for some time. Balfour had been involved in a huge scandal with a married woman the year before and soon afterwards had sold his townhouse in Mayfair, exiling himself to his country estate in Scotland. A few weeks ago, however, he'd written to Iain advising he'd be in the capital briefly and inviting him to dine.
  Iain had to take a hackney cab to Balfour's new address, which was located several miles from Mayfair in an affluent area that was popular with wealthy bankers and merchants. It was hardly surprising, he supposed, that Balfour had chosen to move to this part of town, since he was no longer accepted by polite society. More surprising was the fact that Balfour had bothered to buy a new house at all, given that he

now spent almost all of his time at his new estate in Scotland. Apparently, though, David Lauriston—Balfour's "companion", as Balfour had described him in his letter to Iain—had business in London from time to time, and it was for this reason that Balfour found it convenient to keep a house there.

After paying the cab driver, Iain ascended the half-dozen steps to the imposing front door of Balfour's new home and rapped the large brass knocker. Moments later, he was ushered inside by Balfour's footman, relieved of his coat and hat and led into a drawing room that looked too small to be the main reception room of this large house. Glancing around at the comfortable, masculine furniture, the pile of books on the side table, the half-written letter on the escritoire, he surmised that this was more of a private sitting room. No doubt the formal drawing room would rival the splendid, chilly elegance of Balfour's previous London residence.

"Sinclair, it's good to see you."

Iain turned at that voice to find Balfour standing in the doorway of the drawing room, grinning. He was dressed with less elegance than used to be his habit, his blue coat a little looser than was fashionable, his dark hair grown a little longer than before.

"It's been too long," Balfour continued, walking forwards and stretching out a hand.

"Far too long," Iain agreed, shaking Balfour's hand. He met Balfour's gaze before adding, "The last time was the night of Mr. Lauriston's accident in Edinburgh."

David Lauriston had been badly injured that night. When Iain last saw Balfour, the man had looked half-mad with grief.

"A great deal has happened since then," Balfour said lightly. "You've probably heard."

"I heard about the duel with Kinnell."

Sir Alasdair Kinnell was the man responsible for Lauriston's injuries.

"There was no duel," Balfour said, but he was smiling slightly.

"He challenged you, though."

"He did. But thankfully, honour was satisfied in another way."

"Is that so?" Iain asked, blatantly fishing. "How?"

Balfour just laughed. "As if I'd tell you," he said. "We made an agreement. A *private* agreement." He walked past Iain, heading for the sideboard. "Drink?"

"Brandy, thank you," Iain replied. While Balfour poured the spirit, he added, "I heard Kinnell petitioned his wife for divorce after your little contretemps."

Rumour had it that the contretemps in question was over Balfour swiving Kinnell's wife, though, knowing what he knew of Balfour and his preferences, Iain found that rather difficult to believe. Far more likely, in his opinion, was that the argument was over Lauriston's injuries.

Balfour shrugged and reached for a crystal decanter, filled with amber liquid. "He did. And I'll wager his wife is glad to be rid of him."

"I was surprised to hear he cited you as her lover."

Balfour didn't look up as he sloshed the brandy into two snifters. "Really? Didn't you also hear about the spectacle I made of myself in Culzeans?"

"I heard you publicly claimed you were her lover."

Balfour looked up at that, grinning. "He really had no choice but to challenge me."

Iain raised a brow. "You always were a provocative fellow, though I don't believe you were her lover for a moment. I'm well aware of what fires you up, and it isn't pretty little matrons. I know why you challenged Kinnell to that duel. I was there when he pushed Lauriston under that horse."

Balfour offered him one of the snifters. He looked perfectly calm but for a betraying tic that pulsed, just once, in his left cheek.

26

"I did it for a number of reasons," he said. "Partly for Elizabeth—Kinnell was beating her, you know—and I had my own grievances against the man, from our schooldays. But yes, it was primarily for David." He shrugged, philosophical. "Part of me still wishes I'd put a bullet in the bastard, but there were more important considerations to think about. And I have the satisfaction of knowing I publicly humiliated him. That's something."

"I'll drink to that," Iain said, lifting his glass in an impromptu toast, and Balfour joined him, clinking his glass against Iain's.

"Will Mr. Lauriston be joining us this evening?" Iain asked.

"Yes, once he's dressed," Balfour replied absently. "We've only just got up."

"Is that so?" Iain laughed softly. "Just out of bed, the two of you?"

Balfour looked, quite suddenly, as though he wanted to kick himself and he said, tightly, "If you tease him when he comes down, I'll skin you alive. David's not like you and I—he's *modest*."

Iain laughed again. "He can't be that modest to have held your interest so long. I know how easily you bore, my friend."

Balfour glared at that. "Let me make this clear, before David comes down: what we share"—he glanced up at the ceiling as though he might find the answer written up there—"is a *forever* sort of an arrangement. As good as a marriage, as far as I'm concerned. And I expect you to treat David with the same respect you would show to any man's—" He broke off, frowning.

"Wife?" Iain offered helpfully. "Husband?"

Balfour scowled. "Either," he snapped, then added. "Or both—oh, I don't know!"

Before he had to reach a verdict, the door opened again

and the subject of their conversation joined them—David Lauriston, as handsome and self-contained as that first time Iain had met him in Edinburgh.

Lauriston walked towards them with a smooth, even stride, no sign of any lingering disability from his accident. "Captain Sinclair," he said, smiling, and offered his hand.

"*Mr.* Sinclair," Iain corrected as they shook. He wondered how long it would be before he could say that without a twinge of regret.

"My apologies," Lauriston replied. "Murdo did tell me your news. *Mr.* Sinclair. It's good to see you again. Thank you for joining us."

"The pleasure is all mine." Purely to tease Balfour, Iain let his gaze travel up and down Lauriston's body and, to his amusement, Balfour reacted immediately, clearing his throat and stepping between them. Ostensibly, his purpose was to pass a glass of brandy to Lauriston, but having moved between them, he stayed put, forcing Lauriston to take a step back to accommodate him

Iain glanced at Lauriston to gauge his reaction to the other man's possessive behaviour. Lauriston looked amused but oddly tender too, his gaze fond even as he raised a teasing brow at his lover. As for Balfour, he wore a faint flush across his cheekbones. Of annoyance perhaps, or mortification. Or possibly both.

"So, tell me," Balfour said briskly, in the tone of a man who very much wanted to change the subject. "What decided you upon leaving the army?"

Iain shrugged. "Life as a soldier is very different in times of peace. Not to my taste, I find."

"You miss the battlefield?" Lauriston asked, his tone curious.

"Not the battlefield as such, more the general sense of… purpose, I suppose." He gave a small self-mocking smile.

UNNATURAL

"The truth is, these last few years I've done little but play the part of a court jester for the King."

"Oh, come now," Balfour said. "You don't do yourself justice. The King admires you so much, he takes you into his confidence about all sorts of interesting matters of state. Does that not give you a sense of purpose? At least when you're reporting the results of your observations back to your masters—"

"Murdo—" Lauriston interjected, and Balfour glanced at him, sensitive to the faint note of censure in his lover's tone.

"I wasn't criticising. He's said as much himself in the past," Balfour protested. When Lauriston looked unconvinced, he added, "For God's sake, we've been friends for ages. He *tells* me things."

Lauriston just raised a sceptical brow, which was hardly surprising given that the last time he'd been in Iain's company, Balfour hadn't been terribly friendly to Iain. Then again, on that occasion, Iain had spent that whole evening flirting shamelessly with Lauriston...

"It's true, Mr. Lauriston," Iain said, taking pity on his friend. "Balfour and I actually get on very well most of the time—it's only when you're around that he grows peevish with me."

Balfour laughed at that, a short burst of helpless amusement that made his dark eyes flash and Lauriston's disapproving expression soften a little.

"I still think it's very indiscreet of you to speak of your friend's private confidences in front of me," Lauriston scolded him.

"Well, it's not as though *you'd* say anything to anyone," Balfour grumbled. "I've never met a more tight-lipped man in my life."

"Even supposing," Lauriston said implacably. "You should really apologise."

"Fine," Balfour said, sighing. He turned to face Iain. "I

29

apologise for breaking your confidence in front of my lover, a man who I know will not breathe a word of what he has heard to another living soul anyway." He turned back to Lauriston. "There, will that do?"

Lauriston's cheeks had pinkened at Balfour's use of the word *lover*, but he made no protest. Now he was trying to look severe and failing miserably, his eyes dancing with happiness and suppressed mirth.

"That was an awful apology, but if it satisfies Captain Sinclair, I daresay it will have to satisfy me too." He sent a questioning glance in Iain's direction.

"*Mr.* Sinclair," Iain said again, his light tone belying what that second correction cost him. "And yes, it will do very well, Mr. Lauriston. Now, I do believe Balfour invited me to dinner?"

"He did." Lauriston smiled. "Are you hungry, Mr. Sinclair?"

"Famished."

"Come, then. We have an excellent cook, and I can promise you she's outdone herself tonight."

The dinner *was* excellent. Balfour and Lauriston preferred to dine informally, so the footmen were dismissed once the dishes were brought in, the three of them left alone to serve themselves, an approach that Iain heartily approved of.

The company was excellent too, though it made Iain feel melancholy, seeing his friend's obvious delight in his lover. It wasn't that he begrudged his hosts their happiness. No, the melancholy was all on his own account. It seemed he had a hitherto unacknowledged self-pitying streak that made witnessing their contentment strangely painful.

Balfour and Lauriston were so utterly at ease with one another, every glance they shared was warm with easy intimacy and affection. Iain couldn't help but reflect that he'd never shared such companionship with another—except James Hart, of course, and James was not his lover. James was only his friend. Or had been, until Iain had ruined everything.

Perhaps that was why he felt so sad, seeing Balfour and Lauriston together—because it made him think of James, and of how much Iain missed his friendship. He felt the tug of it now, that invisible thread that connected him to James, an aching sort of pull.

With effort, Iain pushed his melancholy thoughts aside and turned his attention determinedly to his hosts. There was a degree of entertainment to be had from watching the haughty, aristocratic Balfour tending to his lover's wishes with such unexpected and amusing devotion.

Right now, the man was trying to press a slice of black-berry tart on Lauriston even as Lauriston protested he couldn't manage another bite. It was, it seemed, his favourite sweet, and Balfour had especially asked the cook to make it.

"You could still do to put a bit more weight on," he was saying now, adding a pool of custard to the dish.

"Nonsense," Lauriston said. "I've always been lean. My mother and brother are too—it's how we're made. Whether you like it or not, Murdo, I'm a skinny chap."

"*I* think you look just perfect as you are," Iain interjected, letting his gaze travel admiringly over Lauriston's trim form. He had to suppress a laugh when he glanced at Balfour and saw the man's lips were compressed—he really was far too easy to tease.

Despite his protests, Lauriston ended up eating the tart, almost absently, and Balfour seemed to get an odd sort of satisfaction from watching him do so. When he finally pushed his plate aside, Balfour reached over the table, using his thumb to brush a crumb of pastry from Lauriston's mouth, the gesture at once tender and promising. Given the heat that passed between the two men right then, Iain half expected to be handed his hat and asked to leave. But, ultimately, Balfour sat back, though he shifted a little in his seat, making Iain smile to think of what was causing him the need to alter his position.

Lauriston seemed equally affected. He had to clear his throat before he spoke again, and when he did, his voice carried the too-bright note of someone keen to divert attention away from himself.

"So, what are your plans for the future, Mr. Sinclair? Have you thought about life after the army yet?"

"You used to talk about setting up a stud farm," Balfour reminded him.

"I did," Iain agreed. He glanced at Lauriston. "My boyhood passion was horses, Mr. Lauriston. That's why I joined a cavalry regiment."

"A stud farm sounds like a promising prospect, then."

"It might well be," Iain said. "But the fact is, I already have something else in mind."

"Oh yes?" Balfour said. "What is it?"

"It's a rather...interesting post. In India. Madras." He paused, then added, "I'll be there for quite a few years. It's the sort of role that demands a degree of commitment."

Balfour frowned, seeming puzzled. "Are you joining the East India Company?"

Iain considered that. "It's more of a government position, although not an official one. I'll be using an assumed name..." He trailed off.

Balfour's gaze flickered, and Iain saw that he understood. "An agent?" he said. "A dangerous business, that, Sinclair. Do you even know what would be expected of you?"

Iain shrugged. "Does it matter?"

On the other side of the table, Lauriston made a noise of mingled disbelief and irritation. "Of course it matters," he snapped. "What if you're asked to do something morally repugnant?"

"I would be there on a mission," Iain replied evenly, as though the idea didn't bother him at all, though in truth it was something that he'd lain awake thinking about. "Sometimes, completing a mission requires one to follow orders one doesn't like."

Lauriston opened his mouth to reply, but Balfour spoke first. "You're going to take this post, then?"

"Yes. I plan to. I've booked my passage."

"You *plan* to? You don't sound entirely sure."

"No, I am sure. I'm going. Only—"

"Only?"

How to put into words what he'd determined in his own mind this very day? That somehow he couldn't go until he and James had looked one another in the eye and James had forgiven him, and wished him well, and they were friends once more.

"Oh, nothing, it's just that I'm off to Hampshire next week." He smiled. "I don't think it'll feel real until I return."

Balfour considered that. He had a sceptical look about him that made Iain feel nervous.

"What takes you to Hampshire?" Balfour asked at last.

"A house party. The hosts are family friends—Sir Edward and Lady Porter."

"I'm acquainted with Sir Edward," Balfour said. "A very good sort. How do you know him?"

"It's Lady Porter I know, actually—Kate's mother and mine were born in the same village. They were friends when they were girls. Then Kate and my sister Isabel became particular friends at the ladies' seminary they attended, and our families got into the habit of visiting each other every summer." He found himself adding, almost helplessly, "I became quite friendly with Kate's brother, James Hart."

It was a strange relief to say his name aloud, to recognise James's existence in words, but when Balfour's gaze narrowed, he knew he'd been unwise.

"James Hart?" Balfour echoed, frowning. "Wasn't that the name of the fellow who accosted you in Redford's that time?"

It shouldn't have surprised him that Balfour remembered. Iain had realised how very badly he'd betrayed himself that night, and Balfour was not a man to forget something like that.

For an instant, Iain toyed with the idea of lying—claiming that Balfour was thinking of someone else. It would be an easy thing to do. James was a common enough name. But he didn't. He—couldn't. Couldn't deny James's existence. Instead, he found himself nodding and saying, "Yes, that was him."

"You were quite exercised that evening," Balfour said. "I recall you were not happy about him turning up at Redford's."

"No," Iain admitted, rubbing uncomfortably at the back of his neck. "I wasn't happy to see him." He paused, then added defensively, "Should I have been? He was little more than a boy then, and Redford's is a den of iniquity."

"A *den of iniquity*?" Balfour sounded amused.

"It is!" Iain protested. "Have you forgotten what goes on in that back room?"

"No, but I'm surprised to hear you speak of it in those terms—you always headed straight for the back room when I saw you there. Besides he didn't look *that* young."

"He was but three-and-twenty!"

"Three-and-twenty?" Balfour repeated. "Hardly a boy. A man's full-grown at three-and-twenty. Hell, I was three years younger when I first visited Redford's."

"Yes, well, James was probably greener at three-and-twenty than you were at sixteen," Iain grumbled, "so it's hardly the same thing."

Balfour chuckled. "You were certainly perturbed to see him," he said. "You dragged him out so quickly, I doubt his feet touched the ground."

Iain felt his cheeks warm. "Of course I was perturbed," he said. "I went out looking for a man to warm my bed and instead—" He broke off, unsure how to finish that sentence while Balfour canted his head to the side and watched him, curious as a cat. After a long pause, Balfour's puzzled expression cleared with understanding.

"I recall you were arguing that night," Balfour murmured. When Iain didn't contradict him, he added, "Have you spoken to him since?"

God damn the man's perception.

Iain studied the wine in his glass. "No. But I'll see him in Hampshire next week." He paused, then glanced up. "I'm hopeful we can repair our friendship before I leave England."

Balfour's silent gaze was far too knowing.

At length, he said, "I remember that night at Redford's well. It was the same night I decided to return to Edinburgh, to seek David out again. The same night I realised I couldn't stay away from him another moment." He glanced at Lauriston then, and Iain did too. David Lauriston wore a curious look. Perhaps this was a story he hadn't heard before.

"I thank God for that night," Balfour said softly, his gaze locked with Lauriston's, and Lauriston smiled.

Iain looked away from them, swallowing. He felt nothing like Balfour did about that night. In fact, he felt sick whenever he remembered what he'd said to James. How James had looked as Iain's hateful words had tumbled out of his mouth.

Why do you have to ruin everything with this—this ridiculous, childish devotion! Don't you see that it's absurd?

Iain wished he could look back on that night as Balfour did, with gratitude, but he could not.

Only with the coldest and most bitter regret.

5

THEN: 1815

24th March, 1815

Wylde Manor, Derbyshire

James was not looking forward to his sister Marianne's engagement party. His parents had decided to invite numerous friends and family to Wylde Manor for a weeklong house party with a formal ball for Marianne and Thomas on the Friday evening. The Sinclairs were invited, of course. They were invited to Wylde Manor at some point every year, and this time it looked as though Iain, whom James hadn't seen since he'd joined the army two years before, was going to be able to come. Until *bloody* Napoleon had to go and escape from Elba, and Britain declared war again, and it looked as though Iain wouldn't make it after all.

There were worse things than Iain missing the party, of course, such as the fact that it looked as though Iain would be going into battle, and soon. Even though James suspected Iain relished the thought of seeing such action firsthand, the thought made James's stomach twist up. Far preferable to resent the army for not allowing Iain to come to Wylde Manor than to imagine him being bayoneted, or shot from his horse.

The guests arrived in dribs and drabs over the course of the week. Mrs. Sinclair and her two unmarried daughters arrived on the Monday. Mr. Sinclair was not with them. "Indisposed," his wife remarked briefly, seeming not much bothered—James knew that was a reference to the man's drinking, which he'd heard his parents whispering about from time to time. What did bother Mrs. Sinclair was the absence of her younger son, whom she'd desperately hoped to see. But it seemed that the generals hadn't yet decided what to do with his regiment, and so he had to stay where he was for now.

And then, on the night of Marianne's engagement ball, as James was slouching at the edge of the dance floor, a familiar voice murmured behind him, "You look bored out of your mind, Jamie. Why aren't you dancing?"

James whirled round, his grin splitting his face before he'd even seen the owner of that voice.

"Iain!" he cried happily. "I didn't expect to see you!" He clapped his friend on the shoulder, and his smile grew even larger, helplessly stretching so that his face ached with it. "God, it's good to see you!"

Iain grinned back. He was much bigger than he had been last time James had seen him. He was nineteen now, to James's sixteen, and his rangy build had filled out. In his scarlet uniform, he looked impossibly handsome. James found himself drinking in the sight of his friend, his gaze moving restlessly up and down.

"You look—"

Iain appeared amused at whatever it was he saw on James's face. "What? Exhausted? I must admit, I've barely slept these last two days getting here."

"Not at all! You look ready for anything."

Iain smiled, but there was a shadow in his eyes. "I'm afraid I won't be here long—two days at most. I've got to be back in London by Tuesday next. My regiment leaves for the Continent the following day."

James tried to smile against the crush of disappointment. "So soon?"

"I'm afraid so. We're at war."

James swallowed against the lump that rose in his throat. "Well, at least you're here now," he said faintly.

"Yes."

They gazed at each other, till James's mother floated over, distracting Iain by exclaiming over his uniform. She was swiftly followed by all of James's sisters and their friends. After all, they had a dashing cavalry officer in their midst now, and James was quickly sidelined.

Iain's next few hours were taken up with gushing females batting their eyelashes at him, hanging on his every word and shamelessly angling to be danced with. Every now and again, Iain sent James an apologetic look, but James didn't mind, not really. It was good just to know he was *here*. And that tomorrow, James could spend the whole day with him. They could take one of the boats out on the lake and fish, or go for a ride, or maybe a long walk over the hills. It didn't matter what they did, so long as Iain was with him.

Instead of vying for Iain's attention, James set about doing his duty by the young ladies, and pleasing his mother, with renewed vigour. He signed dance card after dance card, committing himself to nearly every set. He was a surprisingly good dancer given how little he enjoyed it, and a popular partner among the younger ladies.

It was only after he was coming off the dance floor, following a particularly vigorous Scotch Reel, that he realised he hadn't seen Iain in a while. He glanced round the ballroom, but there was no sign of him at all.

"Have you seen Iain?" he asked Isabel, Iain's older sister.

"Not for ages," she replied. "He might've gone for a nap—apparently he only had a few hours' sleep last night. He looked pretty well exhausted."

That was true. James moved away, gaze searching the room, but no, there was no Iain to be seen. As it happened, he had a couple of sets free now, and he wondered if he dared escape, just for half an hour or so.

It was easy enough to slip out of the ballroom and sneak into the drawing room that led out onto the veranda and the garden beyond. It was as he was trying to escape through the veranda that he came unstuck.

A body emerged from the shadows, surprising a gasp out of him.

It was Kate. "Where do you think you're going, James Hart?" she demanded. Back in the ballroom, the six-man "orchestra" began to wheeze out another tune.

He didn't bother trying to manufacture an excuse. Kate wouldn't wear it. "I can't bear another minute," he said honestly. "I just need to get out for a breath of air. I'll be back soon."

"For goodness' sake, all you need to do is dance a few steps and bow occasionally! The last thing we need is you vanishing—there aren't enough men as it is, now that Iain's already disappeared."

"Yes, well, he probably needs to sleep after nearly killing himself getting here," James said loyally. "As for me—oh, Kate, I just need to escape for a *tiny* bit. I promise I'll be back in half an hour at the most."

"Mother will be looking for you," Kate pointed out.

James considered that, eyes narrowing. "Hmm. Well, I'm probably not the only one. What are you doing out here anyway?" He looked around, suspicious now. Had someone else been out here with her?

Kate flushed betrayingly, then threw her hands up in the air. "Fine," she declared. "Go and get some air, but don't be long." Then she stalked off, leaving him alone on the veranda.

He watched her go, stifling a laugh, knowing his sister had been up to something. For a moment he was tempted to go after her and tease it out of her, but ultimately, the pull of the outdoors was more alluring, and he set off, running all the way to the bottom of the main garden, just because he could, and because it felt good.

When he got to the end of the garden, his dancing slippers were soaked from the wet grass, but he didn't care, just leaned on the fence and looked out over the little manmade lake his grandfather had created fifty years before, James's favourite place on the whole estate.

He wasn't sure how long he stood there, just looking out over the water, or when he became aware of the presence of others nearby. At first all he heard was a low chuckle of laughter, then the murmur of voices—two at least, or were there three? However many there were, the voices were male, the husky laughter they shared, low and intimate—and growing nearer. James didn't want to see anyone, talk to anyone. He stepped back into the shadow of one of the willows that ringed the lake, hiding himself, and waited for the owners of those voices to materialise, searching his shadowy surroundings with his keen scientist's gaze.

They emerged at last from a clump of trees twenty yards away, two figures, walking side by side. Their shirts blazed white in the darkness making James frown with puzzlement till they drew nearer and he realised they'd been swimming. The wet linen clung to their torsos, and both of them carried some bundled-up clothing under their arms.

It was Iain. Iain and, of all people, Mellick, one of the grooms. Laughing together—like equals.

James realised they were going to pass the willow he stood under. He stepped back, even further into the shadows, moving slowly and carefully so as to make no noise, obscuring himself behind the solid arching trunk of the old tree.

They didn't notice him, just walked on, still murmuring to each other, chuckling softly now and then.

After a little while, James realised where they were going —they were making for the boathouse, growing more careful as they drew closer to the ramshackle building, both of them looking around several times before, one after the other, they entered, and the door closed behind them.

From his place in the shadows, James felt as though his breath had got stuck in his throat. Only when the two men were out of sight behind that closed door did he manage to gasp a breath. He knew what this was, or he thought he did, and now he was feeling too many things at once. Curiosity and excitement, and anger too, that Iain had wanted this more than he wanted to be with James tonight.

But of course, this was different.

He'd suspected as soon as he'd caught that first glimpse of them emerging from the trees, heard the soft, intimate music of their voices. James might have no experience himself, but he'd heard about men who indulged in…unnatural desires. Men who did the very things that he spent hours in his bed at night trying to imagine while he stroked his aching prick.

He would never have thought that *Iain* would want this, though. Iain, who was so manly and vigorous. Iain, who was the most bruising horseman James knew, who could bowl anyone out at cricket. Iain, who could run faster, climb higher, swim more strongly than anyone.

Without consciously deciding to do it, James found himself walking slowly towards the boathouse, his steps carefully silent. He knew these paths like the back of his hand, had been walking them since he was a tiny boy collecting tadpoles in spring, and he made no sound as he approached the wooden structure that housed the rowing boats for the lake.

Silently, he drew closer to the single, small window. A faint glow from within told him they'd lit a candle, a reckless decision since, even standing a couple of paces back from the glass, James could make out the two men inside as they came together.

They put their arms around each other so that they stood chest to chest, and then their lips were meeting—

They were *kissing* each other.

James's chest ached. He couldn't even put a name to the feelings that rushed through him at the sight of Iain Sinclair in Mellick's arms, kissing him with the same heated passion that James had seen between the upstairs maid and the second footman when he'd walked in on them in the stables last summer.

On the one hand, the realisation that Iain did this—this thing that James wanted to do so very badly—was like some great door of possibility opening wide.

On the other...he felt almost sick with the pain of witnessing Iain doing this with someone else.

And alongside those mingled feelings of excitement and pain, there was something else, something infinitely more physical. The crawling, insistent rise of his own arousal.

James watched, dry-mouthed, as Iain stepped back from Mellick and whipped his shirt over his head in a flash of white, revealing the broad line of his shoulders and the perfect planes of his smooth, pale back. When he stepped forwards again, he took Mellick's face into his hands and drew him into another passionate kiss.

Oh, *Jesus in heaven.*

James pressed the heel of his hand over his stiffening cock, the satin of his evening breeches smooth against his skin. He shuddered and bit his lip. He was going to lose himself right here, watching this.

After another minute or so of kissing, Mellick drew his head back, flashed Iain a grin, and dropped fluidly to his knees, busying himself with unfastening Iain's breeches while Iain rested one hand on Mellick's shoulder in a gesture that struck James as unexpectedly tender. He'd heard men talk about sodomites, and they always made the act sound appalling. Violent and brutal. Someone being made to bend and take it. Pain and shame. Who could ever want that?

This was nothing like that.

Once Mellick had unbuttoned Iain's placket, he glanced up again. He wasn't grinning now, but there was still a half smile on his face and his eyelids were half-lowered, giving him a look of languid promise. Slowly, without moving his gaze from Iain's face, he reached inside Iain's breeches and drew out his cock.

For several of James's frantic heartbeats, the groom simply admired Iain's sizeable prick, his frank gaze warm, then he leaned forward, engulfing it in his mouth.

Iain's head went back, eyes closing, lips parting in obvious pleasure.

Oh God.

James rubbed his hand over his breeches a few more times, but it wasn't enough. With a rough exhalation that was part helpless gasp, part protest, he ripped the buttons of his own breeches open and drew out his hard shaft.

Mellick's head was moving up and down. James couldn't see precisely what he was doing, but it didn't matter. He probably wouldn't have looked if he could see. His eyes were all for Iain, for the strong arch of his throat and the abandoned, almost painfully intimate expression on his face. For the way he gripped Mellick's shoulder with one hand and palmed the back of his head gently with the other, canting his hips forwards for more.

Oh God, Iain.

James's hand was moving with a steady rhythm now. As he watched Iain respond to Mellick's attentions, he felt oddly at one with him. Imagined that, somehow, Iain's pleasure was mounting at the same pace as his own.

Strange, to feel so intimately connected to someone who didn't even know he was there.

He saw the pleasure peak and crash through Iain's body. Saw the way his hand tightened, knuckles whitening, on Mellick's shoulder and his whole body seemed to go taut and still, other than his hips, which stuttered in Mellick's firm grip. And then James's own crisis was upon him. He bit his lip against the desire to cry out and, eyes still fixed on Iain Sinclair—now caressing Mellick's hair with seeming affection—stroked himself to a wrenching completion, spilling his seed on the ground like an offering.

After that, everything was different. The instant James's seed hit the ground, it was as though he'd sobered. Suddenly, he was aware of the cold of the night and the wetness from the grass seeping into his evening slippers. The window of the boathouse was grimy, and inside it looked little better.

This was unseemly—sordid and secretive. Pulling out his handkerchief, he cleaned himself up as best he could, hoping he hadn't marked his clothes, and fastened his breeches. When he looked up, Mellick was back on his feet, and Iain was the one lowering himself to the floor.

James's heart twisted at the sight. He didn't want to see any more.

Instead, he spun on his heel and ran back to the house to join the party again.

6

Now: 1824

27ᵗʰ May, 1824

   On the way to Holmewell, Hampshire

By the time Iain was halfway to Hampshire, he was regretting accepting his sister Isabel's offer of a place in her carriage.

The setup was certainly as comfortable as it could be, with blankets and cushions and baskets of refreshments—and thankfully, Isabel's four very loud children were in a separate carriage with their nursemaid—but Iain had forgotten just how much his sister *talked*. She never let up the whole way. She seemed to have decided that, since Iain hadn't attended any Hart family events for a few years, she ought to inform him of every little thing that had happened in the Hart clan since then, as though he might be examined on the topic as soon as he walked through the door. Every baby that had been born—and there seemed to have been legions of them— was identified, along with their godparents and christening arrangements. Every illness and death was covered in excruciating detail, with particular attention given to a bout of mumps suffered by Kate's youngest boy, Harry.

Eventually, though, Isabel turned her attention to the one and only member of the Hart family about whom Iain actually gave a damn.

"Apparently, there's still no sign of James marrying," she said. "Kate says he's on his way to becoming a confirmed bachelor."

Iain schooled his features into a neutral expression. "Well, he's only—what, three- or four-and-twenty?" In truth, he knew James's age very well, but it was better to seem only vaguely interested. "Plenty of time to find a wife," he added.

"He's five-and-twenty, actually," Isabel corrected absently. "But Kate says he's never shown the slightest interest in any young lady."

Isabel's husband, Bertie, gave a tiny snort at that, and Iain glanced at him, wondering what had prompted that reaction. Did he suspect James of being a sodomite? Iain didn't think James was obvious, not in the way of some men he knew, but nor was he as thoroughly...well, *masculine* as Iain. He didn't seem to have mastered the sort of overtly male mannerisms that Iain had. But then Iain had been utterly determined from boyhood to exhibit no sign of his secret inclinations—James did not seem to suffer from the same anxieties.

Sometimes, Iain thought James moved his hands in a suspiciously graceful way as he spoke. And he did have that habit of crossing his legs and leaning towards one in a confiding way when he was talking about something that amused him. Tiny things, really. Nothing to them, only they'd struck Iain on occasion as small betrayals. And perhaps they had struck others similarly.

When they were alone, and James did little things like that, Iain...*liked* it. But when James did those things in front of others, Iain became uncomfortable, and found himself wishing James would be a little more circumspect. But James was different from Iain. Unlike Iain, he didn't spend his every waking hour trying not to betray himself or worrying about bringing shame on his family. He didn't have to be mindful, as Iain did, that if he caused his parents to lose a second son, the cost would be unendurable.

"…because he's so engrossed in his plants. Apparently, he spends all his time at Wylde Manor either out gathering specimens or closed up in his study, peering at them through one of his contraptions."

Belatedly, Iain realised his sister was talking again, and that he hadn't been listening to a word of what she'd been saying—except that last part, which made it clear she was still on the subject of James.

"Is that so?" he replied, aiming for polite interest.

"Yes, indeed," Isabel continued, seeming to warm to her subject. "Kate told me it took all her powers of persuasion just to get him to come to Holmewell this week, and even then, she says he only agreed because there's some butterfly or moth he wants to find while he's here." She laughed. "Honestly, it's such a waste of time, but then his father was the same, do you remember? Always out with a satchel, grubbing around in the dirt to find some old weed or bit of grass."

"His father was a renowned scientist," Iain pointed out. "And so is James. He's published papers."

Isabel's eyebrows rose at Iain's defence of the Hart men. She glanced at Bertie and added in a quieter voice, as though she thought Iain couldn't hear, "He was always protective of James, even when we were children."

"Only because you and Kate and Lucy teased him so much," Iain said. "Someone had to stick up for him. God knows he was no good at sticking up for himself."

Isabel laughed. "Do you remember when you insisted that you and James alone would play cricket against *all* of us girls?" She glanced at her husband. "There were *five* of us and only two of them."

"You weren't going to let him play at all," Iain pointed out.

"We already had even numbers without him!" Isabel protested, laughing. "And of course, the two of you had to win, didn't you?"

Bertie laughed. "I'm not surprised," he said. "Iain was ripping at cricket at school." He glanced Iain's way, his expression a mixture of approval and envy. "You could bowl out anyone—even us older boys."

"Oh, well, he was ripping at *everything*, wasn't he?" Isabel replied, rolling her eyes. "It's hardly surprising that James hero-worshipped him. Do you remember, Iain? He used to look at you as though you'd hung the sun in the sky."

Iain was mortified to feel heat warming his cheeks. "Well, I *was* four years older," he said, turning his head to hide his blush. He stared out of the window at the rolling countryside. The truth was, he remembered too well how James used to look at him, not just when James was a little boy, but later too, when he was a fully grown man. Most especially, he remembered the passionate devotion with which James had looked at him the last time Iain had visited Wylde Manor. And how he'd looked, months later, when he hunted Iain down in London.

The ultimate disillusionment in that turbulent grey gaze.

Could Iain really hope to remedy that?

Perhaps it was a mistake to have come to Hampshire. It was certainly a mistake to have come with Isabel. If he'd journeyed alone, he could have stopped in his tracks and gone straight back to London. Made some pathetic excuse for not showing his face at Kate's party. But there was no doing that now—already the carriage was swinging through the great iron gates of Holmewell, slowing down and halting outside a modern Palladian mansion, the grand house built by Sir

Edward's father on the occasion of being granted his brand-new title thirty years earlier.

Their arrival was chaotic. The other carriage had arrived first, and the children were standing on the steps with their frazzled nursemaid, little Margaret bawling her eyes out. The reason became apparent as soon as they got out—Margaret had been sick on the steps of the house and was demanding her mother. While Isabel comforted her, the other children vied for their mother's attention, tugging on her skirts and badgering her with questions like a gaggle of greedy goslings. The coachmen and grooms began unloading the carriages, only to drop a valise from the roof of the carriage, narrowly missing Bertie, which sent the nursemaid into a fit of mild hysterics and made Isabel fairly squawk with outrage.

It was a relief when Kate's housekeeper emerged and began to take calm control, at least of the servants. She was followed by the lady of the house.

"Izzy, darling!" Kate drifted down the steps into the chaos and made everything right. She entered the fray of children with seeming ease, embraced Isabel, kissed Margaret, greeted the rest of the children with pats to their little heads, bestowed a smile on the poor nursemaid and teased Bertie about the silver hairs at his temples.

Finally, she reached Iain.

"Iain, dear. It's been far too long," she scolded him, squeezing his hands affectionately. "I'm glad you're here at last, though. I'd wondered if you'd come."

He pretended bewilderment at that last comment, as though he hadn't declined her last half-dozen invitations. "I can't imagine why you'd wonder about that," he said. "It's always pleasant to visit Holmewell."

Kate raised an amused brow, but she didn't challenge him, for which he was absurdly grateful.

"Why don't you and Bertie go and have some tea in the drawing room," she suggested. "Your mother's there already.

Izzy and I will follow in a little while once we've settled poor Margaret." She glanced at the housekeeper. "Mrs. Halliday, would you show the gentlemen to the drawing room?"

Iain suppressed the sudden urge to ask if James was in the drawing room, simply nodding instead and following Mrs. Halliday and Bertie into the house.

They were walking down the main corridor towards the drawing room when an unholy shriek split the air. A little girl with a mane of fat blonde ringlets burst out of one of the rooms and into their path, frantically plucking at the back of her dress and squirming. She shrieked again, then screamed, "I *hate* you, Christopher Potts!"

From inside the room came screeches of childish laughter, then a maid hurried out.

"Miss Emily!" she hissed, glancing nervously at the housekeeper and two gentlemen, who now stood in the corridor, staring at the enraged child. "What's this about? What's Christopher done?"

Iain glanced inside the room—there was a table next to the window, set with teacups and plates of sticky buns and other treats. The rest of the furniture had been moved aside, and the large rug that usually covered the floor had been rolled up, leaving lots of space for the dozen or so children in the room to run around and play. Evidently, the children were having their own tea party in there, while the grown-ups enjoyed a more civilised affair nearby.

"He put a spider down my neck!" the little girl wailed. She wriggled inside her dress, trying to pull the fabric away from her skin and shake out the intruder, still evading the hapless maid. "He's *horrid*!"

Iain bit his lip to suppress a laugh.

"Perhaps—" the housekeeper began, stepping forwards, only to be interrupted when a boy rushed out of the room, skidding to a halt in front of her. He was nine or ten, Iain guessed. A sturdy, energetic little boy with a shock of dark hair and a mischievous grin he couldn't quite put away, even as he attempted to look contrite.

"It wasn't a spider, Emily," he said, all in a rush. "I was teasing you. It was just a scrunched-up leaf." He glanced, guiltily, at the four adults staring at him and added weakly, "It was a joke…"

Emily stopped dancing on the spot. She stared at the boy in horror before bursting into noisy tears. The maid coaxed her back into the room, with another apologetic look at Mrs. Halliday, who merely pressed her lips together.

"Master Potts," the housekeeper said, very quietly yet firmly. "That was not well done."

The boy's face reddened. "Are you going to tell Mama?" he whispered. "I'm already in trouble about the china shepherdess I broke this morning."

Bertie snorted at that, and Iain had to look away to hide his amusement. Boys were ever thus, it seemed. His own childhood had been an endless parade of just such incidents.

"If I remember," Mrs. Halliday said quietly, "I shall certainly have to say something to your mother. But perhaps if you play nicely for the rest of the afternoon, it may…slip my mind."

The boy nodded and garbled out his thanks before dashing back into the children's party room and closing the door behind him.

Mrs. Halliday glanced guiltily at Iain and Bertie. Uncomfortably, she said, "Rest assured, I will certainly speak with the boy's—"

"Please don't tell his mother on my account," Iain interrupted.

"Or mine," Bertie added. "Boys will be boys, after all."

Mrs. Halliday paused, then she inclined her head gracefully and set off again, passing another few doors before she stopped at one a little further along the corridor and opened it, stepping aside to allow them to pass through.

This, at last, was the drawing room. There were a number of guests milling around, some sitting, others standing around in groups, chatting. Bertie made for a small group that included Iain's mother, calling out a merry greeting as he strolled towards them. Iain, however, stood frozen in the doorway. He had eyes for only one person.

James stood on the far side of the large room, in front of the window. The sunlight streaming through the glass gilded his dark blond head, granting it the lustre of old gold, and as always, he looked a little rumpled, his cravat a little askew. He was talking, or rather listening, to a paunchy vicar with a prosy look on his face. Judging by James's bored expression, he wasn't much taken with what the vicar was saying.

Iain found himself willing James to look up, to see him. He wanted to see surprise and pleasure transform James's expression, like in the old days. But when James finally looked his way…

…his face *fell*.

Iain felt as though he'd been kicked by a horse, shock drowning out pain till James looked away, as though a stranger, rather than his dearest friend—or at least the man he'd once called his dearest friend—had just walked into the room.

Pain came then, a wrenching ache in his chest that he had to somehow ignore as he finally made his feet move, made himself step into the room and join Bertie and his mother. Bertie's sister Anthea was in the same group, along with her two daughters. The last time Iain had seen Bertie's nieces, they'd been hoydenish children, getting into all sorts of scrapes. Now they were young ladies, uncharacteristically demure in white muslin.

"Iain, darling, you're here!" his mother exclaimed, rising from her chair. She sounded surprised. Had she thought he wouldn't come?

He bowed over his mother's hands, pressing a kiss to each

set of knuckles. "I told you I was coming," he said as he straightened.

"Yes, but"—she paused, her hesitation obvious—"well, I'm glad you're here, at any rate." She smiled brightly.

Her surprise at his appearance irritated him for some reason, though he knew perfectly well the reason for it. For years, his family and the Harts had visited each other's houses regularly. Not only that, but Iain and James, being particular friends, had seen one another separately from these family gatherings.

Until Iain had stopped seeing James or even mentioning him.

After years of going to sometimes extraordinary lengths to make sure he was able to attend any Hart family invitation, over the last several years, Iain had been finding the flimsiest of excuses to stay away.

Evidently, his mother had noticed.

He watched as she settled herself back into her chair and reached for the teapot. She poured him a cup of tea, adding milk before handing it up to him. "James is here," she said, gesturing vaguely at the other side of the room.

"Yes, I saw him," Iain said, sipping the tea. "I'll go and speak to him in a minute." He paused, then asked carefully, "Where's Father?"

"Oh, resting," his mother said airily. "It was a long journey." His poor mother. She'd had years of having to excuse Iain's father's erratic behaviour and inexplicable absences, and he knew it mortified her.

"I'm rather surprised he's here," Iain added. "It's the first time he's been to one of these parties in years, isn't it?"

She gave him an odd look, then said, "He might say the same about you."

There wasn't much Iain could say to that, so he just smiled at her, acknowledging the point, and helped himself to a slice of seed cake.

For the next little while, Iain made small talk with his mother and Anthea, sipping tea and nibbling cake that may as well have been dust for all Iain could taste. But even as he went through these motions, all he could think of was James standing over by the window. As soon as he could decently move on, he did, slowly beginning to work his way round the room. He chatted to the other guests, strolling from group to group, slowly, inexorably making his way towards James. He greeted the guests he already knew with his usual good humour and introduced himself to those he didn't with easy charm. Despite his preoccupation, it wasn't particularly difficult to get through the social niceties. This was, after all, how he spent most of his time in the King's service. It was just a matter of donning the same well-worn disguise he used every day. A mask that had long ago grown so comfortable, he barely felt it anymore.

It seemed to take forever to wend his way round the room, but eventually he was there, stepping up to join James and the prosy-looking vicar who was still bending his ear.

"Hart," Iain called out as he approached. He always called James "Hart" in front of others. "It's good to see you—it's been an age."

James looked up. He said nothing, just looked at Iain with a flat expression Iain had never seen before that made his stomach feel hollowed out.

Oddly shaken by that reaction, Iain turned to the vicar offering him a strained smile. "How rude of me. We've not been introduced. Mister…?"

"Potts," the vicar supplied. The errant Christopher's father? Iain wondered. They shook hands.

After a pause, Potts asked, "And you are?"

"Capt—sorry, I beg your pardon, *Mr.* Sinclair." He offered the vicar an apologetic smile. "I've just resigned my commission, and I am not quite used to my change of title."

"Pardon?"

That came from James. Iain turned back to find James was looking at him as though he had grown another head.

"I've resigned my commission," Iain repeated. "I am no longer in the army."

James stared at him. Eventually, he said, "Well, I confess I'm surprised."

"How long were you in the army, Mr. Sinclair?" Potts asked.

Iain didn't even acknowledge the question, too caught up in James. "Why would you be surprised?" he asked.

"It was the only thing you ever wanted to do," James replied. "It's difficult to imagine you doing anything else."

Their gazes caught and held. There was a beat of silence that stretched too long, until the vicar cleared his throat, reminding Iain abruptly of his presence. The way Iain jerked his head to look at the man—and James did the same—clearly indicated they had practically forgotten his presence.

Potts pressed his lips together, annoyed. "Well," he said loftily. "If you'll excuse me, I'll leave you gentlemen to your conversation." And with that, he swept off.

Iain glanced at James, who frowned at the vicar's back for a moment before giving Iain his attention again, his expression somehow guarded, only the slightest pucker between his dark blond brows. And Iain found, for probably the first time ever, that he wasn't at all sure what James was thinking.

It was a disconcerting thought. He used to find James so easy to read. From boyhood, James hadn't seen the point in subterfuge. He was the most straightforward person Iain knew. Direct, utterly lacking in any guile. As different from Iain as could be, and Iain had loved that about him. Loved that, if he asked James a question, James would answer immediately and with absolute honesty. Loved too that his directness owed nothing to innocence or naïveté but was simply an expression of his essential character.

He'd loved it, and he'd hated it too, because there was no hiding with James.

Until now.

"Have I offended him?" Iain asked as they watched Potts walk away.

"Probably," James replied, then he shrugged. "But I suspect being offended is Mr. Potts's natural state. He'll be pleased to have something to feel aggrieved by, I expect."

It was a typically James thing to say, and therefore reassuring. Iain smiled at him.

"I'm glad you're here, Jamie," he said softly. "I've wanted to talk with you for a long time. When we quarrelled—"

"We did not quarrel," James interrupted. His quick, nervous glance at the other guests was new, unlike him. He lowered his voice still further before he spoke again. His tone was very firm, though, despite its hushed quality. "I offered my heart to you, and you refused me. That is all."

"James, *please*—" Iain broke off when he noticed James's brows lowering unhappily. Only then did he realise that he'd taken a step towards the other man, and that his own voice was probably too loud.

James took a discreet step back. "I have nothing to say to you." He sounded bewildered, as though he couldn't imagine why Iain was standing there in front of him. "We said everything that needed to be said the last time we saw each other."

Iain swallowed hard. "James." He clenched his fists at his sides. "Now is not the time, but please, hear me out privately. I can't bear us not being friends anymore."

James blinked at him. "I'm sorry about that," he replied at last, "truly. But the fact is, *I* can't bear *being* your friend." His tone was kindly, but the words were deadly, and all Iain could do was stare at him in silence, his chest aching.

After a long pause, he cleared his throat. "Well," he said carefully. "I hope to change your mind about that—to show you that my friendship is worth having." He paused. "I hope

I can convince you, James. If I cannot, then I probably don't deserve to call you my friend anyway."

James just sighed. "You're being obtuse. Don't you remember what you said to me the last time I saw you?"

"I remember. I—"

James went on as though he hadn't spoken. "You wanted me to stop embarrassing you with my—what was it you called it? Oh yes. My 'childish devotion'."

Iain winced at that reminder. "James—"

But James was already sidestepping him. "As pleasant as it's been to renew our acquaintance the simple fact is, I see no point in restoring our friendship."

And giving one last polite nod, he walked away, crossing the floor to join another group of guests, leaving Iain standing on his own in the middle of the drawing room.

7

THEN: 1818

23rd September, 1818
  London

As James waited for Lieutenant Iain Sinclair to arrive at the Hart family townhouse one chilly late September morning, he found himself noticing for the first time how very *pink* the drawing room was. The sofa he sprawled upon was upholstered in ivory fabric dotted with tiny pink flowers. It matched the pale pink wallpaper and the rose-pink curtains on the windows. Everything had been chosen by his mother, of course, and pink was her favourite colour.

The fact that he had only noticed this today of all days was not because he was ordinarily unobservant. Quite the opposite. It was because his mother had finally decided to remove the crepe covers from the furniture and have the drapes changed back from the heavy black ones that had covered the windows for the last year since his father's death. His mother still wore her widow's weeds, but the formal period of full mourning was past now—although James wasn't sure his own grief would ever truly be over.

Now that his father was gone, James was, apparently, the head of the family. He didn't *feel* like the head of the family, though. His household was a very feminine one, and he was the youngest person in it, and the only male.

James's mother and four sisters all adored him, but they were about as likely to pay him any mind as they would be to fly in the air. If he governed them at all, it was in name only, as this ridiculously pink-and-white room proved.

In truth, he felt starved for male companionship—or perhaps he was just starved for Iain. He hadn't seen his friend since his father's burial the year before. Since then, he felt like he'd made up two or three years' growth, putting on four inches and filling out his slender frame besides. At nineteen, he felt he'd finally grown up, just when he'd thought he was going to stay short and skinny forever.

He couldn't help wondering what Iain would think of him now, and of course, that thought brought an old and much-revisited memory to the forefront of his mind—of Iain and Mellick in the boatshed at Wylde Manor. Except that now, James imagined himself in Mellick's place, falling to his knees and looking up and…

…and this was *not* the time to be thinking of such things. The last thing he needed was to be sporting a cockstand when Iain arrived…

To distract himself, he stood and went to the mirror over the mantelpiece to fiddle nervously with his cravat again. He'd spent ages trying to perfect a creditable Waterfall this morning but had ended up handling the linen so much, the starchiness had gone out of it. Now it was wilting, and continuing to tweak at it wasn't helping. Ah, well, he was never going to be a dandy, that much was certain. Sighing, he turned away from the mirror and paced to the window that looked out onto the Square.

Where the hell was Iain?

It was a cold autumn day, and everything was grey and dull, from the overcast sky to the rain-slick cobbles. A gusty, unpredictable breeze was sending up bits of straw and fallen leaves from the gutters to dance round the ankles of the few passersby. Everyone was huddled into their coats, shoulders hunched against the wind. All except one man, who came round the corner in a flash of scarlet, tall and upright, splendid in his uniform.

Lieutenant Iain Sinclair strode across the square with purpose, and everything about him was vital and bright.

James's breath caught in his throat at the sight of him. He felt sure there would never be anyone else who would be able to make him feel like this. He'd always admired Iain, since they'd been boys, but after the night he'd seen him with Mellick, three years before, everything had changed. Before then, if James had thought about his friend's distant future at all, it was a future in which Iain had a woman by his side and a full nursery. He would, of course, win the loveliest of girls to be his wife and have the most accomplished and beautiful children.

Except it had turned out that Iain was probably about as interested in young ladies as James was, lovely or otherwise. And if someone like Iain—someone with all the masculine virtues—felt that way, didn't that *mean* something? People always said that men who indulged in forbidden acts with other men were weak, venal, degenerate. But James had been observing Iain for years before he saw him with Mellick, and there was nothing weak or degenerate about him. He wasn't just handsome and accomplished, he was *good*. Brave and kind. Everything a man ought to be.

James had thought about this a lot over the last few years. And ultimately, he had done as his father had always taught him: considered the evidence and drawn his conclusions from that, determining, finally, that there was nothing wrong with

Iain Sinclair. And if that was right—and he felt sure it was—then the next, inexorable conclusion was that there was nothing wrong with James either. That they weren't wicked degenerates, just another sort of person. Classifiable, like James's specimens, with a place on the taxonomic table as valuable as any other sort of being in the world.

Iain was drawing close to the house now, and when he glanced up at the drawing room window and saw James standing there, he lifted his hand in greeting, his bright smile flashing. He'd grown a moustache since the funeral. It was the same glossy dark brown as the hair on his head, and beneath it, his teeth were white and even. James sighed. He really was a handsome devil.

James raised his own arm automatically, loving the way Iain's smile widened a little at the sight, and the glint of humour and affection in the man's eyes as he mounted the steps.

He disappeared from view as he approached the door and James turned away from the window, heart racing, breathless with excitement. His palms felt suddenly damp, and he wiped them on his trousers nervously. It had been a year. Would Iain notice how much he'd changed? He hoped so, even as he dreaded any mention of it.

And then the door to the drawing room was opening, and Iain was striding into the room, his shako under his arm. He cast it aside—tossing it onto the pink-and-white sofa without so much as a sideways glance—then he stepped right up to James and took his shoulders in his hands, leaning back a little to look him over.

"My God, Jamie!" he exclaimed. "Look at you! Christ, if you grow any more, you'll be taller than me, and that will never do!" He grinned at that, lifting his hand to ruffle James's hair with rough affection.

James laughed a little shakily, his mouth stretched help-lessly wide in a smile that would not be contained. He was

61

still a little shorter than Iain, but there were only a couple of inches between them now.

"I've grown a lot this year," he admitted.

Iain laughed and released him. "You look very different. A man now. Not a boy any longer."

James bit his lip against his smile, pleased that Iain saw him as he was.

"And you're at university. Are you liking it?"

"Famously," James said, trying to sound casual. "Would you like some tea?"

"In truth, I'd prefer a tankard of ale," Iain said, still grinning. "This is the first day of leisure I've had in a long while and I'm back on duty tomorrow morning. I didn't even put off time to change my clothes but came straight here. And now—well, since I find you're a man now, Jamie, shall we make merry hell together? I'd as lief make the most of this day!"

"By all means, ale rather than tea," James replied cheerfully, secretly delighted by this turn of events. Iain must truly see him as a man now to suggest such a thing. "Where shall we go?"

Iain's expression turned mischievous. "Have you ever seen a boxing match, Jamie?"

The boxing match was happening in a field at the back of an inn just past the outskirts of the city. Iain suggested James drive them there, and James was happy to agree—it would give him a chance to show off his brand-new curricle.

When he'd first gone to the carriage makers to purchase a gig, he'd been immediately drawn to a flashy high-perched phaeton. Thankfully, he'd taken his older cousin with him, and when Anthony had seen James's choice, he'd laughed, declaring it was precisely the sort of curricle he'd expect a lad of nineteen to choose.

The one he'd ended up purchasing, following Anthony's advice, was plainer and sleeker—lighter too. It drove like a dream, turning on a sixpence, and when Iain clapped eyes on it, his approving expression obliterated any remaining doubts James had harboured about his selection.

Iain gave a low whistle. "What a beauty," he said, his gaze reverent. "I'll bet she handles well." When the groom led James's new bays out of the stable, Iain was even more impressed—well, the man loved his horses, and the bays were a beautifully matched pair. Iain stepped forwards to rub their noses and croon nonsense to them while the groom got them rigged up to the curricle. Only when they were in their traces and ready to go did he jump up beside James, settling himself on the narrow bench.

And then they were on their way, first trotting out of Mayfair, then out of the city altogether, past the outskirts and right into the countryside beyond.

They spoke nonstop as they drove, or at least James did. He told Iain about university and the new friends he'd made, about the dons and their eccentricities, and his first experiences as a young man living on his own. He loved the sound of Iain's ready laughter at his self-deprecating stories, basked in the interest and warmth in his blue gaze.

"And what about you?" he asked at last, realising a little shamefacedly that he'd done nothing but talk about himself since they set off.

"Oh, I'm well enough," Iain said. He spoke with his usual ease, but James still found himself glancing over, alert to the tiny note of reserve in his words. Iain added, "My squadron is being posted somewhere in the north for a while—Manchester, most likely."

"Why there?"

"You'll have heard about the political unrest, I'm sure,"

Iain said, shrugging. "Protests and riots abound. We're being sent to keep order." He sighed then, deeply.

"You don't look very happy about it."

"No," Iain agreed. "I'm not. I didn't join the army to fight Englishmen." He paused. "And certainly not Englishwomen."

James took that in, a little shocked. After a while, he said, "You think there will be fighting, then?"

"Of a sort. There won't exactly be an equality of arms." He shook his head. "My fellow officers keep telling me I'm lucky to be alive after what happened to my regiment at Waterloo, that I should be glad of getting such an easy posting—but I don't find this easy. They expect us to charge on order at crowds of our own countrymen and women." He shook his head and sighed heavily.

James had never seen Iain looking so unhappy.

"Have you ever thought about selling your commission?" he asked.

Iain shook his head. "I couldn't do that," he said.

"Why not?"

Iain stared straight ahead, saying nothing for a long time. James thought he wasn't going to answer at all till at last he shrugged and said quietly, "It's a matter of family honour."

Just that. And somehow James knew it wouldn't be a good idea to ask Iain what he meant. Instead, he nodded and let a companionable silence fall.

Despite the cold, there were plenty of other spectators on the way to the match, so many that the road was badly clogged for the last couple of miles, slowing them down practically to walking pace. Finally, though, they reached the field behind the White Hare Inn, and James brought the curricle to a halt, drawing it up alongside a row of other gigs and carriages behind a sign marked Betting Stand.

"It's so busy." James eyed the crowd in front of them with dismay.

"Lucky we have a nice high curricle to watch from, then," said Iain, whose pensive mood seemed to have lifted now.

"Oh," James replied. "I didn't think of that."

"We'll be further back than the people at the front," Iain pointed out. "But at least we'll see the fight."

"True."

"Right, then." Iain clapped his hands together. "Time to get ourselves some ale and some food! You wait here—I'll be back directly."

With that, he jumped down from the curricle, promising to return directly with provisions. James watched him stroll towards the White Hare Inn, which seemed to be doing a roaring trade. While he waited, he amused himself by watching the antics of the vast crowd of shouting, swearing men that surrounded him. They came from every possible walk of life—from gentlemen to gypsies—and with no women present, none that James could see, anyway, there was a feeling of edgy egalitarianism. It felt as though anything could happen here.

At last, a good half hour after he left, Iain returned, swinging a large, pot flagon of ale in one hand and balancing two hand-sized pies in the other, one on top of the other.

"You'll have to swig your ale from that," Iain informed James, thrusting the flagon into his hands before climbing back up onto the gig one-handed, passing one pie to James and keeping the other for himself. He bit into his own pie with a muffled groan of pleasure and began to chew with relish.

James lifted his pie to his mouth. It was still warm, and the meaty filling smelled wonderful. It was only then that he realised how hungry he was, his belly grouching as though on cue. He demolished the pie in a few mouthfuls, brushing the crumbs from his fingers after.

As tasty as the pie was, the filling had been salty and James reached for the ale as soon as he was done, pulling out the cork and drinking deeply of the dark, hoppy beer. It was strong, far stronger than the ale he drank at home. This was more like stout, treacle brown and sweetish. It tasted good, so James drank more.

"You're fairly getting through the ale," Iain said at one point. He was smiling but frowning slightly too. "It's not a race, you know."

"I'm fine," James protested, slapping Iain on the shoulder. "It's just ale, not spirits."

Iain raised a brow at him, but he said no more about it.

It seemed to take forever for the fight to start. They waited and waited—and drank—as spectators continued to arrive, the field filling up till it was ringed with carriages and there was a crowd seven or eight deep all round. Then, at last, two fighters stepped out onto the grass.

"This is it!" James said excitedly.

"Not quite," Iain replied. "There're two other bouts before the main event. These are untried fighters."

Untried they might be, but their appearance provoked a prolonged betting frenzy, which meant more waiting.

"I'll get more ale," James informed Iain, hopping down from the curricle with the now-empty flagon.

"All right. Get more pies too, if there are any."

The pies were long gone by the time he made it to the front of the line of men that stretched out of the taproom of the White Hare Inn and looped all the way round the courtyard, but the innkeeper filled the empty flagon with more of the dark, treacly beer and sold him a few pickled eggs, which he wrapped in brown paper so James could pop them in his pocket.

By the time he made it back, the first fight was over—there had been a dramatic knockout, apparently—and the second was about to begin. Iain's rapt attention flickered only when James offered him a pickled egg.

"Good Lord!" he said, eyeing the yellowish orbs. "We'll be

taking our life in our hands eating these, Jamie. They look ancient."

"I don't care," James said. "I'm ravenous." He bit one in half defiantly, then practically retched—they were so vinegary, they made his eyes water. Iain burst out laughing at his expression, and then James started laughing too, spraying egg out of his mouth.

He tried to show an interest in the main fight—but no matter how much Iain tried to capture his attention with talk of throwing and parrying and returning, he found it difficult to concentrate. More entertaining by far to drink the ale and watch the crowd, all by Iain's side. That was the real treat for him, just being here, with his friend. The two of them, shoulder to shoulder on the curricle, Iain's flank and thigh warm against James's and his ready, glinting smile flashing under his new moustache. The thrill, each time James drank from the flagon, of placing his mouth where Iain's lips had just been.

It was a wonderful day. Nobody else made him laugh like Iain did, or listened to him the way Iain did. There was no one else but Iain who made James happy just from being able to *look* at him. When he rested his eyes on Iain, he felt warm and glad inside. He couldn't gaze at him the way he wanted to, but there were plenty of chances to steal sideways glances that afternoon. And sometimes, when their eyes met, Iain would give him that special smile James liked to think was just for him. Fond and affectionate. Intimate.

When all the fights were over, James couldn't have said who'd won any of them, but he was so content, he was unable to put his smile away. Iain jumped down from the curricle to go and collect his winnings, promising to be back directly, and James groped around for the ale, finally finding the flagon and upending it one last time, surprised to get naught but a dribble. He lifted the flagon a little higher to peer inside, closing one eye to get a better look, but his concentration was broken when something hit the back of his head, something cold and wettish.

"I said *move your arse*, you fucking molly!" someone shouted behind him. "You're holding everyone up!"

A chorus of jeering laughter followed while James dropped the flagon to the floor of the curricle and pawed the back of his head, his good cheer dissolving on a wave of sour fear and trembling anger. He found his assailant's weapon—a clod of mud—and cast it aside, then looked around for the man who had thrown it at him.

He was in the gig behind James's own, standing up in the driver's seat, brandishing a whip. His face was mottled and slack with too much drink.

"Are you deaf?" he sneered. "Or do you just need your soldier *friend* to come and drive yer gig? Is he another *backgammon player* like you?"

There were shouts of laughter and more jeering at that, and James drew his shoulders back, his anger beginning to overtake his initial alarm now that the drunk was starting in on Iain too.

"Shut your damned mouth," he snapped. "I'll move my gig when it suits me to do it. Be thankful I don't come over there and teach you a lesson."

Mortifyingly, the drunk burst out laughing at that. "Ooh!" he exclaimed in a high feminine voice. "The lad's goin' to come over and 'orsewhip me, lads! Whatever shall I do?"

"Teach 'im a lesson, Ned!" someone yelled out behind him.

"You're right," Ned called back. "He needs to learn some manners." He fixed an ugly look on James, adding, "I saw you making up to your soldier friend. You think you're better than me, but you're nothing but a filthy little sod."

He began to climb down from his gig, and James steeled himself for what was looking like an inevitable brawl, casting his gaze around his curricle for some kind of weapon—until a choked cry drew his attention back to his would-be assailant. He looked up and saw a scarlet-clad figure dragging the man, still mid-descent, from his gig and throwing him bodily to the ground.

Iain.

James gasped and got to his feet, making the curricle rock.

This was Iain as James had never seen him before. His friend was always the very picture of merry good humour, always a smile on his face, a twinkle in his eye. But this man looked dangerous and very angry.

Iain smiled nastily at the man—Ned—who was now sprawled at his feet. "Feeling brave, are you? Come on, then." He gestured at the man to get up for the fight he'd said he wanted with James, but Ned stayed where he was on the ground.

His throat bobbed as he swallowed hard. "I didn't mean —" he began, but Iain cut him off.

"Yes, you did," he said in a tone that was a mockery of encouragement. "You said you were going to teach us some manners, so come on, then. Let's get this lesson of yours." He laughed into the silence that followed, a harsh bark of a sound. "Changed your mind, have you?"

Ned just stared at him fearfully. Iain leaned down, grabbing a fistful of his coat and jerking him forward, raising a fist as though to punch him. Ned cried out, raising his hands to cover his face. "*Please*—" he cried.

Iain laughed again and let his fist unfurl. Instead of punching him, he gave them man a humiliating open-handed cuff to the back of his head before letting him fall back to the ground.

"Fucking coward," he concluded in a disgusted tone.

There were no jeers from anyone else now—the man's friends, if he'd ever had any, had moved on or were staying silent. The bystanders backed away, pulling horses aside and focusing their gazes elsewhere. Iain's lip curled in a sneer that

JOANNA CHAMBERS

encompassed all of them. After one last contemptuous look at the man on the ground, he turned on his heel and crossed to the curricle, unhurriedly climbing up to sit beside James.

Despite all he'd drunk, Iain looked sober, his blue gaze steady and clear. For some reason, that made James feel even more inebriated than he had before. He found he couldn't focus on Iain and had to close his eyes against a sudden swimming sensation, cringing a little when he heard Iain sigh.

"I shouldn't have let you drink so much," he said, his tone regretful. "Come on, I'll drive us home."

He took the reins gently from James's hands.

"You didn't need to save me," James mumbled. "I wasn't going to let him beat me. I can look after myself."

Iain didn't answer that, just gave him a long, hard look. Then he clucked at the horses and flicked the reins, and a moment later, they were on their way. And it was all James could do not to cast up his accounts over Iain's lap from the rocking of the carriage.

8

Almost two hours later, when Iain brought the curricle to a halt outside the townhouse, James was no more sober than he'd been before they'd set off. The ale he'd been supping all day had well and truly settled into his system, and he seemed thoroughly, if happily, foxed.

"Come in," James urged as Iain extricated him from the curricle. "Come and have some dinner, and we'll open a bottle of claret. We've had nothing but a meat pie all day. Although I had that pickled egg, didn't I?" He made a retching face.

"Claret?" Iain exclaimed. "You shouldn't be having anything stronger than tea in your state. Your mother's going to have me up on corruption charges."

James just waved his hand. "Mother's away. Sisters too." He grinned sloppily at Iain. "They've gone to Hampshire for a few days, to Sir Edward Porter's estate. Sir Edward's finally come up to scratch—he's going to propose to Kate. Can you believe he asked me *permission*?" He laughed uproariously at that, and Iain had to laugh too. Porter had to be ten years James's senior and exceedingly high in the instep—the idea of him petitioning James for permission to pay his addresses to Kate was an amusing one.

"What did you say?"

"I said, 'Don't ask me, ask Kate,' of course. She'd've had my hide if I so much as dared an opinion of any suitor of hers!"

Iain chuckled. "Why aren't you in Hampshire too, then?" he asked, handing the reins to the groom who'd appeared to attend to the horses, and steering James towards the front door, which was presently being held open by an impassive footman.

"I'm going tomorrow," James replied. "Didn't want to miss out"—he broke off and hiccoughed—"on seeing you."

Iain didn't know what to say to that, especially when James looked up at him, a stupidly happy expression on his face—happy and hopeful and unguarded. As though Iain was the best thing he'd ever seen. For some reason, that expression made Iain feel both pleased and panicked at the same time. James had been looking at him like that all day, which was doubtless why that loathsome fellow had started in on him, calling him a molly. Christ, when he'd heard that exchange on his way back to the curricle, the anger that had gripped him had been overwhelming. He'd wanted to the pound the man's face to bloody pulp for threatening James.

James, a molly?

Hell.

Sighing, Iain led James up the steps to the house and through the front door, pausing to murmur to the footman, "Which way to Mr. Hart's rooms? I think he needs to get to bed now."

"First floor, sir," the footman replied, swiftly lighting a candle for Iain and handing it to him. "Second door on the right. Do you want me to lead the way?" Iain shook his head. He tried to steer James towards the stairs, but James dug his heels in.

"Tell Mrs. Legget we want a good dinner, Ridley," he said to the footman. "Something *excellent* for Lieutenant Sinclair and myself. And wine!" He chuckled. "Lots of wine."

The footman sent Iain a helpless look at that. Iain just shook his head and smiled, using one hand to turn James back to the stairs and urge him forward. Looking back over his shoulder, he murmured to the footman, "Just some tea and toast."

The footman nodded and slipped away.

Iain walked James up the stairs with a firm hand at the small of his back. James was all over the place, chatty and unsteady on his feet, slurring his words a little. The candles in the wall sconces flickered long shadows up the walls and Iain held his own candle high, illuminating the steps ahead to make sure James didn't trip.

When they reached James's chamber, James shook Iain off and stepped aside, throwing open the door dramatically and gesturing Iain in with a flourish. Amused by James's theatrics, Iain chuckled and entered, moving right into the middle of the room before stopping and gazing around curiously.

Although it was a single chamber, it was a very large room. As well as the usual bedchamber furniture—bed, wardrobe, sideboard—there was a writing desk strewn with papers, a small table with what looked like a microscope and several comfortable-looking armchairs.

Behind him, Iain heard the squeak of bedsprings. He turned to see that James had lain himself down on the bed. He was so still, Iain wondered if he'd passed out. He walked over to the foot of the bed and looked down at the young man lying there, dark blond hair disarranged, boots spattered with mud thrown up from the road. James's eyes were closed but, as Iain stood there, gazing at him, a foolish smile grew on James's face, as though he could feel the weight of Iain's regard. With the careful enunciation of the inebriated, he said, "I'm not sleeping, you know."

"Good. You won't mind taking your boots off, then. You're getting mud all over your clean bedcovers."

"Can't you do it for me?" James wheedled. "The room spins when I open my eyes."

Iain sighed, but he took hold of the heel of one boot, prying it away from James's foot and easing the tight leather sleeve from his slim leg. He repeated the routine with the other boot, set the pair aside, then stood at the end of the bed, looking down bemusedly at his drunken friend.

Beneath the shining black leather, James's legs were clad in plain stockings, the knitted silk smooth over his lean shins and strong, narrow feet. Iain felt a brief but compelling urge to run his hand over one of those feet. To measure the curve of the high arch with his thumb. The thought jolted him and he found himself clearing his throat, almost with embarrassment, which was ridiculous considering some of the things he'd done to a few other gentlemen of his acquaintance. But none of those men had been James. His childhood friend. Someone he'd thought of like a brother for the last ten years.

Most of the time, anyway.

Pushing his wayward thoughts aside, he said brusquely, "Come on, then, let's get your coat off."

"Don't make me move," James pleaded, though he was still smiling. Smiling with his eyes closed. He looked so beautiful lying there on the big bed, with his fine features relaxed and happy and his dark blond hair gleaming dully in the candlelight. Iain found himself imagining what it would feel like to lower his body over James's, to thread his hands into James's dishevelled hair and ravage his smiling mouth with a rough, mauling kiss.

Ah God—as if it wasn't bad enough that he desired men, now he was turning his depraved thoughts to this youngest and most innocent of his friends…

Iain swallowed hard, willing his sudden erection to subside, clenching his hands into hard, painful fists in an effort to distract himself from the tempting man laid out before him.

Exhaling hard, he pressed his lips together and walked round to the side of the bed, hovering uncertainly beside James's head.

"If you sit up," he said, "I'll help you."

"All right," James half groaned, half chuckled. "But you'll have to help me sit up too. My head's reeling."

When Iain sighed, James chuckled again, seeming inordinately amused, and Iain realised the only way the coat was coming off was if Iain wrestled it off him.

"You need a valet," he grumbled, sitting on the mattress beside his sprawled-out friend.

"No, I don't," James mumbled. "I'm no dandy. I can get my own coats on and off and tie my own cravats, thank you very much."

"You can't seem to get *this* coat off," Iain pointed out.

James laughed at that, and Iain couldn't stop a chuckle of his own escaping at the merry sound.

"Come on," he said, leaning forwards and sliding his arms under James's prone body. "Up you get." He levered James back up into a sitting position, holding him steady as James slowly blinked and focused upon him. It was only when James's eyes widened in surprise that the intimacy of their position struck Iain—they were sitting upright, chest to chest, Iain's arms wrapped around James's body, their faces bare inches apart.

For several long heartbeats, they just stared at one another. Distantly, it occurred to Iain that James's ordinarily quiet, grey gaze looked suddenly wild, turbulent as a rainstorm.

"Iain—" James whispered, barely breathing.

Oh hell.

This was wrong, this was *beyond* wrong.

Somehow, Iain managed to drag his gaze away. He pushed James gently back, creating an arm's length distance between them. Looking down, he studied the buttons of James's coat. "Let's get these unfastened," he husked, reaching for the first one.

It was no sort of distraction at all. He could feel James's gaze upon him as he worked the buttons free—the man's attention seemed to thicken the air between them—and when he was done, when he finally looked up again, it was to find James watching him with a raw, hungry expression that was unmistakable.

Iain had no time to move away before James pressed forward, fastening his mouth on Iain's.

Iain froze.

Several things occurred to him at once, first among them that James didn't have the first idea of what he was doing—his lips were stiff and unmoving, his mouth pressing so hard that Iain's lips were crushed against his teeth.

It was an awful kiss.

And yet.

And yet—and this was the second thing—the warm, male body pressing against his own was so beautiful to Iain, and so dear. He'd never felt such a wonderful, *awful* coincidence of feelings for a man he'd been intimate with. The combination of desire and affection—it was heady and frightening at the same time. No way to deny how much, at this instant, he wanted to teach this boy—this man—what a kiss could be…

But damn it all to hell, this was *Jamie*. And Iain knew with sick certainty that he'd never done this before.

Aching with want, Iain wrenched James's wrists from his neck and thrust him away so that he fell back onto the mattress. Then he stood quickly and backed away from the bed.

"That isn't a good idea," he said.

James stared at him, his face a mask of hurt and injured

pride. "Why won't you kiss me?" he said. "I know you like men."

"What?" Iain said sickly.

James's throat bobbed as he swallowed. "I saw you," he whispered. "With Mellick, at the boathouse. On the night of Marianne's betrothal ball."

Mellick.

Iain dredged his memory for the name—it felt like ages before he finally remembered who James was talking about. Then it came to him—the dark-haired groom from Wylde Manor.

The boathouse.

James had seen them there, together.

Iain turned away, stomach churning, guilt already pricking at him. The incident with Mellick had been years ago. How old had James been then—fifteen? Sixteen?

Iain rubbed his hand over his mouth, his mind racing as he tried to recall the details. Christ, but James had idolised him back then—hell, he still did, if the expression on his face when Iain had arrived here this morning was anything to go by. Had James kissed him just now because he thought Iain wanted him to? To earn Iain's favour?

The very thought made his blood run cold.

"I hope you don't think," he said carefully, still turned away, "that just because I have…indulged in such things with others, that I was looking for that from you."

The silence behind him was deafening. It went on so long that at last he had to turn round and look.

James was lying on his back on the bed again, but now one arm was thrown over his face.

Iain stepped closer, wary. "James?"

"Go away," James said thickly from under his arm.

Was he…*crying*?

Iain sat gingerly on the mattress. Slowly, he stretched out a hand and gently moved James's arm aside. Sure enough, his face was streaked with tears.

"What's wrong?" Iain whispered.

"What do you think?" James snapped, pulling his arm back and covering his face again. "Just go away if you don't want me!"

"James, it's not that I—" He broke off before he could finish the sentence—because *wasn't* it that? As desirable as he found James, Iain didn't want to lose his dearest friend, and he surely would if he allowed anything to happen between them, especially when he was very far from convinced that James knew what he was about. He couldn't allow his drunk friend to confuse what might be no more than innocent hero worship with the much darker kind of desire that he'd witnessed between Iain and Mellick.

"Please go away," James mumbled under his arm, dark blond head moving from side to side. "I'm not so drunk that I don't know how humiliating this is."

"James, don't—that is, you shouldn't confuse our friendship with what you saw between me and Mellick. You and I —" He stopped, unsure how to go on, then tried again. "Men like Mellick—I never spend more than one night with them. Hell, it's usually not more than an hour or two, and when it's done, it's done. I don't see them again." He swallowed. "It's just something I need to do every now and again."

James flinched—Iain saw it, despite the arm still covering his face. "You make it sound so cold." His voice was muffled, but Iain could hear the bewilderment in it.

"I know," he admitted. "But when I do that, it's only because of bodily urges. I don't want…" He trailed off.

"You don't want that from me," James finished flatly.

Iain swallowed again and was glad that James wasn't looking at him now, that he wasn't able to see that betraying signal.

"No," he lied. "I don't want that from you, Jamie." Then

he added, more truthfully, "Your friendship is important to me. I don't want to lose it."

For a while, James just lay there, absorbing Iain's words. Then, slowly, he uncovered his face and sat up without so much as glancing at Iain. He looked utterly done in, and when he swung his legs over the side of the bed, he put his elbows on his knees and leaned over tiredly, one hand rubbing the back of his neck, eyes on the floor.

After a brief silence, he said quietly, "I understand."

Do you? Iain thought, but he didn't say the words aloud.

James sighed heavily. "And you're right," he said. "I'm drunk and I need my bed, so perhaps"—he paused—"perhaps you should go now."

Iain cleared his throat. "Yes," he said at last. "It's about time I left anyway."

He walked to the door of the chamber, but as his hand closed over the doorknob, he paused. Turned to look over his shoulder. "I'll write to you once my new posting's confirmed," he said. "To let you know my direction."

Finally, James looked up, and their gazes met. James's was wary.

Iain gave him a crooked smile. "I expect you to write to me often."

James snorted at that, and the familiar sound settled something in Iain.

"I don't know why I bother writing to you at all," James grumbled. "You're terrible at writing back."

"I'm not a good correspondent," Iain admitted, "But I love to receive your letters, and I keep them all. I read them often."

James looked faintly surprised at that. "Do you?"

Iain felt a little foolish, but he made himself admit the truth. "Yes. I do."

James smiled. It was a sad sort of smile, not like his usual one at all, but at least it was a smile. "I don't want to lose your friendship either, Iain," he whispered. "It's the most important thing in the world to me."

Despite everything, something inside Iain sang with pure happiness right then, hearing those words. To know that this friendship was as vital to James as it was to him.

"I'm glad to hear it, Jamie," he said softly. "Good night."

9

Now: 1824

27th May, 1824

Holmewell, Hampshire

James didn't usually spend much time dressing for dinner, but on this particular evening, he found himself behaving like a girl at her first ball, discarding no fewer than three coats before settling on his dark blue superfine and going through several neckcloths before he was finally satisfied with the knot of his cravat. Now he was fiddling with his *hair*, something he never did.

It was absurd, and it was Iain Sinclair's fault. Turning up at Kate's after years of silence, just when James had begun to get used to his absence. And of course, it was bloody Kate's fault too—for not telling James that Iain was coming.

Of course, she'd probably guessed James wouldn't have come if he'd known.

James huffed out a sigh and turned away from the mirror.

He hated that he cared how he looked. Hated even more that, when Iain had walked into the drawing room this afternoon, James's gaze had gone straight to him, drinking in the sight of him. He'd been stunned by the difference in him. Oh, not in his appearance—he wasn't changed much in that respect. It was that…he didn't seem happy. James had always loved the twinkle in Iain's blue eyes, but today, even when he'd been talking to the other guests, even when he'd been smiling and laughing, he'd looked strangely grave. James was used to seeing laughter lines at the corners of those eyes, a twinkle in their blue depths. Not today, though. Today Iain had been as serious as James had ever seen him.

I can't bear us not being friends anymore.

That was another thing James hated. That when Iain had made his plea—*please…hear me out*—James's heart had leapt with happiness, and a part of him had just wanted to forget everything that had happened between them, to accept the friendship Iain was offering him again and tell himself it was enough.

Except, it wasn't enough.

James had finally learnt that lesson—and a long and painful lesson it had been: that sometimes half a loaf was worse than no loaf at all.

He glanced at the clock on the mantel. It was past time to go down for dinner. All this fiddling with his appearance was no more than sheer procrastination. No matter how long he stood here in front of the mirror, at some point, he was going to have to go down and face the other guests.

Sighing, he turned from the mirror, put his shoulders back and left his bedchamber, making his way to the drawing room, where the guests had been instructed to gather before dinner.

At the top of the stairs, he encountered Mr. Potts with his wife. Mr. Potts tightened his lips minutely and gave him a slight nod, still offended, it seemed, from earlier. James smiled anyway, then bowed politely in Mrs. Potts's direction.

"Good evening, ma'am, you're looking well this evening." He smiled serenely as she twittered her thanks, then turned to her husband. "And Mr. Potts, I apologise for this afternoon. I hope we will get a chance to continue our conversation this evening."

May God strike him down as an inveterate liar.

Mr. Potts appeared to soften a little at that, inclining his head a tad more generously this time. "Perhaps so, Mr. Hart," he said, his careful tone suggesting that, whilst he might be a little mollified, James was not yet entirely forgiven.

Suppressing a smile, James offered Mrs. Potts his arm to escort her downstairs, leaving her husband to follow behind.

Mrs. Potts was a matronly woman with an alarmingly huge bosom, who looked as though she could be anywhere between forty and fifty years. When James politely asked about her connection to Edward, it transpired that she was one of Edward's three older half-sisters from his father's first marriage and his senior by a dozen years. She was also the only one of the siblings who had been unable to attend Edward and Kate's wedding five years before, which was why James hadn't met her previously.

Mrs. Potts explained that, whilst her mother—the *first* Lady Porter, she emphasised—had borne a number of daughters, she had failed to produce a son before her untimely death. The second Lady Porter had fared a great deal better, producing Edward a bare ten months after the wedding.

"But would you believe, Mr. Hart," she continued in a low voice as they strolled into the drawing room, "in the twenty years of marriage that followed Edward's birth, there was never so much as a whisper of another single babe!" She sniffed, a disapproving sound. "In fact, Edward's mother spent nearly all her time in London after that, while Papa was always here at Holmewell—he was a very devoted father. He always professed to be fond of her, though, despite the fact that she was remarkably…well, free in her friendships, shall we say. For a married woman, I mean."

"I've always found Edward's mother to be very kind," James said mildly. "And she has always spoken of your late father with great affection, at least in my presence."

There was a brief awkward silence, then Mrs. Potts said coolly, "Well, I'm sure I wouldn't dream of contradicting you, Mr. Hart." Her faintly acid tone suggested just the opposite. "Please excuse me," she continued, extricating her arm from James's. "I see my sister is trying to catch my attention."

"Of course," James murmured politely, and she stalked off. He couldn't deny he was glad to see her go.

Having freed himself of Mrs. Potts, James joined a small group of young ladies that included his cousin Sylvia, and her particular friend, Miss Alicia Whyte, a very pretty if somewhat hoydenish young lady with an unfortunate braying sort of laugh. The young ladies found his complete idiocy concerning all matters pertaining to fashion and society highly amusing, and there were a few flirtatious looks from one of them, a slight, dark girl with a secretive smile, Miss Helena Dobbie. James pretended not to notice her interest in him. He had long ago learned that encouraging flirtation from young ladies was a recipe for disaster. Now he generally treated any unmarried females he came across like troublesome younger sisters. He tended to find that quashed any romantic thoughts they may be harbouring about him fairly promptly.

After a few minutes, Iain strolled up to join their group, tall and elegant in his black-and-white evening clothes, his thick brown hair glossy as a chestnut, a smile firmly in place beneath the waxed points of his moustache that didn't quite, James thought, reach his blue eyes.

God, just the sight of him made James's chest ache.

"Good evening," Iain said, smiling round the circle of feminine faces before finally settling his gaze on James. "Hart, will you do me honour of introducing me to these lovely young ladies?"

Somehow, James managed to dredge up a smile of his own, one he hoped wasn't as strained looking as it felt, and made the introductions. The difference between how the young ladies reacted to James and how they reacted to Iain was palpable. James might have snagged the attention of one of the group, but when Iain arrived, each and every one of them perked up. They began vying for his attention, their gestures becoming more flirtatious and a competitive spirit coming to the fore. The laughter from their group increased in volume, attracting glances from the other guests, mostly of smiling indulgence, though Mr. Potts looked noticeably pained.

James lapsed into silence, not that anyone noticed except Iain. He glanced at James from time to time, his gaze faintly troubled, before being distracted again by another breathless, feminine question. When James murmured an excuse and tried to draw away from the group, Iain put his hand on James's arm, holding him back with a surprisingly firm grip.

"Don't go, Hart," he begged. "You cannot leave me alone with the ladies. They will eat me alive!"

The young ladies squealed with laughter and protested loudly, but through it all, Iain's hand stayed on James's arm, warm and firm and unyielding, even when James tried to surreptitiously pull away.

He was relieved when the dinner gong sounded. Iain had to let him go then.

Kate had seated Iain at a number of places distant from James, thankfully. Too far to make direct conversation easy. She hadn't been entirely kind, though. He had the flirtatious Miss Dobbie on his right and the somewhat deaf Lady Jenner on his left. On Lady Jenner's other side was Iain's father, and from what James could make out, he was making no effort to talk to the querulous old lady at all, his entire attention taken up with emptying his wineglass as frequently as possible. Consequently, James had to divide his time between fending off the advances of the determined Miss Dobbie and shouting himself hoarse at Lady Jenner.

As dinner went on, however, the elder Mr. Sinclair became more talkative, even voluble. He began in a jolly enough mood, but his mood deteriorated when he started a long debate with Mr. Laughton, a Member of Parliament, about the act that had been passed the year before giving judges the power to commute death sentences for most offences.

"I cannot believe you voted for this travesty, Laughton," he said in a loud voice, drawing glances from some of the guests at the other end of the table. "The threat of the noose is the only thing that keeps us being overrun by criminals altogether. Without that deterrent, many more of these rogues will come out of the woodwork, mark my words. No decent Englishman will be able to sleep easy in his bed."

Laughton smiled patiently through his ranting. "In fact, Sinclair," he said, "the opposite is true. Now that judges have the ability to commute sentences, juries will be more likely to convict. Have you any idea how many criminals escape punishment because juries are unwilling to send them to their deaths for petty crimes?"

"I've never heard such nonsense!" the elder Sinclair spluttered. "And you call this progress?" In his agitation, he knocked over a glass of wine, causing the lady to his left to squeal and rear back in her chair. A footman moved forwards to clear up the mess and remove the upset glass.

James glanced at Iain. He was watching his father with a resigned sort of dread that James recognised, a dread that struck him as all of a piece with the unhappiness he'd seen in the man's eyes earlier.

"It's not just thieves and murderers," Sinclair went on, his tone haranguing. "It's fraudsters, smugglers, *sodomites*—"

"Father!" Isabel interrupted. "Please, this is hardly suitable for the dinner table."

She turned her head to glare at poor mild-mannered Bertie, who shuffled in his seat and mumbled, "She's right, sir. Ladies present and all that."

Sinclair opened his mouth, probably to argue with his son-in-law if his belligerent expression was anything to go by, but happily, the footman chose that moment to deliver a clean glass to him and pour him more wine, distracting him. Laughton took the opportunity to change the subject, looking to his right to catch Iain's eye.

"So you have resigned your commission, Mr. Sinclair. What will you do now?"

Iain shrugged. "I shall have to give it some thought."

"Ah yes, he has turned in his regimentals," Iain's father interrupted. "The first officer of our family to do so less than halfway through his military career."

The old bastard. This was always his way with Iain. James had witnessed it many times before, the persistent criticism, often delivered with seeming good humour.

James glanced at Iain. His jaw had tightened slightly, but other than that, his expression was mild. He was good at hiding his reaction to his father's barbs but James knew they bothered him.

"I thought you'd be pleased, Father," Iain said lightly, "since you were of the view that I was no better than a glorified footman in the King's service."

"*Iain*—"

That was Iain's mother, her voice pleading, face drawn and unhappy, but for some reason, Iain's comment just made his father laugh.

"Did I say that?" he chuckled, raising his wineglass to his lips. "I don't remember."

Hardly surprising, James thought, since the man was probably three sheets to the wind when he said it.

"Well," Iain's father continued blithely, "it's true enough. From what I can make out, you do nothing but attend social engagements and provide your opinion on His Majesty's clothing. Three years of balls and parties should be sufficient for any man."

James winced. The contempt in the man's voice was plain to hear, and no matter how unconcerned Iain looked to hear his words, James knew they wounded him. All his life, Iain had striven to make his father proud, but there was no pleasing him.

If Sinclair had intended to give his son a set-down in front of the other guests, however, it certainly hadn't worked. The revelation that Iain had been in the King's service had the other guests agog, and soon he was being quizzed about His Majesty's famously lavish entertainments while the elder Sinclair fell into morose silence and applied himself more assiduously to his wine.

As dinner drew to a close, the younger ladies begged Kate and Edward to permit some parlour games.

"I'm not playing any damned games," Iain's father grumbled. "I've been looking forward to a quiet glass of Port."

More like a bottle, James thought sourly. He'd suffered through postprandial Port with the elder Sinclair before. Anything was preferable.

"You shall have your Port, Mr. Sinclair," Kate said politely. "It will be served directly. But there's no reason, is there, that the young people can't play a few games if they particularly want to? What do you think, Edward?"

She sent him a significant look and he nodded. "Excellent idea," he agreed, smiling.

"I must say, I'm not at all sure I agree." This was Mr. Potts. "Playing fast games only leads to—"

"Oh, nonsense," Kate interrupted briskly. She offered

Potts a wintry smile. "Besides, you needn't be troubled, Mr. Potts. You're perfectly welcome to stay here with Mr. Sinclair, and any of the other gentlemen who are disinclined to join in."

"I wouldn't dream of leaving you alone to chaperone all the young ladies," Potts replied in a repressive tone.

Opposite James, Sylvia rolled her eyes, and he bit his lip against a laugh.

In the end, most everyone elected to play parlour games, apart from a few of the older ladies who withdrew to take tea, and some gentlemen who didn't want to miss out on their Port. Kate led the way back to the drawing room to get started. They began with a game of charades—even Potts couldn't object to that, though he did remark at one point upon the young ladies' "unfeminine shrieking", a comment that earned him a glare from Kate and some muffled giggles from the young ladies in question.

When everyone grew bored of charades, Miss Whyte suggested Kiss the Lady You Love Without Anyone Knowing. Potts immediately protested, and this time, though she looked irritated about it, Kate had to agree with him.

"I have an idea," she said. "Let's play Hide and Guide and Seek. James, isn't it a perfectly splendid game?" A half-dozen pairs of eyes turned to him expectantly.

"I've never heard of it," one of the young ladies said.

"That's because it's a Hart family game," James explained. "We played it all the time when we were children. It's just like Hide and Seek, only you play in partners, and when it's your team's turn to seek, one of you guides and the other seeks— the seeker has to wear a blindfold and obey the guider's instructions."

Iain met his gaze over the young ladies' heads. "James and I were the unvanquished champions," he said, grinning.

"Oh, hardly!" Kate exclaimed, though her protests were drowned out by the young ladies all noisily agreeing that it sounded famous. The very mention of blindfolds had them all atwitter.

When they all calmed down, Kate began to organise them. "There's quite a lot of us, so we'll have lots of teams," she decided. "All right, I know. Let's have one team of hiders and one of seekers for each room. We'll draw lots for who hides and who seeks in each one. If the seekers find the hiders in the allotted time, the hiders will have to pay a forfeit and if they fail, vice versa."

The young ladies began bouncing with excitement at the thought of forfeits.

"Right, then," Kate announced. "Everyone who wants to play, pick a partner."

Sylvia and Miss Whyte both ran towards Iain in a most unladylike fashion.

"Oh, now I *must* protest!" Potts cried. "You cannot be thinking of letting young ladies play such a game partnered with young unmarried gentleman?"

Kate laughed. "Why? Do you think they should be partnered with the *old married* gentlemen?"

Potts began to splutter, and Edward had to step in to smooth things over. "Come, Alfred," he said, clapping his brother-in-law on the shoulder, "Kate didn't mean to scandalise you—she's only teasing, aren't you dearest one?" He sent Kate a significant look, and she tried to look serious, only to start laughing again.

Edward rolled his eyes at her and turned back to the outraged vicar. "No need for alarm," he continued. "There's no question of ladies and gentlemen being partnered with one another—even the married ones. We'll pair ladies with ladies, and gentlemen with gentlemen, all right?"

James had to suppress a chuckle when Potts immediately declared himself satisfied and suggested partnering Edward with himself—Edward's expression was priceless. His own amusement was curtailed, though, when a voice behind him said, "Partner me, James? We have our record to uphold after all."

It was Iain, of course, his smile strained and uncharacteristically nervous.

As much as James might want to refuse him, he knew it would be foolish to do so—what would the other guests think if they heard him resisting such an innocent suggestion? Besides, now that he and Iain were standing together, everyone was already assuming they'd paired up, and were partnering themselves accordingly.

"I—ah, I thought I might sit this out," he tried weakly. Disappointment flashed over Iain's face, and immediately, James felt a pang of regret, swiftly followed by another of anger. *Why* was he so soft when it came to Iain Sinclair? He needed to toughen up. Remember just how much pain Iain had caused him over the years.

Unfortunately, Sylvia overheard his pathetic excuse.

"Oh, don't be a spoilsport, James!" she pleaded. "If you don't play, we'll have odd numbers and Mr. Sinclair will have to sit out! Everyone else is paired up now." Several more young ladies joined in, chorusing her plea.

"Come on, Hart," Iain said. "You can turn *me* down, but you can't disappoint the ladies, now, can you?"

"Oh, fine," James grumbled at last. "I'll play."

Ever officious, Kate soon had everyone lined up and lots folded up on a plate to be selected from.

"You pick," Iain said when Kate asked them choose. James selected one of the folded up paper lots and opened it.

"*Library*," he read aloud. "*Hiders*."

Edward and Potts drew the seekers' lot for the library, which Potts looked disappointed about. James wondered if he'd been secretly hoping to get the chance to accidentally fondle one of the young ladies while blindfolded.

"All right, hiders," Kate called out. She was holding Edward's pocket watch aloft. "Get ready to go to your allotted rooms. When three minutes is up, the first team of seekers will begin searching—we'll do each room in turn because it's more fun that way. Ready?" She paused, eyes on the watch, tracking the hands. "Go!"

Iain grabbed James's sleeve and began pulling him towards the door.

10

James and Iain dashed out of the drawing room with the rest of the hiders and plunged down the corridor. Sylvia and Miss Whyte peeled off first, entering the music room, then Iain and James were next, diving into the library a few doors further down, while the other teams scrambled past them.

Iain slammed the library door closed, and they both began to look round frantically—there were quite a few places to hide, but most of them were pretty obvious: behind one of the wingback chairs, under the desk...

"Behind the curtains," Iain said.

James glanced at the floor-length curtains that covered the bank of windows to their left. "Too obvious," he replied. "That's the first place they'll look!"

"Not there—" Iain replied. He pointed at the other wall— at the small, round window, high up on the wall behind the desk. "There."

"Oh bloody hell," James muttered, but he couldn't help but smile.

"Come on, it's perfect." Iain grinned. "No one will think to look up there."

In an instant, he was standing on the chair behind the

desk and swinging himself up onto the narrow ledge. The window was fully circular, though its outermost edges were obscured by a pair of short velvet drapes. It'd be awkward, standing there, waiting for someone to find them, but it could be done.

And anyway, it was too late to protest now. The first three minutes would be coming to an end imminently. Iain leaned down to offer his hand to James.

"Quick!" he said. "Before they come."

Ignoring Iain's hand, James scrambled up onto the ledge beside him, teetering a little when he turned to face Iain, who immediately reached out a hand to steady him. James instinctively pulled back, even though it made him wobble more.

Iain sighed and withdrew his hand. "Brace yourself against the glass," he advised. "It's safer that way. The ledge is very narrow."

James nodded and did as Iain said, leaning against the cold glass, and immediately felt steadier.

"All right?" Iain asked. When James nodded, he leaned outwards again, taking hold of the edges of the drapes and yanking them together, shutting out the candlelight from the library and enclosing them in sudden darkness. He settled back into position opposite James, mirroring him.

"When you hear the door open, you need to stay absolutely silent," he whispered.

"I *know*," James muttered, his tone exasperated, feeling all of ten years old again.

The stirrings of the seekers emerging from the drawing room began to reach them, then—voices laughing and the sound of feet walking down the corridor. As the group drew closer, James tensed, but they passed by, chattering, heading for one of the rooms beyond them apparently.

"They must've decided to start at the far end of the corridor," James murmured.

He caught sight of a glint of white from Iain—a ghost of smile perhaps. "Or they're picking names out of a hat again."

The only illumination reaching them now came from the near-full moon that hung outside the window, fat and pale gold. James's vision began to adapt to the darkness. He could make out the outline of Iain's head and the broad shape of him leaning against the window.

"How long did Kate say the seekers would be allowed to try to find us?" Iain asked.

"Three minutes."

"That's ages! They'll find us easily—there's hardly any hiding places in here."

"It's amazing how quick the time goes when you're blind-folded and a lot depends on how good the guide is," James pointed out.

They were murmuring under their breaths, and it made every word that passed between them feel absurdly intimate. *Everything* felt absurdly intimate—the tiny space they were inhabiting, and the words that were spooling out in whispers between them. The very air that they were sharing in their little cubbyhole.

The intimacy was almost unbearable, and a part of James wanted to thrust the curtains aside and jump down to get away from it. Stalk out of the room and start packing his port-manteau right now.

Another part of him wanted never to leave.

The silence between them grew heavy, thick with unsaid things—at least it felt that way to James. Perhaps, though, he was imagining the tension. Perhaps—probably—Iain was feeling perfectly relaxed, just leaning against the window in the moonlight, waiting to be found. James was so suddenly certain of that, that the words that drifted out of the darkness towards him utterly confounded him.

"I've missed you, Jamie."

The words were whispered so softly that James wondered if he'd really heard them or if he'd just imagined them.

"Sorry?" he said stupidly.

"I've missed you," Iain repeated. "Missed our friendship."

James swallowed, unsure how to respond. Iain sounded sad—bleak, even—but James couldn't see his expression to verify that. All he could see was the gleam of the man's eyes in the darkness, like a ripple across a pool.

"I've missed you too," he said at last, honestly. "But you know why I broke off our friendship. I can't bear being around you when—"

"You won't have to be around me," Iain interrupted. "I'm leaving England. I'm sailing to India at the end of the summer."

"*India?*" James hated the devastation he heard in his own voice, plain as day in all this darkness. He added weakly, "I thought you told Laughton you didn't know what you'd be doing."

"Yes, well, I have my reasons for that." There was a brief silence as James tried to take that in, then Iain added softly, "I accepted Kate's invitation because I didn't want to leave England without us having made peace with each other. With all this…anger between us."

James searched the darkness between them, willing himself to see Iain's expression, but there were only maddening hints. Something about the precise angle at which he held his head that spoke of a heaviness upon him. The sorrow in his voice. The thickness of the emotion in the air between him.

"Leaving England," James echoed redundantly. His voice was tinged with disbelief, and distantly he wondered at himself, at the sudden grief that was swamping him. He had been the one to cut off all contact two years before, the one to say he wanted to never see Iain again. Yet now, when he was about to get his wish, the thought caused a pain so sharp, it was as though the last two years hadn't happened at all.

Perhaps a little part of him had always believed that, one day, Iain might come round to his way of thinking. He knew —had always known—that Iain cared for him. He knew too that the man desired him physically. And if Iain didn't feel the same desperate love for James that James felt for him, neither were his feelings those of mere friendship. But they were not equal to James's feelings.

"Yes," Iain said. "I've been offered a post in India. It's not with the army, but it's similar in a way. I will be living under another name."

"Subterfuge?" James guessed, dismayed. "Spying and such?"

A huff of amused consent. "That sort of thing. You can see why I didn't want to talk about it at dinner."

"Yes," James said, adding helplessly, "That's dangerous work."

Even in the darkness, he saw Iain's shrug, the broad outline of his shoulders shifting briefly upwards in a familiar gesture of unconcern. People thought Iain Sinclair was reckless. Devil-may-care. They looked at him and saw the brave cavalry officer. The daring captain. Sometimes James wondered if he was the only person that the saw the desperation under the courage. The lack of self-care that made Iain strangely invincible. Since the first time they'd met, all those years ago, James had known it was a mask.

"I know how angry you were the last time we saw each other," Iain murmured. "And I don't blame you, Jamie. But I'm asking you to consider forgiving me. And perhaps even writing to me again."

Oh, the letters James had written this man over the years. The outpourings he'd sent. About his home and his family, his father's death, his passion for science, his little discoveries and his travels all over the country for specimens. All his hopes and fears and passions.

And all his embarrassing feelings for Iain, buried in every line...

I wish you could've been there...

Perhaps next time we can go together?

I'm so looking forward to seeing you in the summer...

"Write to you?" he said now. His voice was suddenly too loud, and he lowered it to a whisper to add, "Why should I, Iain? You were never much good at writing back. Everything was always one-sided with us."

Iain exhaled another of those little huffs of air. This one carried no amusement, but rather regret. It was extraordinary, James reflected, what could be communicated without words or facial expression, though perhaps the meaning of such tiny sounds and gestures was discernible only when one knew the person very well. When one could read the smallest movements of their body.

Or perhaps he was being foolish and imagining a connection that simply wasn't there.

"What if I promise to write to you from India?" Iain asked. "Since I'll not be living under my own name there, I'll have to be careful, but there will be ways of getting letters to and from my friends and family, from time to time."

James's gut clenched at those words and at what they hinted at—the risks Iain would be living with, day in, day out. He pressed his head hard against the window, as though the physical sensation of the cold glass against his skin might somehow distract him from the turmoil that Iain was causing him.

"Will you write back to me?" Iain asked softly. "Let me know how you are?"

There was a blockage in James's throat that he couldn't get a word past. It seemed to swell painfully when he swallowed against it, and heat was building behind his eyes, prickling there. The shame of tears threatened, and he fought to get himself under control.

"James?" Iain's voice was soft with disappointment. Pleading. "Won't you answer me even?"

James couldn't hold back the small, choked noise that escaped him then. It was only a little noise, in its way, but in the dark, in this strange little cocoon they'd made for themselves, it was naked and raw. It carried all his grief and anger and bewilderment and put them on painful show.

Yes, he still cared for Iain. Still loved Iain. And Iain must know it.

It was humiliating, to care so deeply for someone who did not reciprocate those feelings beyond friendship. For someone who could talk so casually of leaving England forever and never seeing James again, when that thought was enough to break James's heart—again.

"Jamie—"

The darkness moved. The darkness that was Iain's body shifted towards him on the narrow ledge. Iain braced his hands on either side of James's head, one flat against the cold glass that James's cheek was pressed up against, the other gripping the curving edge of wall. He was so close that his breath stirred James's hair, and when James turned his head, his nose brushed Iain's cheek.

Now, they were eye to eye. Now James could see him. Iain's eyes gleamed in the darkness, and the moon washed the planes of his face with its cold, gentle light.

He watched James for long, unmoving moments.

Didn't Iain know what to say?

"What?" James prompted, and still Iain didn't speak, just stood there, so vibrantly alive. The glass of the window was cold against James's left side, but all down his right flank, Iain was warm. For the first time in two long years, they were in contact again, careless of the rules of a world that said that men did not touch each other in such a way.

"I want you to forgive me."

The words were carried out on a whisper. They touched James's own lips.

"Forgive you?" James repeated, puzzled. "For what? Rejecting me?" He shook his head minutely. "You don't need to apologise for not wanting me, Iain."

Iain bent his head a little so their foreheads met. It had the effect of lowering his gaze, shielding him from James's scrutiny when he said softly, "No, not for that. I did want you. For hurting you."

James closed his eyes, and for a little while, he just stood there, allowing himself the luxury of this rare physical contact, conscious that this might be the last time they would ever be so alone, so intimate. Finally, though, he had to open his eyes, had to go on. "All right," he said wearily. "If you feel you need my forgiveness, you have it."

Iain sagged a little against him. "Really?" he breathed. He sounded surprised, as though he hadn't expected to win the point so easily.

James nodded. "I wouldn't want you to leave England forever with a loose end trailing," he said, trying and failing to inject a little humour into his tone. "This way, you can depart with a clear conscience, can't you?"

"I'm not sure you can grant me a clear conscience," Iain said. "But if I can depart knowing I have your friendship again, I will be happier than I can say."

James frowned at that. "I—I don't know about friendship, Iain. Forgiveness for the past is one thing, but—" Before he could complete the thought, the door rattled and swung open, and a crowd of people swarmed into the quiet of the library, all giggling and talking.

"Mr. Sinclair!" one of the young ladies called out. "Mr. Hart! We've come to find you out, wherever you're hiding!"

"Come on, Mr. Potts!" another one said, giggling. "Put on the blindfold!"

"Oh, really I don't think… Wouldn't it be more sensible for me to be the guide?" That was Potts, that unmistakably pompous self-important tone. "I am, after all, a guide of men in my role as a vicar."

A chorus of objections shouted that suggestion down.

"You lost in the coin toss," a firm male voice—Edward—said, cutting through the babble. "You're the seeker. *I'm* the guide."

"Oh, but Sir Edward—"

"Oh, just get *on* with it! You've only got three minutes—I'm going to turn the timer over in half a minute, whether or not you've got the blindfold on." This last was Kate, all firm and no-nonsense.

During these noisy exchanges, Iain and James remained nose to nose, sharing the same air as they breathed, neither of them daring to speak. The silence between them was fragile, the veil of darkness they wore a flimsy protection from the clamouring world just beyond the drapes.

James wasn't sure what made him do what he did next. Perhaps he was goaded into it by the thought of the world and its insatiable demands of proper behaviour, or perhaps it was Iain's plea to return to the platonic safety of their childhood friendship.

Or perhaps he just *wanted* it.

Whatever the reason was, he lifted his chin and pressed his mouth against Iain's, raising his right hand to curl his fingers round the back of Iain's neck and pull him closer.

For one frozen moment, Iain was all shock and resistance, but when James pulled him in closer and stroked his tongue over the firm seam of Iain's lips, James felt a deep shudder rack the man's body. And then Iain was pressing against him harder, lifting his hand from the window pane to thread his cold fingers into James's hair, deepening the kiss further.

I did want you.

And God, his mouth. So smooth and pliable, the soft

bristle of his moustache teasing the edge of James's lips. And the scent of him, the headily familiar trace of neroli oil from his hair pomade. His heat, his strength as he pressed his long body against James's, and every bit of him, everything that James had *missed,* all of it so welcome after these years of estrangement.

James hadn't been entirely chaste since they'd last seen one another, but his occasional encounters didn't alleviate his basic loneliness one bit, merely slaked his lust from time to time. And right now, the reason for that was painfully clear— that his loneliness wasn't caused by being alone, but by the absence of Iain, by the absence of the one person who knew him better, *liked* him better, than anyone else.

It was a realisation that made his blood run cold. Made him tear his mouth from Iain's and end their kiss, turning his face back to lean it against the window again, to stare out into the darkness, horrified by his own thoughts.

Iain had never offered him more than friendship. The occasional letter.

And it wasn't enough.

Beyond the curtains, the babbling voices of the crowd of seekers quietened down to some muffled giggling.

"Walk forwards till you get to the desk," Edward instructed. Shoes shuffled on the wooden floor and one of the young ladies giggled.

Iain took hold of James's chin between his thumb and forefinger and turned his face back so they were looking into each other's eyes again. He stayed silent, but his eyes held a question that James could see, even in the darkness. James shook his head, trying to turn away again, but Iain wouldn't let him. He looked puzzled and angry. He let go of James's chin and pointed at James's chest, before jerking his thumb at himself, his movement seeming almost angry.

You were the one who kissed me, he seemed to be saying.

"Two minutes," Kate announced beyond the curtains.

The other guests began calling out suggestions while Edward tried to give Potts instructions. It sounded as though the vicar was getting confused. He managed to knock over what sounded like a whole shelf of books. They clattered noisily to the floor, causing Mr. Potts to let out a decidedly unmanly squeak and the young ladies to shriek with amusement.

With twenty seconds to go, Kate began a countdown, and the rest of the guests joined in while Edward sent Potts to search behind the desk, just below them.

"Where the hell can they be?" Edward exclaimed. "There's not even any good hiding places in here!"

"Four, three, two, one—time's up!"

"They can't be in here!" Edward protested.

"Come out, you two! You've won!" Kate sang out.

Iain stared at James for an instant, then he pushed away from him and leaned forwards to wrench the curtains apart.

"We're here!" he announced, grinning merrily, and jumped down, leaving James stranded on the ledge.

As soon as Iain was back on the ground, the young ladies surged forwards to meet him, all of them talking over each other.

"Oh, that was so clever!"

"How ever did you think of such a hiding place, Mr. Sinclair?"

"What forfeit are you going to choose for Mr. Potts?"

He let them swarm him, laughing as he answered their questions, as he teased them and flirted with them. He was putting on his usual show, the dashing, merry cavalry officer.

No sign now of the man who had whispered, *Forgive me.* Of the man who'd kissed James with passion and desperation.

No sign of the real Iain Sinclair at all.

11

Then: 1821

2ⁿᵈ June, 1821

Wylde Manor, Derbyshire

Iain had elected to ride all the way to Wylde Manor, sending his luggage ahead of him. As much as he'd enjoyed the ride—he was, after all, a cavalry officer, as at home in the saddle as on his own two feet—he was glad to finally arrive. Dusty, tired and saddle sore, he had already decided that the first thing he'd do would be to ask for a hot bath in which to soothe his aching muscles.

Within two minutes of stepping inside the front door, however, when he was just about to express his wishes to James's efficient housekeeper, a familiar voice distracted him from his determined course of action.

"Iain, by God! You made it a day early. What luck!"

Iain looked up to see the source of that voice, his friend, standing, smiling, at the top of the staircase, and his heart leapt with uncomplicated happiness, a grin spreading over his face as he watched James's swift descent.

"I rode like the very devil to get here today," he admitted as James reached the bottom of the stairs and they strode towards each other, reaching out to clasp one another's hands. "All to have an extra day and night here. I hope you are suitably grateful."

"Oh, I am," James said brightly, "I am." He kept hold of Iain's right hand in his own and stepped in a little closer to clap his left hand to Iain's shoulder, looking straight into his eyes. For a long moment, they said nothing, just looked at one another, grinning like fools.

The self-conscious discomfort that had dogged their first few meetings following the disastrous night when James had tried to kiss him had long passed, thank God.

"It's been too long," Iain said at last.

"Far too long," James agreed. "Ten months, is it? But God, it's good to see you now. You're looking well, old boy."

"As are you," Iain replied, grinning. James was wearing what looked to be his oldest, most comfortable clothes, and his hair had grown too long—he'd tied it back at the nape of his neck with a black ribbon in an old-fashioned style. All in all, he was very far from the fashionable ideal of a gentleman. Yet somehow he looked perfect, effortlessly handsome with that bright, happy smile and his grey eyes shining with undisguised pleasure.

"I look like a country yokel," James said ruefully. "But I don't mind. I'm quite happy in my baggy breeches."

"You do look a little yokel-ish," Iain agreed, chuckling. His laughter was more of a spontaneous bubbling of happiness than an expression of mirth, and James seemed unperturbed by it. He chuckled too, his grey gaze moving over Iain's face with a pleasure he took no pains to hide.

"Christ, look at us," he said at last. "Standing here like a pair of idiots. I was just about to walk out to Shipley Edge. Care to come with me?"

And just like that, Iain forgot the bath he'd been dreaming of, forgot his aching thigh muscles and tense neck. "I'd love to," he said promptly. "Can you spare me five minutes to change my clothes?"

James chuckled. "Take a half hour if you like," he said. "I don't mind waiting for you."

"I won't need more than a few minutes," Iain assured him. "My luggage arrived this morning. Your housekeeper tells me it's already been hung up for me."

With one last grin, he clapped James on the shoulder and dashed upstairs. He didn't need a footman to guide him. Mrs. Morrison had already confirmed he was in the same room he'd been put in the last two times he'd come. The chamber was, as she had promised, all ready for him, his clothing hung up in the wardrobes, a fresh ewer of water sitting on the sideboard and a vase of purple irises on the small table next to the bed.

Iain stripped off his dusty riding clothes and filled the basin with water, dampening a cloth and running it quickly over his face, neck and chest, under his arms and over his groin. And then he was dragging out fresh clothes and dressing at breakneck speed before rushing back downstairs.

James was waiting for him in the hallway, scribbling in a notebook.

"Ready?" Iain called out as he walked towards him, causing James to start and look up. His sudden helpless smile made Iain happy.

"Absolutely," James replied, closing the notebook. "Come on, let's be on our way."

They fell into step together, heading for the front door again, nodding at the footman who opened it for them to pass through.

"So what are you looking for today?" Iain asked, certain there would be something.

"Anything of interest," James said, tucking his notebook into the small leather satchel at his hip. "But most especially *Ophrys apifera*, more commonly known as the bee orchid."

"A bee *orchid* rather than a bee?"

Iain's voice was tinged with surprise—James's particular interest was insects, not plants.

"Yes, I've become rather interested in a particular group of plants which seek to draw insects to them by mimicking the anatomy of the animal in question. The bee orchid is one such plant."

"And where will we find it?"

"Chalky ground," James replied promptly. "Of which we have plenty round here. Well, four miles or so hence. Are you up to eight miles this afternoon?"

"I think I can just about manage that," Iain replied drily, faintly affronted by the question.

James laughed. "Don't be offended, it's just that you've already had a long ride today. I thought you mightn't be in the mood for more than a stroll."

"I'll be fine," Iain insisted. "Come on." And with that, they started down the long drive that led to the manor gates.

It was a beautiful afternoon, warm and sunny. A perfect afternoon for a walk. They strolled along country paths, enjoying the cool shade cast by the trees, and exchanging family news.

Every now and then, they paused for James to examine a plant or take a sample of something to look at later. He had all sorts of little tools in his satchel—an eyeglass for observing the tiniest of details, a little cutting tool that was part blade, part scoop. Soft cloths for storing any specimens he took away with him and, of course, his notebook, which he used not merely for notes but also for quick sketches, sometimes of a whole plant, other times just one part of it.

After a couple of miles, they turned off the main path, climbing over a stile to access the narrower, steeper track that led to the top of Shipley Edge.

"Come on," James said as he jumped to the ground. "We've been dawdling a bit. Let's pick up the pace."

Iain nodded and followed James over, easily matching his brisk pace. James thought nothing of walking fifteen, even twenty miles in a day, so eight miles was a mere stroll to him. As for Iain, he was equally used to strenuous exercise, albeit he tended to spend more time on horseback than on foot.

"So, how goes army life?" James asked as they half walked, half clambered over a rocky section of the track. "I know you hated being posted in Manchester. You've sounded happier in your recent letters. Are you enjoying your vaunted new post, guarding the King?"

"Better than Manchester," Iain admitted. "Though in truth I've been growing a little bored lately. The King is not an easy man to be around."

"He seems to have taken to you."

"He has," Iain replied, not bothering to hide his surprise. "I don't know why, to tell you the truth. He is a rather strange fellow."

James just laughed at that. "It'll be the same reason everyone likes you."

"*Everyone* doesn't like me," Iain said drily. "I can assure you of that."

"Most people do," James said, and when Iain looked at him, raising his brows in exaggerated disbelief, he added, "They *do*. You're blind if you think otherwise. I think it's because you seem so merry all the time. Always so—oh!" He broke off suddenly. "Oh, do look! Birdsfoot trefoil!"

He shrugged his bag off his shoulder and crouched down to take a closer look.

While Iain waited for James to finish with his newest

discovery—a modest yellow flower of tiny proportions—Iain pondered the man's words.

Although it was absurd to suggest he was universally liked, it was true that he tended to get along with most people, and he couldn't deny that the King seemed to have formed a certain attachment to him. Over the last few months, Iain had gradually become an unofficial part of the King's personal guard, and very recently his role had begun to morph again so that now he was more of a personal attendant—part of the King's inner circle. It was a turn of events his army masters thoroughly approved of. They liked to know everything that was going on, and having a man so close to the King was extremely useful.

My dear young friend.

That was what the King called him.

In all honesty, though, it was a friendship that was beginning to weigh on Iain. The King was given to emotional outbursts and lengthy periods of wallowing over his hurt feelings. At such times, he liked to have his friends about him, to seek their counsel and give vent to his emotions. Repeatedly.

It was—boring.

Today, though, Iain could only be glad of his privileged position. It was, after all, entirely due to the King's intervention that he was here at all. Technically, he was still on duty, but when he'd told the King about the dear friend who had invited him to visit and who he would not otherwise see for the second year in a row, his sentimental master had all but ordered him to be on his way.

I shall manage without you for a week or two, Captain, he'd said in a martyred tone. *Go. Visit your friend with my blessing, and when you come back, you may accompany me to Brighton.*

So, here Iain was, at Wylde Manor for two whole weeks. No duties or obligations. Just long, leisure-filled days. With James.

Heaven.

James straightened from his examination of the tiny flowers. "Such a pleasing little plant," he said happily.

"You've not taken a sample," Iain pointed out, gesturing at James's empty hands.

"Gosh, no, I must've looked at hundreds of these in my time. They're pretty common. I'm sure I've shown you them before. Don't you remember?"

Iain shook his head. "I can't say I do, but in fairness, you've probably shown me scores of little yellow flowers over the years."

"It's not just a little yellow flower!" James protested. He bent and picked one of the tiny blooms, then stood up again, stepping closer to Iain to show him. "Look at the shape of those petals."

"It's doesn't look much a bird's foot to me," Iain said, considering the puffy curves of the little flower, neat as a lady's slipper.

"'Birdsfoot' isn't a reference to the flower," James said. "It's the seed pods." He pointed at the plant again, and Iain saw what he was talking about, a star of five brownish seed pods that looked like nothing so much as a chicken's foot. The pods even had little points on the ends, like claws.

"Oh yes," he said, bending down for a closer look. When he glanced up at James again, he saw the man was smiling at him almost indulgently. "I never notice these things," he said. "Except when you point them out to me."

"That's what I like best about being a naturalist," James said. "I have all these little secrets that no one else knows about." He gave a wry chuckle, then said, "Come on, let's find this bee orchid. I'm sure there are some on the other side of the hill."

They set off again, as briskly as before, but they got all the way over to the other side of Shipley Edge with no sign of any bee orchid. It was only when they were on their way back to the house, when they were just about to cut into the woods behind Wylde Manor, that James stopped in his tracks.

"There's one!" he exclaimed, slipping the satchel from his shoulder and crouching down.

Iain squatted down beside him, curious.

The bee orchid was an odd little thing. Its pretty purple petals were like a set of fairy wings surrounding the central part of the flower that looked like nothing so much as a bee's rear end, nuzzling in to collect nectar. Iain squinted and looked more closely, fascinated to see that what looked like the swollen abdomen of a good-sized bumblebee was in fact another petal, ingeniously rounded.

"How extraordinary!" he declared. "It looks like a real bee when you first look."

"Yes," James said, turning his head to look at him. He smiled delightedly, his whole face lighting up with the pleasure of discovery. "Isn't it outrageous?"

Iain frowned. "I don't understand, though," he said. "Won't it put the other bees off? Thinking there's a bee in there already, getting the nectar?"

"Not at all—the idea is that male bees want to copulate with it!" James laughed.

Iain frowned even harder. "But hang on, you told me that worker bees don't copulate or—"

"That's honeybees," James interrupted, shaking his head. "The sort of bee that this plant is trying to attract is solitary. Not the sort that make honey or live in colonies."

"Oh. So the male bee comes along and tries to have his way with that petal—"

"*Labellum*," James corrected. "That's the proper botanical term."

Iain rolled his eyes. "He tries to swive the *labellum*," he continued, "and…what?"

"And he gets the pollen from the flower on his body and carries it away with him. And thus the orchid reproduces.

That's what's supposed to happen anyway, if the right sort of bee is around."

"That's sneaky," Iain said, grinning.

"Oh, nature is very sneaky," James replied. "There are lots of plants and animals that mimic things. Some, like the bee orchid, seem designed to attract, others to repel—to put predators off eating them. Still others are concerned with blending in with their surroundings. It's difficult to fathom how such seemingly perfect design came about in the humblest of living things—an insect, a wildflower, a little bird." He smiled at Iain. "Of course, many would say that it's all part of the good Lord's grand design."

"Don't you think that?"

James was silent for a long beat. "No," he said at last. "I think that's too easy an answer. Though I do think there's a reason for everything. That's why I'm a scientist, I suppose. To try, in my small way, to contribute to the discovery of the great *Why* of it all." He turned his attention back to the bee orchid and frowned thoughtfully.

After a minute, Iain said, "Well? Aren't you going to dig it up?"

James worried at his lower lip with his teeth, a habit of his when he was undecided about something.

"I don't like to dig up specimens when there aren't many around," he said. He dug into his satchel, drawing out his notebook. "I think I'll draw it instead, if you don't mind waiting."

"Of course not," Iain said. "I'm happy to lounge in the sun for a while."

He settled himself on the grass while James rummaged in his satchel, stretching out and leaning back on his elbows, tipping his head back and closing his eyes. Relishing the warmth of the sun on his face. He felt like he'd spent more time indoors these last five months than in the five years previous. The King was not a lover of the outdoors.

While he basked, James sketched. At first James sat, cross-legged, his drawing book resting on his knees, but after a while, he adjusted his position to lie on the ground beside Iain, flat on his belly, his chin propped up on one hand, while he drew with the other.

At length, Iain sat up, leaning over to examine James's work.

"Not bad," he said, tilting his head to one side as he examined the drawing.

James screwed up his nose. "Not good enough, though."

He'd told Iain years ago that he wasn't a natural artist, but he'd worked hard with a drawing master to achieve a degree of competency, maintaining it was important for a scientist to be able to accurately sketch his specimens.

"It's better than I could do," Iain pointed out.

"Well, that's not saying much. You can barely draw a circle. There are infants who draw better than you."

"How dare you!" Iain exclaimed, all mock outrage, shoving at James's shoulder.

"*Oi!*" James protested as his pencil flew across the page, right through his careful sketch. "You bloody oaf!" he cried, but he was grinning.

Casting his notebook and pencil aside, he launched himself at Iain, using the element of surprise to knock him over before trying to wrestle him into submission.

Iain began laughing as James tried to pin him, and it was a laugh that came right from the pit of his belly, filling his whole body with mirth, an expression of the happiness that had been building in him all day.

"Submit, villain!" James cried.

These days, he was as tall as Iain, with shoulders that had broadened considerably over the last few years, and lean, wiry muscles. His grip was strong too, firm on Iain's shoulder and hip. But he didn't have Iain's bulk—or his fighting skills—so when Iain finally overcame his mirth enough to fight back, it wasn't long before he dislodged James, flipping him onto his back so hard that the wind rushed from him with a pained huff and he was gasping for air and laughing at the same time.

"Unfair!" James gasped when he could finally speak, the single word carried on a gurgle of pained hilarity.

"Submit," Iain demanded softly, looming over him. "I have you fast. You'll not escape."

And then the oddest thing happened. One moment, they were in fits of laughter; the next…something between them shifted. James's chuckles faded to a smile, and his grey gaze softened with affection. Iain's breath caught in his throat to see the tenderness on James's face. Worse, his cock, pressed hard against James's thigh, stiffened. He felt sure James must feel his excitement and the sudden flush that crept over the other man's cheeks seemed to confirm his fears. He watched, fascinated, as James's oil-black pupils expanded, their darkness eating up the calm grey of the surrounding irises, and for an absurdly long moment, they just stared at one another. As much as he knew he ought to, Iain couldn't look away. His friend's dear, beloved face—all mirth melted away now— held all of Iain's attention, and desire pulsed through his body, insistent as the pounding of his blood in his veins.

They were still gazing at one another when, with a *whoosh*, like a great sucking breath, a dozen or more birds rose out of the trees at the edge of the wood, making them startle and jump apart. A few seconds later, came the unmistakable sound of human voices.

They scrambled to their feet, dusting themselves down. James was just putting his drawing things back in his satchel when the walkers who had disturbed the birds emerged from the edge of the trees. Two ladies—more of the Harts' guests, Iain guessed.

"Hello there," James called out to them, waving. They greeted him with waves of their own and warm smiles.

114

"Good afternoon, ladies," James said as they drew near. He executed a brief, clumsy bow—the man had never had much time for elegant manners.

"Good afternoon, Mr. Hart," the older lady said, nodding at him in a friendly way and sending Iain a quick curious look. "Have you and your friend come out to enjoy the air as Agatha and I have?"

The younger lady said nothing, but she sent James a bashful look through her lashes that Iain noted James entirely missed.

"Yes, it's far too lovely a day to stay inside," James replied. He gestured in Iain's direction, adding, "May I introduce my friend, Captain Sinclair? Would you believe he arrived only this afternoon, and despite having ridden all day, immediately agreed to walk out to Shipley Edge with me?"

"Without even so much as a cup of tea first?" the older lady asked with mock astonishment. "Oh, now that is heroic!"

Everyone laughed politely, and the introductions were duly made. The older lady was Mrs. Lamb, a friend of James's mother. It transpired she knew Iain's mother too and asked warmly after Mrs. Sinclair's health. The younger lady was Mrs. Lamb's niece by marriage, Miss Kirk. When James suggested they walk back through the woods together, the ladies happily agreed.

Iain quickly offered his arm to Mrs. Lamb—although he had something of a reputation as a hardened flirt, he always made sure to assiduously avoid the company of any marriageable young women who might be looking for a husband. It was only once they were on their way that he realised he'd made a mistake. His decision meant he had to spend the entire walk back watching James escort Miss Kirk, and by God, but the girl milked every second.

Iain scowled as James guided her over the uneven path, noting sourly that she leaned far more heavily on his arm than was remotely necessary. When they crossed the stile at the tree line, she actually asked James to lift her down from the wooden step despite the fact she must've climbed over without any assistance only a few minutes earlier. It was all Iain could do not to roll his eyes at Mrs. Lamb, who, despite being at least three decades older than her niece, was able to hop down perfectly well, declining Iain's offer of assistance with a chuckle.

Iain found himself deciding that the Kirk girl was an irritating chit. He hated the soft, breathless way she spoke, leaning close to James's ear every time she had something to say to him. And her silly helplessness was plainly put on. At the very same time that she was stumbling her way over a few exposed roots, hanging on to James as though for dear life, her aunt was informing Iain that the girl was a bruising rider who thought nothing of racing her mare, Artemis, along the long Northumbrian beaches at a breakneck gallop.

At last they were back at the house. As soon as they were inside, Mrs. Lamb indicated that she and Miss Kirk ought to have a lie down before dinner, oblivious to her niece's annoyance at that announcement. That left Iain and James alone in the hallway again, back where they'd been stood just a few hours earlier.

"A lie down," Iain said scornfully, once the ladies were safely out of earshot. When James laughed softly, he added, "That girl was hanging on your arm so hard, I thought she was going to pull it out of its socket."

"Don't be unkind," James chided him. "She's really very nice."

"My sisters don't behave like that," Iain replied churlishly. "Nor do yours."

James just shrugged. "Anyway," he said, "if there's one person who really *ought* to have a lie down before dinner, it's you. You'll be falling asleep by eight o'clock at this rate."

"You're probably right," Iain admitted, rubbing the back

of his neck. His shoulders and thighs ached from the long ride. "Perhaps a short nap before dinner."

James smiled at him, his expression wistful. "I wish I could join you," he said.

For a moment, Iain couldn't look away, struck dumb as a rush of mental images flooded his mind: James walking towards Iain as he lay in bed, loosening his cravat as he drew near. James lying down on him, his cock as hard against Iain's thigh, as Iain's had been earlier. James's soft grey gaze on Iain's face, his breath ghosting over Iain's lips as he drew close…

"What did you say?" Iain said faintly, and was that his voice? He sounded stupid. Dazed.

"I wish I could have a nap too," James said. His tone was prosaic. Apparently, he was unaware of the wave of desire that had just swamped Iain. "A little snooze would be just the thing right now, but I really ought to write my notes about the bee orchid while they're still fresh in my mind, and I promised Mama I'd be in the drawing room early tonight, to entertain the ladies before dinner."

Ah.

Iain cleared his throat and smiled tightly. "I see. Well, I'll leave you to your duties then," he said, adding after a pause, "Sorry I ruined your drawing earlier, old man."

A stupid thing to say. It only reminded him yet again of that all too brief tussle in the grass, and his painfully hard cock pressing insistently against James's thigh. Iain's cheeks warmed at the memory—Jesus Christ, was he *blushing*?

If he was, James hadn't noticed. "That's all right," the man said easily. "It wasn't nearly good enough anyway. Besides, Miss Kirk's agreed to come out and sketch it for me tomorrow. She's an excellent artist, apparently."

The urge to sneer at that was near overwhelming, but by some miracle, Iain managed to resist, instead saying something about Miss Kirk's artistic abilities being a happy coincidence before heading for the stairs to return to his chamber for his long-awaited nap, James's wish that he experience "sweet dreams" ringing in his ears.

He didn't have any dreams, though, sweet or otherwise. Instead, he spent the next two hours staring at the ceiling, reliving those minutes in the grass earlier, over and over, wondering if he'd imagined James's response to him.

5th June, 1821

Wylde Manor, Derbyshire

When James walked into the breakfast room early on Tuesday morning, it was to find Iain sitting at the table alone, drinking coffee and staring unseeingly at the *Times*.

"Good morning," he said cheerfully. "You managed to get up, then?"

Iain sent him a pained look. "It's far too early. I'm meant to be having a restful country break, didn't you know?" He gulped down the rest of his coffee, then poured himself another cup, yawning.

James chuckled and wandered over to the sideboard, which was groaning with food, to fill a plate.

"At least we'll be able to escape on our own for a few hours this way," he said as he served himself some kedgeree.

Somehow, Agatha Kirk had learned that it was James's habit to breakfast at the unusually early hour of eight in the morning, and ever since, she'd been appearing for the breakfast every morning at the same hour. Worse, she invariably invited herself along to whatever James was planning to do that day. It was putting a complete damper on Iain's long-awaited visit. In desperation, James had cornered Iain while Agatha was showing off her pianoforte skills the previous evening and asked him to meet James for breakfast at the even earlier hour of seven this morning.

"So," James said, settling himself into the chair opposite Iain's and shaking his napkin open. "What do you say to going riding with me this morning? Just you and me for a few hours? No one else."

Iain grinned. "That sounds perfect. Do you promise no Miss Kirk?"

James laughed. "It's why I asked you to get up at this god-awful hour. Where shall we go?"

"How about Rowley Tor?"

James paused. It was a fair way. Over two hours out there and the same back—and they'd have to rest the horses in between. Even if they were on their way promptly, it would likely be midafternoon before they were back—and James had promised his mother he would be an attentive host to the Lambs and their niece.

"We could go for a dip on the way back, at that swimming hole in the woods you showed me last year..." Iain's tone was wheedling.

James glanced out of the window. The cloudless sky promised another glorious day. "A swim would be bliss," he admitted. And besides, Iain was his guest just as much as Agatha Kirk—more so, in fact, since Agatha had been invited by his mother, whereas Iain was all James's responsibility. And so far, James had been an exceedingly neglectful host to his friend.

"All right," he said decisively. "Let's pop over to the stables once I've eaten this and see what's what." Iain's wide grin was all the reward he needed.

They finished their breakfasts quickly after that and headed out for the stables. James's favourite mare, Treacle, a good-natured if frisky beast, stuck her head out of her stall and whickered softly at him. James went to her and rubbed her nose, fussing over her while Iain looked over the other horses, finally selecting a young, headstrong gelding named Hector.

Less than half an hour later, the horses were saddled and waiting at the front of the house, a simple lunch packed inside their saddlebags.

James mounted first—for all her playfulness, Treacle had a sweet temperament and was fairly easy to handle. Hector was a different story. He was nervous and jumpy, tossing his head and whinnying even as the groom patted his flank soothingly. Not that Iain was intimidated. James had yet to see the horse that his friend could not win over, and Hector was no exception. The man spent a few minutes murmuring to the animal, stroking him soothingly till he ceased his stamping and quieted. Then he swung himself up into Hector's saddle with easy grace, settling the horse's renewed jitters with a few soothing noises and pats, moving all the time as though he and the horse were one, his knees nudging the beast's sides, his hands gentle yet firm on the reins till the gelding calmed.

James rolled his eyes. "Bloody typical. That horse doesn't like anyone, but already he's in love with you."

"Oh, he's just a big show-off." Iain grinned, patting Hector's neck. "He's happy because he knows how much I admire him."

"Mr. Hart! Oh, do wait!"

The voice that interrupted their conversation was a young feminine one that already had James's heart sinking before he'd turned in his saddle and seen its owner, standing at the top of the steps of the manor house.

Agatha Kirk.

She was looking fresh and lovely in a pale green muslin dress, her smile bright as she waved at them.

"I say," she called down to him. "Are you and Captain

Sinclair going riding? We could all go together, if you don't mind waiting a little longer?"

Dismay hit James hard—he could hardly say no. He opened his mouth to reply, steeling himself to express agreement in a way that didn't betray how very irritated and disappointed he felt. But before he could get a sound out, Iain was speaking.

"I'm afraid not, Miss Kirk," he said abruptly. "We have to leave now. We're riding all the way to Rowley Tor, you see, and can't afford to lose any time. Sorry."

He didn't sound remotely sorry, and James felt an uncomfortable mingling of mortification and relief at having the decision taken so resoundingly—and rudely—out of his hands.

At first, Agatha Kirk just gaped. Then she shut up her open mouth like a trap and eyed Iain for a long, steady moment before turning her gaze back to James.

"Oh well," she said sadly. "Perhaps another day, Mr. Hart?"

"Of course," James said, relieved by her gracious acceptance of defeat, even as he knew he was being manoeuvred into something else he wouldn't want to do.

She smiled shyly and added in a hopeful tone, "Tomorrow?"

"I shall look forward to it," he lied. Beside him, Iain muttered something under his breath and set Hector to walking down the drive.

Agatha looked pleased, smug, actually, her Cupid's bow mouth twisting up betrayingly, and for the first time, James felt something for her—a bolt of pure dislike—that went beyond the mere dread with which he'd regarded her to date. With a final curt nod, he wheeled the mare around and set off after Iain at a trot.

"Do not even consider going riding with that chit without

me and another female," Iain said when James caught up with him. His voice was tight with annoyance. "She's a manipulative little snake. One wrong step and you'll find yourself so neatly trapped, there'll be no getting out of it. You'll be halfway up the aisle before you can stammer out an excuse."

James shuddered at the thought. "I'll be the soul of discretion. I have no wish to be caught in the parson's mousetrap by Agatha Kirk."

"No, she'd lead you a dog's life, that one," Iain agreed. "I can tell by that mean little mouth of hers." He made a prissy face at James, pursing his lips together and looking down his nose, and James laughed.

"Thank you for stepping in," he said after a beat. "I'd've felt obliged to agree to her suggestion."

"That's all right. I know your mother's expecting you to be a gentleman, but she can't be surprised at me being a boor. After all, I'm a military man and quite unused to delicate female company."

"That's the fattest lie you've ever uttered," James said drily, "and Mama'll know it too. You may as well prepare yourself for the fact that you'll be getting a scolding over this."

Iain chuckled. "That's all right. I'll make it up to Miss Kirk by insisting on joining her riding excursion tomorrow and sticking to you both like glue."

James laughed again.

"Come on," Iain said then, smiling at James wickedly. "Race you." He touched his heels to the gelding's flanks and leaped ahead, and with a whoop, James leaned forwards over Treacle's neck and bounded after him.

They couldn't have picked a better day to go for a ride had they planned it in advance. The sun shone bright and warm in a cloudless azure sky.

"What a glorious day," James said, tipping his head back to enjoy the sun on his face. Beneath him, Treacle's broad back rocked as she walked slowly along the path.

"Perfect," Iain agreed. He let out a happy sigh that made the warm, contented feeling in James's chest grow.

They were on the uphill stretch now, on a wide path that let them walk the horses side by side.

"I'm glad you managed to put Miss Kirk off," James said. "She's been rather…persistent."

Iain snorted. "I acted purely out of self-interest. She's been hanging around you like a bad smell since I got here. I've barely had a chance to talk to you."

It was true. The girl was everywhere James turned.

"You do realise she sees you as husband material?" Iain said.

James sighed. "I know," he replied. "I've already had words with Mama about inviting her here without my knowledge. I've told her in no uncertain terms that I've no interest in the girl."

Iain just pressed his lips together in a firm, unhappy line.

"What?" James said. "Why are you looking like that?"

For a moment he thought Iain wasn't going to answer him, but after a pause, he said, "If you're not interested in her, you shouldn't encourage her."

James blinked, taken aback both by the accusation and by Iain's brusque tone. Iain, meanwhile, stared straight forward, his expression unreadable.

"I've not been encouraging her," James said, annoyed. "But she's a guest of Mama's. I can hardly ignore her."

Iain turned his head, meeting James's gaze. There was a faintly disapproving tightness to his jaw, a slight frown between his brows.

"I'm not suggesting you be rude," he said. "Merely that you stop paying her particular attentions."

"Particular attentions? I haven't—"

"Yes, you have. You took her out walking to see your bee orchid. You sat watching her draw for a whole afternoon. Don't you realise that a young lady would consider that a mark of particular attention?"

"Her aunt was with us!" James protested.

Iain ignored that. "You accepted the drawing from her," he said, adding to James's list of crimes. "A personal gift."

James stared at him, an oddly panicky feeling gripping him now. Did Agatha Kirk think he'd been paying her attentions? So far as he was concerned, he'd merely been polite.

All at once, Iain sighed, and his condemning look fell away, though his frown stayed in place. "I just want you to be careful, Jamie. It's not your fault that she's set her sights on you, but she has. She sees that you're handsome and eligible, and she's the sort of girl who's used to getting what she wants."

James found himself swallowing hard.

She sees that you're handsome...

"Perhaps I shouldn't be warning you off," Iain went on. "Perhaps she would make you a good wife." He smiled crookedly at James, though his usually merry blue eyes were sad. "What do you think, Jamie? Could you see her as mistress of Wylde Manor?"

The feeling of warm contentment James had had all morning dissipated. Suddenly, James felt sad, intensely so.

He shook his head firmly. "I don't want a wife," he said huskily.

"No?" Iain asked. "Don't you think you'll be lonely as a bachelor?"

"I'm not lonely now," he said. "I've got my family, and friends." He paused. "I've got you."

"You don't see me very often," Iain said softly.

"No," James agreed. "Not nearly as much as I'd like to."

There was a long moment—as Iain's blue gaze clouded with what looked very like real pain—when James felt as though he was staring right into his friend's soul. Then, Iain broke eye contact and picked up the reins he'd been holding loosely in his hands, digging his heels into Hector's sides to increase the horse's pace and draw ahead of James.

"Come on," he called over his shoulder. "We'll soon be at the Tor."

Sighing inwardly, James urged his own horse on. The path had begun to narrow, though the incline had lessened, and for a while, they rode at a reasonable trot, James on Iain's heels. He found himself dwelling on what Iain had said about being lonely without a wife, wondering what Iain had meant by that. Was he was talking about the everyday companionship of sharing another's life, making a household together? Or was it the deeper intimacy of the marriage bed he was referring to?

When it came to his household, James was perfectly content. Now that his sisters were all married, his mother spent much of her time in London, but whenever she came to spend a few weeks at Wylde Manor, they rubbed along pretty well together—except when she invited prospective brides to visit, that was. Even when she was away, the house ran like clockwork thanks to Wylde Manor's excellent servants, leaving James free to spend most of his time on his scientific pursuits. It was a life that contented him, for the most part.

The question of intimacy though, that was something that had been occupying his thoughts a great deal recently. Was something, in fact, that he'd been planning to ask Iain about at some point…

They dismounted at the top of Rowley Tor. A pair of kestrels was circling overhead, and James bent his head back, shielding his eyes with one hand to watch them.

"What are you looking at?" Iain asked as he checked over Hector's legs.

"Kestrels," James replied softly. He pointed. "Look."

Iain strolled over to stand beside him, following the direction of James's gaze with his own. For a while they just watched the little raptors as they wheeled and dipped and hovered in the cloudless sky.

"That one's seen its dinner," James said after a while, pointing at one of the birds. The sleek little bird was poised on a wind current, its gaze very fixed on the ground. James fancied he could feel it, quivering with intention, and wondered if Iain felt that too, or if that was something that you only perceived when you'd watched kestrels as often as he had.

Sure enough, after another few seconds, the kestrel swooped, plunging swiftly to the ground, straight as bullet. When it rose up again, an instant later, it had a creature in its talons—a field mouse by the look of it.

"It's fierce for such a little thing," Iain said wonderingly.

"Small as it is, it's a predator through and through," James replied. "And now it has a good meal to eat."

Iain lowered his gaze and glanced at James. "Speaking of meals—are you hungry yet?"

"Getting there," James said. "But I thought we might eat after our swim, if you can wait a bit longer."

"Agreed," Iain said, pulling himself back up into the saddle. "Besides, we'll be halfway back to the house by then, so the horses won't have too much work left to do."

They set off again, descending the south side of the Tor this time. It was steeper but shorter and led onto a broad, flat path the horses could take at a comfortable trot.

"May I ask you something?" James blurted out after a while.

Iain glanced at him, curious. "Of course."

James felt his cheeks flush. "The thing is—well, how do

you—obtain male company?"

"Company?"

James cleared his throat. "Carnal relations, I mean." When Iain just stared at him, looking vaguely horrified, he felt his cheeks heat still further. "Don't pretend you go without," he added. "I shan't believe you."

To his credit, Iain didn't even try. He cleared his throat. "What do you want to know?"

"Well," James began, "Some men keep mistresses, don't they? Do you have a—an arrangement like that with anyone? A man, I mean?"

"No," Iain said. Again, he looked curious. "Why? Do you?"

"No," James replied. "I wouldn't be asking if I did—though it sounds like a good solution to me."

"A solution to what?"

"To—well, meeting one's needs. It is not an easy thing, to find discreet partners. I would prefer a regular arrangement."

Iain frowned at him. "Have you sought out such an arrangement?"

"I wouldn't say—" James began slowly, but before he could go on, Iain was interrupting.

"Jamie, you really do need to be careful—"

"I *am* careful," James insisted.

Iain didn't look reassured by that. He shook his head and exhaled hard. "Don't you realise there are people who prey on men like us?" he said. He was agitated now. "People who would rob you, assault you, blackmail you. Once they have you in a compromising position—" He broke off.

"I'm not a fool, Iain," James replied, frowning. "I'm careful. And the truth is—well, I've only had a handful of encounters with other men."

"A 'handful'? How many is that?" Iain demanded.

James raised his eyebrows. "Four, if you must know."

"Who with?"

"None of your bloody business!" James snapped.

Iain's shock at James's angry tone was palpable. He reared back in his saddle a little and for several long, silent moments said nothing. Then he shook his head, almost imperceptibly.

"You're right," he said. "I'm sorry. I just—I just hate to think of you putting yourself at risk. It worries me. You're too trusting at times."

"You don't need to be so protective," James replied woodenly, staring straight ahead. "I'm not as foolishly naïve as you imagine."

Silence fell, the only sound now the clopping of their horses' hooves on the hard-packed mud path.

Then, into the quiet, James said, "There have been only two men. One was a university friend—three of those four encounters were with him. The last was with a man I met at Kate's house last year. One of Edward's cousins." He shrugged. "I liked him. I wondered if it might be possible to have something more with him, but the opportunity to discuss the matter never came up. It got me wondering, though, what other men like me do." He glanced at Iain. "Men like us."

Iain returned his look warily. He said nothing, but his expression said he was listening.

James sighed. "What I'm trying to say is that I've never solicited a stranger. Never paid anyone—for that. But, well, I suppose I can see how tempting that could become." He swallowed. "It's been almost a year since I met Freddy..."

He looked pleadingly at Iain, begging silently for understanding, and Iain didn't turn away, though he dropped his gaze and rubbed uncomfortably at the back of his neck.

"It can be tempting to be foolish," he said at last. "That's why I have a place I go to. A safe place."

James swallowed. "What place?"

"It's a club, of sorts. Somewhere like-minded men go, to meet one another. To meet each other's needs."

"What's it called?" James asked. "Does it have a name?"

Iain gave a small smile as though amused by the question. "Redford's," he said. "It's in London. Membership is by introduction only—the members rely on each other's trustworthiness."

"Do you—that is, do you...*pay* for the company there?"

Iain stared at him, and James wondered if he was offended. He didn't sound it though, when he finally said, "No. I could if I wanted to, but I prefer to deal with men like myself."

"Men like yourself?"

"Men who want a straightforward sort of thing. No buying or selling. Just getting what we want from each other, then parting."

"Do you ever go with the same man?"

Iain just shook his head, and his expression didn't invite further questions on that point.

After a moment, James said diffidently, "Perhaps you could nominate me for membership?"

"Absolutely *not!*"

James blinked, taken aback by Iain's swift, uncompromising reply. "What? Why not?"

Iain scowled. "I just—" He broke off.

"Just what?"

"I don't—hell, I don't like the thought of it!"

"The thought of what?"

"Of *you*, in Redford's. Looking for that." He was staring forward, not even looking at James now.

"Why not?" James demanded.

"I don't know," Iain said irritably. "I just don't like it."

James stared at his friend's grim profile. "You go to this club regularly by your own admission," he pointed out.

"I do."

"You go with other men—never the same one twice."

"Correct," Iain gritted out.

"So why should you mind the thought of me doing the exact same thing?"

Iain said nothing, but a muscle in his jaw flickered.

"Why don't you want me to go there, Iain?" James demanded again, irritated by the man's hypocrisy. When Iain didn't answer, he pressed on angrily. "I think you look at me and see a boy, but I'm two-and-twenty—"

"I don't see you as a boy," Iain broke in. "I can assure you of that much."

James didn't know what to say to that. Didn't know how to interpret Iain's quiet, almost resigned tone.

For a long, silent moment, their gazes held as he puzzled over it.

Briefly, he wondered if Iain's odd reaction was down to the fact that the thought of James with another man bothered him—but that was a silly idea. Iain didn't want James like that. Never had.

I hope you don't think that just because I have indulged in such things with others, that I was looking for that from you...

No, that was a preposterous idea.

Yet now he found himself remembering that odd moment yesterday afternoon, when they'd wrestled in the grass. He'd been sure he'd imagined the flash of desire in Iain's blue gaze, the hardness of Iain's body against his own.

But had he?

It was half an hour later that they entered the woods that backed onto the manor house and walked the horses to James's favourite swimming place, a small, deep pool, fed by a tiny waterfall. In the winter, the foss gushed, icy cold, but at this time of year, its flow was diminished to little more than a trickle and the surface of the water was glassily still.

"That looks heavenly," Iain said as he dismounted. "It's a

long time since I've been swimming."

They let the horses drink their fill first, feeding them each an apple before tying them up and leaving them to graze under the willows that fringed the banks of the pool. The willows provided a welcome barrier between the water and the woods beyond, lending them a little privacy as they began to undress.

It was only then, as they began to shed their clothes, that James felt suddenly and oddly shy. It was the silliest thing. He hadn't felt shy the last time they'd swum here, not much more than a year ago. Not that he hadn't been aware of Iain—in truth, he would *always* be aware of Iain, always be drawn to sneak looks at the man's powerful physique—but this time...

I don't see you as a boy. I can assure you of that much.

"Come *on*, Jamie!"

Iain's voice, excited and urging, distracted James from his thoughts. He glanced over to see that the man was already half-naked, jacket, shirt and waistcoat all carelessly discarded on the grassy bank. He was, in fact, down to his boots and breeches—apparently he wasn't bothered by the situation at all.

James's mouth dried to see the dappled sunlight kissing Iain's smooth skin. His heart beat a little faster as his wistful gaze took in the muscled planes of Iain's powerful torso, the intriguing patterns of the dark hair that swirled over his chest, around his nipples and all the way down to his navel. James had only a light line of hair from belly button to crotch, and none at all on his chest, which was pale and marble smooth.

And Christ but he was *staring*.

"All right, all right," he called, turning away and beginning to loosen his cravat, hoping that Iain didn't hear the catch in his voice.

Forcing himself to concentrate on removing his own

clothes, he made sure to miss the sight of Iain stripping away his boots, breeches and undergarments, but when he heard Iain's whoop and the enormous splash that followed, he turned back, laughing hard when Iain yelped, "*Fuck*, that's cold!"

Iain's dark head bobbed up and down in the middle of the water a few times as he treaded water briefly, then he lunged up and dived under, emerging half a minute later on the other side of the pool with a gasp.

"Come on, get in!" he yelled, shaking his hair out of his eyes and sending water drops flying. "It's bloody lovely in here!"

James was down to his smallclothes now, and he quickly stripped that final layer away before wading into the pool, gasping when the water kissed his balls, and again, more loudly, when it moved further up to his waist.

"Jesus Christ!" he exclaimed accusingly. "It's hardly fucking lovely!"

"Oh, stop being feeble!" Iain laughed. "Get your head under, then you'll be fine."

"I'll give you feeble!" James cried, all mock outrage, and with a big gulp of air, he arrowed his body into the water, leading with his outstretched arms. Once under, he stayed there, swimming all the way to Iain underwater.

The water was clear, and he easily made out Iain's circling legs as he approached, grabbing one with two hands and quickly tugging him under before lunging to one side. He swam several strong strokes in the opposite direction before bursting from the surface with a laughing gasp to watch as Iain spluttered his way back up, coughing and cursing.

"Ah, so that's how it's going to be, is it?" Iain cried once he'd righted himself. "Prepare to be routed!" He launched himself at James with a roar, and James darted away, cackling with laughter.

They wrestled and played like puppies in the water,

ducking each other mercilessly. Iain was stronger, but James was quicker in the water, so they gave each other a good run for their money before they finally flopped onto the grassy bank side by side, panting and exhausted.

They'd inadvertently found a patch of sun created by a gap in the trees, and James was glad of the warmth on his chilled skin. He draped his forearm over his eyes to block out the light and sighed with contentment. The grass beneath him was soft and cool, the sun above, warm as honey.

And Iain was beside him.

James turned his head to look at his friend and smiled. Iain was stretched out in the sun, lazy as a lion, eyes closed, mouth faintly smiling, entirely oblivious to being observed.

Ah, but he was a lovely looking man.

And drowsing a little now too, if James wasn't much mistaken.

James propped himself up on one elbow and let himself look. Let himself just have this moment, since Iain was sleeping. Watching Iain was pure pleasure for him. The man had long been perfection in James's eyes. Skin the colour of warm cream stretched over the muscular perfection of that well-honed body. Iain had the broad chest, flat belly and narrow hips of a beautifully formed male. James's gaze moved further down to the thatch of dark hair at Iain's crotch, and the impressive half-hard shaft that rested there.

James swallowed, unable to tear his gaze away. Iain's cock was fascinatingly different from his own, not quite as long, but thicker. Straighter too, not like James's, which curved distinctly to the right.

His mind flooded with a score of lurid imaginings. What it would feel like to take that thick shaft in his hand? In his mouth? What it would feel like thrusting into his body? He'd never—

"Jamie?"

His name on Iain's lips was murmured, blurred with

sleep, and when James glanced up, it was to find the other man's slumberous gaze upon him.

James's heart missed a beat.

There was desire in Iain's eyes—this time he was sure of it. And it was a desire that matched his own. Remarkable. Amazing.

In that instant, nothing moved. Somewhere nearby, an insect droned, but everything else was still and waiting. Poised. This was a moment in which something could happen; a moment in which James could act, or not.

He chose to act.

He reached out and stroked his thumb slowly over Iain's lips, mesmerised by the twin sensations of smooth lips and the faint bristle of moustache against the pad of his thumb. The whole time he held his breath, watching Iain, waiting to be rejected. But the rejection didn't come. Instead, Iain went very still below him, his eyes tracking James's movements.

Iain remained still when James shifted to lean over him, moving slowly so as to give the man the clearest warning of his intentions. He was ready to be stopped, ready to be pushed away, but when he slowly lowered his head, his eyes shifting from Iain's intense blue gaze, to his beautifully carved lips, there was no resistance at all. Quite the opposite —when James touched his mouth to Iain's, the man's lips clung to his own, making James moan with pleasure and press closer to deepen the kiss, relishing those masculine whiskers against his own beardless face.

Iain's body was still cold from their swim, but his lips were warm, and his tongue, when it slid between James's lips to enter his mouth, was hot and sleek, a startling contrast to his chilled skin.

Iain raised his right arm, sliding it round James's neck to draw him closer while anchoring his other arm around James's waist. Then, without warning, he flipped James onto his back.

That quickly, Iain was the aggressor, groaning into James's mouth before plunging his tongue deep inside. All James could do was open to him, and he did it as thoroughly as possible, welcoming whatever the man was finally prepared to give him, wrapping his legs round Iain's waist as he arched up against him, dizzy with the pleasure of their kiss, unable to believe this was really—finally—happening.

When Iain began to pull away from him, James's heart sank, and he closed his eyes, waiting for the inevitable words of rejection and regret. Instead, he felt the weight of Iain's forehead touching his own, and his own name being whispered against his lips.

"*Jamie.*"

When he opened his eyes, it was to meet Iain's very blue gaze.

"This is madness," Iain whispered. "But there's only so much temptation a man can take—"

James's heart swelled with gratitude at those words. He was not alone, then, in his desire for Iain. Iain wanted him too.

He arched up, capturing Iain's lips again, and Iain groaned in mingled submission and dominance, letting James lead the kiss, even as his hands began to take control of James's body, stroking over his flanks and buttocks, squeezing and caressing. James found himself surrendering to that sure determination, accepting Iain's silent demands, his thighs finally falling open to welcome the firm stroke of the man's hand on his shaft. He gasped, his body bucking in Iain's arms, his voice husky with incoherent pleasure as Iain kissed his way up his throat, along his jawline, pausing to murmur in his ear, "Christ, Jamie, I imagined having you just like this, last night in my bed…"

James moaned at that, at the thought of Iain thinking of him as he lay in his chamber, just down the corridor from where James slept, but he couldn't find words to respond. The pleasure Iain was wringing from his body with his lips and his hands was maddening him, clouding his brain and turning him into nothing but want and need. When Iain pressed his own body closer to James's, his thick shaft rubbing directly against James's, they both shuddered, and when Iain wrapped his hand around both of their cocks and began to work them in a slow, devastating rhythm, James whimpered, burrowing his face into the crook of Iain's neck.

"Iain—God, *please!*" he begged. "It's too much. I'm going to spend—"

"Do it, Jamie," Iain breathed in his ear. "Let me see you lose yourself."

"I—oh God—"

His crisis was upon him before he could say anything more. It was all terribly, embarrassingly quick but it was difficult to care when he was coming harder than he'd have thought possible, ten times harder than he had during last year's encounter with Freddy Greaves. He came so hard, he felt like he was being turned inside out, but it was all right because Iain had him safe. His arms were strong and certain round James's body, and even as James spilled, helplessly, he knew Iain had him.

It took him long moments to come back to himself, for the fog of pleasure clouding his mind to dissipate, and all the while, Iain's hand was still moving, using James's spend to bring forth his own shuddering climax, his groan of satisfaction in James's ear causing James to hunch a shoulder against the nerve-prickling pleasure induced by his deep voice.

"Jamie. God, *Jamie…*"

After a minute, Iain rolled off James's body, collapsing beside him in the grass. James didn't dare look at him yet, but he couldn't keep the grin off his face—he'd never been so happy in his life. He wanted to stay like this forever. Everything he loved was here: Iain and the sun-warmed earth, the sounds of a hundred little creatures all around him, none of them caring a damn what the two men lying in the grass had just done together.

It felt so very, very right.

Until…hell, was that *voices*? And the sound of horses' hooves?

He glanced at Iain, eyes wide. Iain had gone white. "Bloody hell," the other man hissed. "Quick, get up!"

Heart suddenly thumping, James jumped to his feet and began searching for his drawers. He managed to stumble into them and find his shirt just before the small group of newcomers entered the clearing, walking their horses in single file.

Thankfully, the rider at the front of the group was a gentleman rather than a lady—Mr. Lamb.

"Hold up, there, Lamb!" Iain called out, raising an arm. Somehow he managed to inject a smile into his voice, as though he was amused rather than horrified at being discovered lying naked in the grass. "We've just been swimming! Keep the ladies back, will you? We're not quite dressed yet!"

Lamb laughed out loud at the sight of them, Iain in nothing but his drawers and James clutching his shirt to his chest like a maiden aunt. Then he called out over his shoulder, "Stay back so they can get dressed. And Agatha, for God's sake, close your eyes in case you see anything you oughtn't!"

The Lambs and Miss Kirk retreated from the clearing, giving them privacy to dress. The sudden flood of relief that swamped James as he watched them disappear from view was so intense, it had him shaking. They really hadn't thought that James and Iain were doing anything other than swimming. Thank God.

James looked over at Iain, grinning with relief. He was expecting to see a matching expression on the other man's face. But Iain didn't look the least bit happy or relieved.

In fact, he looked wrecked.

13

Mr. Lamb rode up front on the way back to Wylde Manor, then James and Mrs. Lamb, leaving Iain and Miss Kirk to bring up the rear. Iain had made sure it happened that way—he wasn't about to let Miss Kirk get her claws into James again, not after what had just happened. God knew what James might let inadvertently slip—he didn't seem to have any instinct for self-preservation.

Jesus, his expression when he'd first clapped eyes on Lamb—guilty as sin and twice as shocked. Just remembering made a horrible gnawing anxiety eat at Iain's stomach.

"Have you and Mr. Hart been friends for very long?" Miss Kirk asked politely.

Iain glanced at her. She had a good seat, and her hands were light and easy on the reins of her grey mare. He noticed that she patted the animal's neck frequently and with real affection. It made him feel a little less hostile towards her, though he still didn't trust her an inch.

"Since we were children," he replied.

"You are close," she observed, and her gaze was calculating. He felt instinctively that she was implying something. She was not, he decided, an ignorant young lady.

"We are," he agreed. This time he deliberately smiled, letting his gaze drift over her a little, as though he had just noticed how pretty she was. He had made no attempt to charm this young woman so far, but when he made the effort to charm ladies, he was generally successful. He'd been credited with numerous female conquests over the years, though in truth none of them had ever amounted to more than innocent flirtation.

It may be no bad thing to curry a little favour with Agatha Kirk. And to lure her away from James.

Miss Kirk did not return his smile. Her gaze was steady. "Do gentlemen generally swim naked together?" she asked coolly.

From another young lady, the question might have seemed fast, or maybe even silly. From this one, it was a challenge. Perhaps even a threat.

I see you.

Iain put his smile away. "Yes," he said crisply. "When young ladies whose sensibilities have to be considered are not present, they do."

After that, they said no more to one another. They rode all the way back to the manor house in silence, the last of their small group to trot into the stables.

James was chatting to one of the grooms when they arrived. He looked up as they clattered in, his grey gaze going straight to Iain, his smile wide and happy. It was as though Miss Kirk wasn't even there. He just...didn't see her.

Iain glanced at the girl and saw that her lips were pressed together in an unhappy line. Her obvious annoyance troubled him. He'd realised a long time ago that when you preferred men, it was best not to have enemies if you could possibly help it, and he made it his business to avoid incurring anyone's resentment. When people looked at Iain, they saw a man who was charming and feckless, but the truth was, he was always watching, always weighing, always aware of the reactions of those around him.

Not like James. Oblivious James, who was still looking at Iain with that warm, happy expression.

Who was still to so much as *glance* at Miss Kirk.

"Would you be kind enough to help me dismount, Mr. Hart?" she said. She was using her helpless voice again, and it took real effort for Iain to control the urge to sneer, sour antipathy filling his belly.

James glanced at her then, finally. "Oh, Miss Kirk. Of course." He stepped forward and lifted his arms to her.

Absurdly, Iain found he couldn't watch. Instead, he busied himself with dismounting from Hector, then leading the horse away to check its legs and speak with the groom who approached to take over the animal's care. All this he did while determinedly ignoring the polite conversation between James and Miss Kirk, though her soft, delighted laughter grated on his nerves.

When Iain was done with the groom, he left the stables and began striding up the gravel path to the house. He felt ready to fly apart. Now that he was finally alone, the events of earlier were playing over and over in his mind—that first tentative kiss from James and how quickly Iain had succumbed to it, the passion that had flared between them, a passion Iain had long feared—rightly, it seemed. He'd never known anything like that sort of *immersion* in another person. It had overtaken him completely at the swimming hole, consuming him utterly. What if the others had arrived a few minutes earlier? Would Iain even have heard their approach? He doubted it. There had been a real danger of both him and James being exposed today, and the fear that realisation sparked in him near hollowed him out.

He had almost reached the house when he heard James calling to him.

"*Iain*—wait!"

Damn.

He stopped in his tracks and turned. The other man was jogging towards him, grinning, though his grin faded as he drew nearer, his expression growing wary at whatever he saw on Iain's face.

Iain hated himself a little for being the cause of that, even as everything in him knew that he had to start squashing James's dangerously obvious happiness.

"What do you want?" he said shortly as James finally halted in front of him.

James frowned. "What's wrong?"

"Nothing. I just want to know what you want." He sounded abrupt and annoyed. Cold.

James straightened slowly, his gaze tracking over Iain's face. At last he said, "This afternoon. You probably know I've wanted that to happen for a very long time."

Iain closed his eyes. "James—"

"No, let me speak," James interrupted, and Iain looked at him again, reluctant to hear what the man had to say even as he knew he had to let him say it.

"It's not just that I wanted what happened to happen," he said. He swallowed hard then plunged on, "It's that I want what we already have—this thing that's been building between us—to be more than friendship." He stopped then, and smiled tentatively, reaching out to touch Iain's arm.

Iain couldn't help it—he shook James's hand off and took a step back. "Don't touch me."

James paled, and Iain felt like he'd just stuck a knife in him. But he made himself press on anyway, hack the whole limb off.

"Why do you think I never go with the same man twice, Jamie?" His voice was harsh, unfamiliar even to his own ears.

James just stared at him dumbly.

"It's because doing otherwise is dangerous," Iain bit out. "If you start something like this up with a friend—can you imagine how easy it would be to give yourself away? The hundred ways that can happen, with a look, a touch?"

"We'll be discreet," James blurted. "We'll hardly be the first men to have to hide our feelings in public."

Iain huffed out an astonished laugh. "Well, you certainly weren't discreet earlier today!"

"What do you mean? I've done nothing that would attract attention!"

"Yes, you did," Iain condemned. "Earlier in the woods, you acted like a guilty schoolboy, not like a man who'd merely been swimming."

"For God's sake, Iain! I was embarrassed at being caught naked and worried about one of the ladies seeing me—anyone would have acted the same!"

"Would anyone have openly stared at me in the stables like a lovesick puppy? And in front of Agatha Kirk, no less? I swear that girl suspects something…" He turned his head, casting a glance down the gravel drive to check there were no observers to their argument. They probably looked like they were having a lover's tiff.

There was no sign of anyone, but Iain stepped back from James nonetheless, putting a little more distance between them. He saw James notice, hating the hurt expression in his eyes.

"All right," James said slowly, his gaze very steady. "I think you're being a little excessive, Iain, but I can appreciate why you're concerned. I can be more careful, more discreet. But please, just give this a chance before you—"

"No." Iain shook his head to emphasise the firmness of his resolve. "No, Jamie, we're not going to repeat what just happened. You're my friend, and I will always"—he broke off before making himself go on honestly—"I will always have a deep regard for you. But I can't give you what you're asking for. It's too risky for you."

James stepped forward, moving into the space Iain had so painstakingly created between them.

"Too risky for *me*?" he exclaimed. "Don't pretend this is anything to do with me. *You* are the one who is afraid here, not me! You, the big, brave cavalry officer!" He made a sound of disgust.

"Less than a minute ago, you were assuring me you could be careful," Iain said tautly. "Well, look at yourself now, Jamie. If anyone came upon us now, they would wonder what on earth you're in such a passion about. And this is exactly my point. This is why it's so dangerous to mix up physical desire with real emotions."

James opened his mouth to reply, then closed it again. He swallowed hard, his Adam's apple bobbing visibly in his throat, and attempted a wobbly smile.

"Listen to me. This is the wrong place for this discussion," he said. "Let's go back to the house. We can talk privately there."

Iain shook his head. "There's nothing more to talk about."

"How can you say that?" James whispered.

Iain stared at him for what felt like the longest moment of his life. James's grey eyes were wide and pleading, and that dark blond hair that Iain's fingers had been buried in such a short time ago was tumbling over his brow into his eyes. Old gold. He wanted to reach up and brush the stray strands back. Wanted to pull James into his arms and chase away that injured look.

He wanted things that it was unwise to want.

"I think I'd better go back to London," he said at last, wearily.

James looked stricken. "What?"

"First thing tomorrow."

"But you only just got here."

"I know, but I can't stay now. It's best for both of us that I go. You must see that, Jamie."

"No, I don't see that. Not at all. I see that you want to avoid talking with me in private. That you—"

Iain interrupted angrily, throwing up his hands. "Why is everything so difficult with you? You are always pushing. Always wanting things from me that I simply *cannot give*!"

"I have never asked you—"

"Yes, you have!"

Suddenly Iain realised that he was the one shouting now, and that he was breathing heavily with temper and frustration, his blood up. He stared at James's mouth and was appalled to discover he wanted nothing so much as to crush his own against it. He closed his eyes, forcing himself to calm.

When he opened them again, he said flatly, "You asked this afternoon when you decided to kiss me."

James's expression was disbelieving. "You kissed me back," he pointed out. "In fact, let's be very clear. You kissed me back, and then you turned me over and lay on top of me and took control of what we were doing. Jesus *Christ*, Iain, don't pretend you didn't choose what happened between us! For pity's sake, have some pride, man."

A hard flush warmed Iain's cheeks at that reminder. "I didn't mean to suggest it was all you," he said. "Of course, I take responsibility for my part in it. I don't *blame* you for what happened—"

"*Blame* me?" James said incredulously

James looked so shocked, Iain wondered if he'd misheard what Iain had said.

"I just said I *don't* blame you."

James still didn't say anything, but he looked stricken.

"Jamie," Iain said firmly, fixing the man with a steady look. "Listen to me, I *don't* blame you. It was as much my fault as yours. No, more so, in fact. I was the one who…" He trailed off as he saw that his words weren't helping at all. "What's wrong?"

"It's not only that you don't want to do this again, is it?"

James whispered. "You regret what we just did. You're already wishing it hadn't happened."

"I—"

And right then, Iain was lost for words.

Did he regret it?

The afternoon's events flooded his memory, each sensation bright and vivid. The scent of the cool, crushed grass beneath them, the uneven warmth of the dappled sunlight on their bodies. The feel of James in his arms, his skin smooth beneath Iain's hands, his lean body tensing with passion and need. The slick pulse of his spend as he finally came. The soft, happy look in his grey eyes afterwards.

"No, I don't regret it," Iain whispered. But James didn't hear him. He'd turned on his heel and begun to walk away several moments before. When Iain made his soft, inaudible confession, it was to the man's retreating back.

James's gait was swift and angry as he strode down the drive, his shoulders stiff with injured pride.

Best let him hold on to that anger, Iain thought. It would be a better bedfellow than heartache.

And hopefully in a few months, when James—when both of them—had calmed down after today's events, they could be friends once again.

14

Now: 1824

28ᵗʰ May, 1824

Holmewell, Hampshire

The morning after that game of Hide and Guide and Seek, Iain wakened early—or rather, gave up at last on trying to sleep.

He'd lain, wakeful all night, thinking of those dark minutes behind the curtains in the library with James. Of their kiss. He'd touched his own mouth as he lay in bed in the darkness, trying to summon up a better memory of the press of James's lips and the sweet sweep of his tongue, but the physical sensation had been translated in his memory into something more elusive and ephemeral—something that could stir but never satisfy.

Better to chase that memory, though, than to allow himself to dwell on the others. Like the wary reserve on James's face, an expression Iain hadn't seen before, and one that he wished he could banish forever. James's nature was to be direct and open—it was Iain who had taught him to be distrustful and careful. Before he left Holmewell, he wanted to do something to repair what he'd done. He just wasn't sure what. Before he'd come, he'd hoped that an apology, a heartfelt one in which he took all blame upon himself, would be enough to restore things to how they'd been before. But now he realised that wasn't going to be nearly enough.

Last night, James had, with typical generosity, accepted his apology, granting him forgiveness without hesitation. Yet nothing had changed, not really. Not when James remained unwilling to restore their friendship, and Iain's apology had done nothing to erase the sadness from his eyes.

Plainly, Iain had expected too much. It stood to reason that it would take time for James to trust him again, but in a matter of weeks, he would be on his way to India, and God only knew how long it would be before he returned to England.

Well, all he could do was try again. Kate had planned a picnic down at the river this afternoon, with games for the children. It would be just like when they were boys. And perhaps—just like in those old days—they could sneak off together for a while.

With renewed determination, he got out of bed, ringing for hot water. Within half an hour, he'd shaved and dressed and was on his way to the breakfast room. His plan was a simple one—to find James and shadow him for the rest of the day, whatever he might be doing.

The breakfast room was empty when he entered. The footman informed him that he was the first of the guests to rise, which surely meant that if he waited long enough, James would eventually appear. With that heartening thought, he helped himself to some coddled eggs and ham and sat himself down at the table.

The next guest to arrive for breakfast, annoyingly, was Mr. Potts.

"Good morning, Mr. Sinclair," the vicar said, smiling in a way that managed to suggest smug superiority and oily ingratiation at the same time.

Iain nodded in response. "Morning, Potts. You're up early."

"Yes," Potts agreed as he filled his plate. "Mr. Hart and I are going on a little expedition."

"Mr. Hart?"

Had James willingly agreed to spend time with the pompous vicar?

"Didn't he mention it to you?" Potts replied, taking a seat across from Iain. "I assumed he might have done, since the two of you seem to be such *particular* friends."

Iain sent the vicar a quick glance, wondering what he meant by that. He knew Potts had been put out the afternoon before at having his conversation with James interrupted by Iain's arrival. Was it merely that still?

"No," Iain said carefully. "He didn't mention any expedition. Isn't there to be a picnic today?" He looked away as Potts cut a kidney in half. He'd never been able to abide offal at breakfast.

"I understand the picnic's this afternoon," Potts said as he buttered some bread. "Mr. Hart was telling me after dinner yesterday evening that he planned to spend this morning looking for a particular species of butterfly. Apparently, if we walk up the hill, there's a place in the woods just beyond, where there's a good chance of seeing it. Since I'm something of a naturalist myself—though more of a botanist, in truth—I told him I'd be delighted to join him for the morning."

So, Potts had invited himself along—well, two could play at that game.

Iain forced himself to smile. "Butterflies, eh? Sounds fascinating. Do you know, I think I'll come along too. It's not as though I've got anything else to do." When the vicar opened his mouth to protest, Iain quickly added, "After all, it's not

149

often a layman like myself gets the opportunity to join *two* learned gentlemen on a scientific expedition."

Potts closed his mouth but still frowned. Pleased by the flattery, Iain guessed, but still unhappy at the thought of Iain joining the outing. After a while, he said uncertainly, "*I* don't mind, but I'm not sure that Mr. Hart will be agreeable."

"What wouldn't Mr. Hart be agreeable to?" another voice asked from the doorway.

James.

Iain looked up from his breakfast and smiled at his friend, but James's gaze was fixed on Potts, eyebrows raised in question.

The vicar opened his mouth to speak, but Iain got in first. "Mr. Potts is wondering how to tell you that I've just shamelessly invited myself on your butterfly expedition. He didn't want to say yes without your agreement, but you would not forbid me to come, would you, James?"

James's cheeks pinkened at Iain's use of his first name. Iain usually called him *Hart* in front of others, reserving *James,* and especially *Jamie,* for when they were alone. This casual use of his Christian name in front of Potts made plain to the vicar that Iain considered James a particularly close friend. No one would be surprised by such familiarity given how long they'd known one another, of course, but before now, Iain had always been careful to avoid the intimacy in public.

Now he wondered why he had been so absurdly strict about such a silly thing. It felt good to use James's given name. He found he wanted to say it again, to use the blatant privilege over and over, as if he was making a claim.

"Well?" he said, grinning at James, putting him firmly on the spot and feeling reasonably safe that the man would be too polite to refuse such a modest request from an invited guest of his sister's. "May I come? I'm not as knowledgeable as either of you, it's true, but I promise not to interrupt when you start talking about clever stuff."

James's blush faded. He looked irritated now, those beautifully carved lips pressed together in a firm line. "Of course you may come, Sinclair," he said at last, his use of Iain's surname very deliberate, Iain was sure. He strolled over to the sideboard to investigate the contents of the various silver dishes lined up there, adding over his shoulder, without looking round, "I'm hardly going to refuse to allow you to join us purely because of your admittedly profound ignorance."

Iain couldn't help but laugh at that, tickled by the man's cheek, despite recognising James's irritation was very real. He turned in his chair to watch James fill his plate. "What kind of butterfly are we looking for?" he asked.

"*Gonepteryx rhamni*," James said absently. "The common brimstone."

"What does it look like?"

"The common brimstone is not one of the Lord's more beautiful creations," Potts interjected. Iain jerked his head round to look at the man. He'd all but forgotten Potts was there.

"With its wings closed," Potts continued, "it looks like nothing so much as an old leaf."

James joined them at the table, smiling briefly at the footman who arrived at his elbow with the coffeepot. "I think it's beautiful," he disagreed. "It's no peacock butterfly, true, but the accuracy of the mimicry—it's extraordinary. The shape and hue of the wings, the veins, and those little brown spots and edges. It's perfectly realised, Mr. Potts. You must agree."

"I don't doubt the accuracy of its mimicry," Potts conceded, raising another greyish slice of kidney to his lips.

Iain leaned back in his chair. "I remember your interest in mimicry," he said to James. "Do you remember showing me that bee orchid the last time I was at Wylde Manor?"

The last time he visited James. Neither of them was likely to forget that in a hurry.

James smiled tightly. "Yes, of course. That was when I was first becoming interested in mimicry."

"Ah, the bee orchid!" Potts said. "Now you have piqued my interest, Mr. Hart. My own principal area of study is botany, you see."

"Well, I'm afraid we won't see any bee orchids where we're going today, Mr. Potts," James said, smiling coolly. "We're bound for the woods, and as you will know, being a botanist, bee orchids prefer a meadow."

"That's a shame," Potts said. "I should very much like to see one."

"Well, there's no need for you to miss out," Iain said, spotting a chance to get James alone. "I'm sure Hart here can direct you to the likeliest place to look for them."

Potts sent him a suspicious look, as well he might. "That's all right," he said. "I can look for bee orchids another day. We're staying a se'nnight, so I shall have plenty of opportunity to explore the estate."

"*You* could go and look for bee orchids, Sinclair, if you prefer." James didn't even look up from his kedgeree to deliver that set-down.

"Oh no," Iain replied promptly. "I wouldn't miss seeing your leaf-butterfly for the world."

If he had to endure Potts to have James's company, so be it.

James had decided, when he retired to bed last night, to avoid Iain as much as possible today, so it was aggravating to have his decision so thoroughly undermined before he'd so much as finished his breakfast. What was the point in stirring up the dying embers of their friendship now? They'd be going cold soon enough anyway, when he left England.

That thought made his stupid heart contract, which in turn made him feel wildly angry, and he increased his pace so that he was not far off running up the hill, leaving Iain—whom he'd abandoned with Potts a few minutes before—even further behind.

Served him right for insinuating himself where he wasn't wanted, James thought savagely. He could hear the drone of Potts's voice behind him as he lectured Iain about something or other, and it filled him with absurd satisfaction to know that Iain was probably having to listen to the self-aggrandising monologue that James had been subjected to the previous afternoon.

The vicar was not a modest man. In fairness, his botanical knowledge was reasonably good, but James found the man's determined lack of curiosity tedious. Potts thought—had said so repeatedly the previous afternoon—that the sole purpose of all the astonishing diversity in the natural world was to demonstrate the glory of God. That was it, as far as he was concerned, and there was no more to say. When James had mentioned Monsieur Lamarck's theories, Potts had waved his comments off dismissively, saying merely, *Who can divine the Lord's purpose, Mr. Hart?*

Oddly enough, what the Lord's purpose might actually be was the one subject on which Potts appeared to have no view.

James found it equally irritating that Potts seemed unable to see the loveliness in anything that was not obviously beautiful. He liked flowers—pastel-pretty blooms—but grasses, sedges, lichens, none of those held any real interest for him. Nor did insects or other small, humble creatures. Certainly not a butterfly that looked like a dying leaf. He hadn't invited himself along on this outing because of any real curiosity about the common brimstone, only to talk about himself and show off his knowledge of plant anatomy and Linnean names to James.

James soon reached the top of the hill, pausing for a little while to get his breath back from his swift climb. The day was still and humid, the silent promise of rain permeating the warm, oppressive air. There was no birdsong to be heard at all, and overhead, the sky wore a cloak of grey clouds that hung low and heavy in the sky. Already, James felt sticky in his clothes, but he didn't care. It was good to be out. It always lifted his spirits to have earth and rocks and grass under his feet.

He set off again, hopping over the stile and starting down the path to the woods, but after a minute more of walking, he slowed to a reluctant halt. Neither Iain nor Potts knew which way he intended to go, and if he went much further ahead, he'd be out of sight. Briefly, he wondered if he could give them the slip and pretend later he'd thought they were right behind him. After all, the purpose of this morning's outing was to observe the butterflies' behaviour. He already had all the drawings he needed, as well as specimens he'd collected and carefully preserved. Today, all he wanted to do was sit quietly and watch the brimstone in the wild, and he knew it was unlikely he'd get a chance to do that uninterrupted with Potts there. James would be amazed if the man could go a minute without speaking.

He was mulling over his options when Potts's faraway voice hailed him.

"I say, Mr. Hart!" he cried. "Do wait for us!"

James sighed. He should've gone on ahead while he had the chance. He turned on his heel to see that Potts was in the midst of climbing the stile, Iain standing behind him on the other side of the fence. James began to walk back towards them, trying to suppress a smile as he watched Potts swinging his plump legs over the top of the stile in an odd, straight-legged fashion. Evidently, his breeches were too tight.

It wasn't easy to hold back the unkind urge to laugh, especially with Iain standing there, looking distinctly amused.

"You were getting quite far ahead there, Mr. Hart," Potts scolded him as he finally stepped down from the stile. "And Mr. Sinclair and I aren't at all sure which part of the woods you're heading for."

Now that Potts was finally over the fence, Iain vaulted it, not bothering with the stile at all. Potts sent him a brief look of disapproval, then turned back to James.

"Is it much further?" he asked, adjusting his bulky satchel on his shoulder. He'd insisted on bringing all manner of equipment with him, expressing surprise that James wasn't bringing anything but a pocket notebook.

"Perhaps another hour of walking," James said. He and Iain could cover the distance much more quickly but Potts was really rather slow. "But only about half of that is uphill."

"An *hour*? Uphill?" Potts looked horrified. "And you've brought no provisions?"

"Provisions? What for?" James asked, puzzled. They'd be joining the other guests for the picnic in a few hours' time.

Potts didn't immediately answer James's question. He seemed to be thinking. Then he frowned—a little overdramatically, James thought—and looked skyward, stretching one plump hand out, palm up. "Oh, I say, did you feel that? I'm *sure* that was a raindrop."

"I didn't feel anything," James said honestly.

"Nor I," Iain added, yawning. "Shall we proceed? The butterflies will be getting ready for bed before we see any at this rate."

"I am quite sure that was rain," Potts insisted. He sent James an apologetic look. "I am afraid I cannot risk catching a chill, Mr. Hart. I have a weak chest, you know. The last time I had a cold, I was in bed for a fortnight. I really think I should return to the house."

A faint thrill of happiness coursed through James at the

thought of being alone with Iain, and he pressed his lips together, annoyed at the automatic reaction. There was nothing to be gained by his being alone with Iain. They had said everything that needed to be said last night. James had forgiven Iain, and that was as far as he wanted to go. No more friendship, no more letters. What was the point anymore?

"Must you go, Mr. Potts?" he asked, a little desperately.

Potts sent him a sympathetic look. "I fear so. I'd be happy to discuss your observations this afternoon, though. If the picnic is called off—as I suspect it may be—we could talk over afternoon tea." He offered James a glib little smile, then turned back to the stile without further ado and began the tortuous business of climbing back over.

Behind him, James laughed nervously. "You're not really going back just because of a few raindrops, are you?" he asked. "Even if there's a downpour, there are places to shelter. Come, Mr. Potts. Where's your spirit of adventure?"

Potts stilled in the act of climbing the stile, sending James a martyred look over his shoulder. "You are very young, Mr. Hart, and happily for you, quite without obligations. I, however, do not have that privilege. I have a wife and family to think of, and, of course, my flock. If I do not take care of my earthly body, how can I expect to take care of their eternal souls?"

This was another of the vicar's rhetorical questions, judging by the way the man immediately turned away without waiting for a response. James glanced at Iain, who chuckled softly, rolling his eyes, and reluctantly, James's lips twitched in response.

"Well, I'm very glad to have amused you both at least," Potts said stiffly. Evidently, he'd managed to complete his descent more quickly this time. He was standing on the other side of the fence now, watching the wordless interplay between them.

"Jesus Christ," Iain muttered, rolling his eyes again.

"*If* you could possibly refrain from *blaspheming*, Mr. Sinclair, I'd be obliged," Potts bit out. "Unless you had forgotten, I am a man of the cloth!"

"Since you remind us at least once every five minutes, I hadn't forgotten, no," Iain drawled, his sarcastic tone making the vicar's face purple up.

"Oh, for goodness' sake," James muttered. "Iain, do stop baiting Mr. Potts. And Mr. Potts"—he turned to the vicar—"I will be very happy to discuss butterflies, botany, or indeed anything else with you this afternoon over tea, but for now, I'm proceeding as planned. Will you be all right getting back to the house by yourself?"

"Of course," Potts said coolly. "I do hope you do not get caught out by the weather, Mr. Hart. Though I must say, I fear you and Mr. Sinclair may end up getting quite drenched." And with that gloomy prediction, he was off, bumbling down the hill, his fat satchel bumping against his ample hip.

"Thank God," Iain sighed once he was out of earshot. "What a pompous ass that man is! You should've heard what he was saying on the way up here—he fancies himself as quite the botanist. As though he could ever hope to know as much as y—"

"What are you playing at?" James interrupted icily.

Iain looked almost comically surprised at that. "What do you mean?"

"All the times you've told me off for being obvious, for being *indiscreet*," James accused hotly. "Yet this morning, you couldn't have made it more obvious to Potts if you tried that you wanted to join us—and as if that wasn't bad enough, you made it even more obvious just now that you didn't want him to stay. What happened to being careful, Iain? Does that not concern you anymore, now that you're going to India?"

"James, for God's—"

"But then, why worry about consequences that won't

affect you?" James continued, throwing his hands up in the air. "After all, *I'm* the one who'll have to live with any rumours you spark with your behaviour, aren't I? Not you."

"I thought you didn't care about that sort of thing," Iain threw back at him. "You're the one who said I was excessively discreet, yet the instant I *stop* being so discreet, you're the first to complain!"

"How dare you!" James hissed. "Despite your accusations, I never did or said anything in front of anyone that would have called the nature of our friendship into question. You were the one who saw dangers that weren't there. That's quite different from your behaviour just now—deliberately goading a man you *know* to be petty and interfering, just to amuse yourself. If I'd done that a few years ago, you'd've been furious with me, but now that you're off to India and *you* won't have to come across him again, you don't care!"

He was breathing heavily by the time he finished that speech, fury suffusing him, a slow-burning anger fed by years of lingering resentment beginning to fire in his veins.

Iain didn't say anything for a long time. His blue gaze tracked over James's face, as though he was reading him, like a schoolboy faced with a page of Latin, brow furrowed with concentration. At last he sighed and looked away, raising a hand to rub the back of his neck as he stared down the hill.

"I'm sorry, Jamie," he said softly, his tone resigned.

Just that. Nothing else.

James wasn't entirely sure what Iain was saying sorry for. For his behaviour just now, or years before? Perhaps it was both. James decided not to ask. Instead, he gave a sigh of his own.

"Oh, come on," he muttered. "Let's find these butterflies."

15

Holmewell's woods were more extensive than Iain had realised. James led him over the hill and down a winding, descending path. It rained a little as they walked, but the thick canopy of leaves overhead kept them dry.

Eventually, the ground evened out, and after a while, they entered a glade that made Iain catch his breath.

"Good lord," he whispered.

The trees were more widely spaced here, allowing a little light to dapple through, and the ground was a sea of bluebells, a rolling wave of purple, washing through the wood.

A bluebell wood.

James glanced at him, smiling. "Beautiful, isn't it? Kate likes to keep this secret."

They were the first words James had spoken to him since they'd set off again, and the tightness in Iain's chest eased a little at the soft, friendly pitch of his voice.

"I can't believe you were going to bring Potts here," he said.

James's mouth hitched up and Iain's stomach lurched to see that familiar, quietly amused expression.

"I'd planned to take *him* somewhere else." James said.

"But since he decided to leave us to it, I was able to go back to my original plan."

Iain smiled, warmed by the idea that James didn't mind bringing *him* here. "Does that mean I'm forgiven for riling him up?"

James sent him a strange look, then gave a short laugh. "Yes, all right," he said. "Why not? Let's have all the injuries between us forgiven before you go, every one. A clean slate for us both, eh?"

And that was enough to have Iain's chest tightening again, just at the thought of leaving England's shores. Leaving James behind.

He swallowed hard. "I don't think I've anything to forgive you for," he said. "But I'll gladly take your forgiveness, since you offer it so generously."

James gave a sigh. It made him sound weary. "I don't know about you not having anything to forgive. I probably expected too much of you. Asked more than any man could reasonably be expected to give. It's just that I"—he closed his eyes before adding huskily—"I *wanted* you. Not only as a lover in the flesh, but in every way. Someone to share my life with, the way Kate and Edward share their lives." He gave another of those short, unamused laughs that tore at Iain, and said wryly, "And I can just imagine what's going through your mind right now."

"Can you?" Iain said, and his voice sounded broken, rusty.

"You think I want the impossible," James said, smiling sadly. He turned away, casting his gaze over the clearing, then pointed. "Let's sit over there. If we're quiet, I'm fairly sure we'll see some butterflies. One of the curious things about brimstones is that they particularly favour purple flowers, so they should love this place."

He set off in the direction of a fallen tree lying amongst the bluebells, and Iain followed in his wake.

You think I want the impossible.

But the truth was, what James wanted—someone to share his life with—wasn't entirely impossible, was it? The evening he'd recently spent with Murdo Balfour and David Lauriston had shown Iain that. They had each other, though Balfour had had to wilfully destroy his own reputation to secure their future. Iain felt a sudden pang of something deep and aching, sadness perhaps, envy certainly, as he remembered that night. As he remembered the striking coincidence of love and desire between Balfour and Lauriston. That sort of connection had always seemed impossible to Iain, even frightening. Unnatural desires were bad enough, but they could be managed. Once the heart was involved though, a man could be so easily destroyed. Could so easily bring dishonour and shame on his family.

Nevertheless, now he found himself wondering...*was it possible?*

As Iain followed James through the clumps of nodding bluebells, that question echoed through him, over and over —*was it possible?* The words were a litany inside him as he walked, as the sea of indigo flowers gently undulated around him and their sweet, light, unforgettable scent drifted on the air. Iain was following James again—as he always did. Always coming back to James, in the end, forced to return by the invisible thread that bound him to this man.

Would a whole ocean be enough to snap that thread?

When James finally settled himself down on the broad log of the fallen tree, Iain sat beside him, marvelling inwardly at the calm silence between them when he felt as though his mind was all a-clamour, every nerve vibrating with the new truths he was discovering.

The fallen tree they sat on might be dead now, but it still held the warmth of a once-living thing. He felt whatever residual life it had sink into him, felt too the tremulations of life on the air, from the bluebells and the trees and all the creatures in the wood. He was part of this. Alive with it, and in it, with James.

He turned his head, meaning to say something of this to the man in his thoughts, but he stopped himself when he saw that James was already transfixed, that his watchful gaze was steady on something in the sea of flowers before them. God, but Iain loved that look on James, the expression he wore when all his formidable attention was caught, hooked by something that interested him.

What a thing it was to be the subject of that attention. To be seen like that, and known. James was the only person in the world who saw Iain. Who knew his heart. There were others who knew parts of him, even secret parts. But none who knew all, bar James. In the years they'd known one another, James had studied Iain as thoroughly as one of his specimens, and with the same curious-for-the-truth eye.

And of course, Iain had studied James back. The face he looked at now was as familiar to Iain as the one he looked at in the mirror each morning—more so, for he knew James's fleeting expressions better than he could ever hope to know his own. In profile, James's face was lovely to him. Straight nose, determined chin. Fine, dark blond brows. James's upper lip protruded just a little as his front teeth bit softly into his lower lip—a sign that the man was concentrating. Iain smiled helplessly. He wanted to raise his hand and smooth it over James's old-gold hair, trace his thumb over the edge of James's small, neat ear. Lean forward and kiss…

James seemed to sense his attention then, but instead of turning, he slowly stretched out one arm to point. "Look," he whispered. So Iain did.

It took him a little while, but then he saw it, only two feet away. It looked like a leaf hanging from the edge of a clump of bluebell heads. Until it opened its wings and flapped off, flitting around for a little while before landing again on another flower. He saw then that there were several of them.

They were feeding in a determined way, flitting from flower to flower, collecting nectar.

Iain wanted to ask his usual stupid questions, but he could see that James wanted to watch quietly, so he held his peace, contenting himself with observing, dividing his time between the butterflies and James, letting himself have the simple pleasure of sitting in harmony with his friend.

They really were extraordinary little creatures. It wasn't just that their wings were leaf-green, they even carried a pattern of distinct veins and had points at each corner tip just like the point of a leaf. They were spotted and edged with subtle marks of brown, as though to mimic rot, and when they hung from a flower to feed, they looked just like a stray leaf caught up by a stirring breeze.

For a long time, Iain and James sat there, silent and still. The only sound either of them made was the occasional notation James scratched into his notebook. Iain didn't mind sitting quietly. If there was one thing the army had taught him, it was endless patience—soldiers were forever waiting around. And just having James at his side felt like a kind of reward, something to absorb and enjoy. Something to remember.

Eventually, James shifted and glanced at Iain. "Shall we walk a bit more?" he asked. "I think there might be some alder buckthorns further along—that's where they tend to lay their eggs."

"I'd like to see that," Iain agreed, rising. During their period of silent observation, his clamouring mind had quieted and now he felt oddly content, more at peace than he had in ages. Perhaps it was being in the wood, surrounded by nature, but Iain felt oddly sure that it was being with James.

"The butterflies were feeding," he observed as they strolled.

"Yes, they feed a lot at this time of year. They're not long out of hibernation."

"They hibernate? How do they manage that when the leaves have fallen from the trees?" Iain asked. "Where do they hide?"

"They hibernate in evergreens," James said. "Somewhere they can burrow into and sleep undisturbed. Ah, look, here are a few buckthorns." He stopped in front of what looked like an indeterminate wall of greenery. How James could tell these were buckthorn bushes rather than some other kind of shrub, Iain didn't know.

"This is where they like to lay their eggs," James continued, squatting down to peer at the underside of the dense clumps of leaves. "When the caterpillars emerge, they eat the buckthorn and pupate here. Ah, here we are. Come and see this."

He beckoned to Iain, who obediently dropped to his haunches to look. The eggs were more obvious than he expected, hanging from the underside of the leaves like milky tears, just three of them and well spaced out.

"There aren't many," he pointed out.

"Yes, and they might not even have been laid by the same female," James said. "The brimstones tend to lay only one egg at a time." He rose gracefully to his feet and said, "Let's see if we can find any pupae."

He checked over the clump of shrubs thoroughly but ultimately shook his head. "There's none here that I can see, but there are more buckthorns further along. Come on."

They checked several more shrubs before James finally found what he was looking for.

"That's a pupa?" Iain exclaimed, leaning closer. It looked exactly like a brand-new, tightly furled leaf, readying itself to stretch open.

"Isn't it lovely?" James murmured, his gaze rapt. "As the pupa matures, a spot will appear here." He pointed to the side of the green casing. "It's the same spot you see on their wings when they emerge. This is a very early pupa, though."

"They're always hiding," Iain observed.

"Yes, through the whole life cycle," James agreed.

"I bet they sometimes wish they could just stop," Iain mused. "It's tiresome, always having to be careful."

James glanced at him sharply, but Iain kept his gaze fixed ahead, though James's gaze upon him was so heavy, he could feel it like a physical touch.

After a while, James said softly, "Life is not safe. Hiding means survival for them. And that's the business of all living things, isn't it? Surviving, I mean." He paused. "Potts thinks these creatures are here to satisfy the whims of his God. I don't agree. I think they're here because of their own burning need to live." He glanced at Iain and smiled. "Science will explain it all, one day."

"I don't think Potts would like the sound of that," Iain replied. "He prefers to look for the answers in his own Book."

"Yes," James agreed. "But he only has one book to look in, and it never changes, so I doubt he'll find any new answers there." He turned and began to walk away, calling over his shoulder, "Let's start walking to the river. The picnic will be starting soon."

Iain started after him, and they began to walk back towards the main path.

"So, how long till you leave England?" James asked when they'd been walking a few minutes.

"I'm due to sail in two months' time."

"How long is the passage?"

"I hope not much longer than four months, but it could be five, or even six."

James was silent for a little while, then he said quietly, "That's a long time to be at sea."

"Yes." Iain sighed. "And I'm not what you'd call a keen sailor."

"You don't like it?"

"Not much. I tend to get quite seasick. I'm hoping I'll get

used to the motion, though, what with the journey lasting so long."

"I don't get seasick," James said, "but when I'm out there —truly at sea, I mean, with no land in sight—well, I don't like that much, I must say. Though I'm glad I've experienced it."

Iain recognised the feeling James described only too well. The great, vast loneliness of being at sea, cast out onto the ocean with nothing to protect you but the boards of the ship beneath your feet and a few scraps of cloth to catch the wind.

"What is it that you're glad to have experienced?" Iain asked, curious.

James's didn't look at him. His gaze was fixed ahead. The expression on his face—what Iain could see of it in profile— was dreamy, a little unfocused. As though he was looking inward.

"Most of the time, you go through life without realising how small and unimportant you are," he said. "Without seeing what a tiny fragment of all life on earth and in all history you represent. How fragile your human body is, how easily broken it is." He did look at Iain then. "I sailed to Ireland a few years ago. It was a terrible crossing. There was a storm, and we were badly tossed about. I thought we were all going to die—though when I told the captain afterwards, he seemed to think that was terribly funny." James gave a rueful smile at that before going on. "I went onto the deck for a while during the storm, and the waves were huge. When I looked out over the ocean, all I could see was water, stretching forever in every direction. I remember I looked up and saw a kittiwake flying high above us, and I imagined what we must look like to it from up there. What a tiny, fragile little basket of sticks I'd entrusted my safety to. It was terrifying."

"And you were *glad* to have experienced this?" Iain said, raising an eyebrow.

James laughed softly. "Yes, it was strangely liberating. Oh, there was a sort of sadness, I suppose, in comprehending the fragility of life, but at that instant, I understood in a way I never had before how precious my small life was. That if I didn't make the most of it, that if I didn't choose to do the things that excited me, took the…comforts that I needed, then I would simply—never have those things. Would die without having lived." He smiled, a little sadly. "That was when I decided once and for all never to marry. As soon as I got home, I told Mother. Did I ever mention that to you before?"

"You told me you'd decided it," Iain said. "But not the reason why. How did you tell her?"

"She was going on about some young lady she wanted to introduce me to, and I found myself saying it—that I couldn't consider marriage to any woman, that I had no inclination or wish for such a thing." He shrugged. "As you'd imagine, she was upset, but she's come to realise I'm not going to change my mind." He paused, then added pensively, "Sometimes I think she knows about my…preferences, though we've never discussed them, obviously."

Not like Iain and his father, then.

"Once a sod, always a sod."

Just then, there was a low, threatening rumble overhead. They both looked up at the ominous sky.

"Looks like the rain might be coming after all," Iain said.

Even as he said it, the sky was darkening, black clouds rolling quickly in. Another rumble of thunder, and the first drops of rain came, spattering against the leaf canopy above.

"I think this is going to be a downpour," James said. "We should shelter. Come on, there's a place near here."

He turned around, leading Iain back the way they'd just come, except instead of taking the path that led to the bluebell glade, he selected another, less obvious path that snaked left. This path was so overgrown, it was almost unnoticeable, and it twisted and turned its way to a clearing that was even more surprising than the one filled with bluebells, because this one had a cottage in it. It was small and painted white, and it had a neatly thatched roof. Iain didn't bother asking who lived here—the cottage was too pretty and well kept, and these woods too private, for it to be anything other than a rich man's folly.

The rain was driving down heavily now. Iain sheltered under the lintel of the front door while James dashed round the back of the cottage, returning half a minute later with a key held triumphantly aloft. "Kate showed me where this was the last time I was here," he said as he fitted it into the lock and opened the door.

"Mind your head," he warned, ducking his own as he walked into the cottage ahead of Iain.

It was pretty inside too. A wealthy man's idea of a simple life—everything plain yet deeply comfortable. The wingback chairs on either side of the fireplace suggested companionable evenings in front of the fire, and Iain could imagine a pair of lovers sharing a tasty meal at the small sturdy oak table by the window where he and James set down their wet hats.

It looked as though there was another chamber off this main room. Curious, Iain crossed the floor—half a dozen paces did the job—and opened the door, halting in the doorway at the sight of the surprisingly sumptuous bed, draped in blue silk, that dominated the tiny bedchamber.

"Kate told me Edward's father had a lover," James said behind him. "This cottage was their place. Kate said no one knew who she was."

"Perhaps 'she' was a 'he'," Iain murmured. "Perhaps that's why he was so discreet."

"I wondered about that," James admitted. After a brief silence, he added, "Just last night, Mrs. Potts was telling me that Edward's mother spent all her time in London while his father stayed at Holmewell. She suggested that Mama Porter was off having *affaires* with half of London while Papa Porter was virtuously celibate here. I wondered if she knew about this place."

Iain glanced over his shoulder. "Mama Porter or Mrs. Potts?"

"Both." James smiled. "Either."

Iain turned back to look at the blue expanse of that big empty bed. "It's possible they had an agreement," he said. "Many married couples are pragmatic like that." For some reason, James's words from before came back to him.

"If I didn't choose to do the things that excited me, took the… comforts that I needed, then I would simply—never have those things. Would die without having lived."

Edward's father had come here to be with his lover. Male or female, who knew, but Iain fancied from everything he saw around him that it was someone the man had loved. Someone with whom he had taken pains to make a cocoon from the world. Safe and hidden.

The sudden, salty lump in his throat surprised him. He swallowed hard against the obstruction, staring at the bed, intensely aware of James standing at his shoulder, of James's gaze upon him.

Right then, a bolt of longing hit him, deep in his gut, as sudden as the lump in his throat and equally unwanted.

He'd told himself he'd come to Holmewell to make things right with James. To make peace with him. Perhaps to try to snap that invisible thread between them.

Yet now he felt things were messier than ever, and as though it wasn't one thread that connected them but a thousand, and all of them tangled up and knotted.

An apology wasn't enough to sever those threads. All the forgiveness in the world wouldn't do it. Only a blade, a sharp one, to slice through it all in one clean sweep. Or…

…was it possible?

Iain felt as though the storm that raged outside, lashing the little windows of the cottage with pitiless rain, raged inside him too, churning in him, making him dizzy with purpose. Should he slice himself free of the thread that bound him to James or…

Was it possible?

There were so many risks, so many ways to be found out. Worse than death to be publicly dishonoured—that was what he'd always thought—and it was right, wasn't it? It wasn't just himself he had to consider, after all. He had his family to think of too. People who trusted him to uphold the family honour. He couldn't betray that. Bad enough that he'd left the army. The least he could do was go to India and make an attempt at serving his country in some other way.

Christ.

He whirled round in the doorway, catching sight of James's startled expression as he stepped forward, seizing James's upper arms and shoving him up against the wall.

"I can't do this," he managed, the words coming as hard as if they were being torn out of him, torn from his own flesh. "I can't have you, and I can't *not* have you." He groaned, letting his head fall forward, forehead knocking hard against the wall beside James. "I can't love you."

He felt James's body stiffening under his hands. "You *don't* love me," James said sharply.

"But I do," Iain whispered. "And it's killing me, Jamie."

There was a moment of profound silence before James said, "No." He began shaking his head from side to side. "No," he said again. "This is what you love." Crudely, he reached forward, rubbing his palm over Iain's half-hard cock, making it thicken, and him hiss in a breath. "And no sooner have you had it than you want to be set free with good grace. For me not to hold you to anything after." James pressed his hand there again as if to emphasise the point, sliding it up and down, making Iain buck helplessly against him.

"James, please, I—"

But James cut him off ruthlessly, lifting a hand to the back of Iain's neck to jerk their mouths together in a hot, savage kiss.

His tongue was sinuous and sleek and seeking, his lean body hard and unyielding, giving no quarter. The fierce desire his kiss provoked in Iain was almost unbearable. Iain hadn't wanted this, but he *needed* it, needed it like a drowning man needs air. His hands went to James's hips, dragging him closer as he groaned into the man's mouth, opening himself to James's devouring kiss, only to stagger back when James pushed his hands between them and thrust Iain violently away.

For an instant, James just stood there, chest heaving, expression shocked and angry, then he said, almost brokenly, "Why are you doing this to me, Iain? Will you not be satisfied until you have destroyed me?"

Iain felt winded, as though he'd taken a solid punch to the gut. At first, he could do nothing but stare at James, reaching for him only when James began to turn away. "Jamie, please, how can you think that I'd want to destr—"

But James just pushed past him, grabbing his hat from the table as he made for the front door of the cottage and hauled it open. Outside, the rain came down in sheets and the thunder rolled again, heavy and ominous.

"Jamie, please," Iain said again, grabbing for him, but James shook him off with a rough sound of disbelief.

"Don't follow me," he said. "Don't ever follow me anywhere again."

And with that, he ran off into the storm.

16

THEN: 1822

16th April, 1822

Black Boar Inn, London

Iain was drunk. Gloriously drunk.

He'd had barely a minute's peace for days. Caught up in one of his self-pitying glooms, the King had demanded Iain's constant attention, till Iain was nearly driven mad with it. He was desperate to leave the King's service, but his army masters wouldn't have it. As long as Georgie wanted him, he was stuck there.

Tonight, though, he'd escaped with an invented story about a sickly aunt, tugging shamelessly on the King's heart-strings to persuade him to agree, only to embark on a tour of his favourite public houses before ending up here, at the Black Boar, a place where, unbeknownst to most of the patrons, men like Iain came to find companionship.

Over the heads of the more oblivious customers, signals

were exchanged, too subtle for an ordinary man to notice—not to mention Iain in his present state.

He sniggered at that thought and upended his tankard, pouring the last of his ale down his throat.

"Another, Cap'n?" the man beside him asked, hiccoughing as he elbowed Iain in the side. He was a new friend, this one. Not bent, unfortunately, since he was comely, in a rough sort of way. Not really Iain's type, though. He liked them prettier, and fair. Fair like—well, that one over there.

Iain's gaze snagged on the back of a man's head on the other side of the dim room. He'd just walked in with his two companions and was in the process of removing his hat. His hair gleamed like old gold in the dim light, picking up the sparse candlelight. His friends were beardless lads with nervous, eager smiles, but Iain wasn't interested in them. His attention had been caught fast by the fair man. With his height and those shoulders, he reminded Iain of James Hart—but it couldn't be Jamie, could it?

"Cap'n!" the man beside him repeated, jostling him with that elbow again. "Come on—do you wan' another?" He paused and seemed to think carefully. "Or we could get some gin."

Iain dragged his gaze back to his companion, forcing himself to concentrate on what the man was saying. He blinked hard, thinking back to what they'd just been talking about. "Wha' were we goin' to do?" he said, a distant part of him wincing at how slurred his words were. He sounded like his father, a thought that made his gut churn. Then he remembered. "Weren't you going to get some playing cards?"

His new friend—Charlie?—frowned at that, then grinned. "Yes—you're righ'," he said, standing up and clapping Iain on the shoulder. "I'll go and see what I can rustl' up. Cards and"—he hiccoughed—"gin. I think gin for cards, don't you, Cap'n?"

He didn't wait for a reply but weaved away, disappearing into the press of bodies.

Iain's head swam, his vision blurring. Christ, how much had he had? He pulled out his pocket watch, closing one eye in an effort to focus on the hands. After a few seconds, his eyes adjusted, and he saw that it was almost eleven o'clock— he'd been drinking hard for five solid hours.

He didn't care. He was glad of it, glad of the oblivion and tired of feeling bored and miserable. Tired of watching every word he said, tired of having to spend his days charming everyone he came across. He felt more like the King's fool than his guard these days. The King wanted Iain in his personal entourage because he was handsome and merry and people tended to like him easily. He expected Iain to be always amusing, ever ready with a bon mot and a compliment for the ladies. Ready to talk to anyone he was seated next to at dinner, no matter how dull, how rude, how incapable of comprehending the English language. Always on hand to listen to the King's complaints and self-pitying monologues, always available to soothe George with platitudes about how well thought of he was, how loved by the people.

He'd been stuck in the King's service for over a year now, and there was no sign of him getting back to his regiment any time soon. He felt like a fraud wearing his uniform. His sword would be rusting in its scabbard.

Iain's gaze crept back across the room to the young men standing at the bar. They were talking animatedly and laughing loudly, an attractive group. He suspected they were bent, and when he saw the shorter, dark-haired one brush against the tall, fair one, he was sure of it. Infuriatingly, the fair man still hadn't turned round, and Iain found himself willing him to do so, as though he could make him move merely by desiring it hard enough.

"Come on," he muttered under his breath, "come on."

As though he'd heard Iain, the fair man finally shifted,

turning round and leaning his elbows back against the rail of the bar. The lurch of excitement that racked Iain's body when he caught sight of his handsome *familiar* face had him rising to his feet before he could think better of it.

It *was* James Hart standing there.

Iain hadn't seen him since the previous summer, a silence having settled between them since Iain's last visit to Wylde Manor and the argument they'd had after that…incident down by the swimming hole. Iain had left early the following day, not even waiting to say good-bye properly.

Suddenly, that seemed so very absurd.

He was crossing the floor of the inn before he could think better of it, his long legs eating up the space between him and James. He saw the moment that James noticed him, the instant smile that lit up his handsome face before an uncertain expression Iain didn't like chased it away.

"Jamie!" Iain exclaimed as he drew close. "It's really you."

He could feel James's companions' eyes upon him, but he didn't so much as glance at them—his attention was all for James, who was now looking at him as though he were a ghost.

"Iain," the man said faintly, allowing Iain to take his hand in a firm grip and to clap his other shoulder in a display of easy friendship that belied all the complicated feelings between them.

"Jamie," Iain said again. Just that.

For a long moment, they just stared at one another, and even though James looked a little troubled, his grey gaze was still the most wonderful, welcome, *restful* thing that Iain had seen in a long time. It soothed all the jagged parts in him so that it felt like, right now, standing here holding James's hand, he was experiencing the first peace he'd known in ages.

And then James was clearing his throat and extricating his hand from Iain's grip, looking away from him to catch the eyes of his companions.

"Gents, this is my…friend. Captain Iain Sinclair." James gestured at him, a small, almost embarrassed gesture that Iain found he didn't like, and when James glanced at him again, his expression was careful. "Mr. Alun Lloyd, and Mr. Philip Carstairs," he intoned politely, indicating the two gentlemen beside him. "Friends from university."

Carstairs glanced at Iain from under his sandy lashes, offering a subtly provocative smile. "Delighted to meet you, Captain." He was a decent enough looking fellow with his sandy hair and compact frame, but he couldn't hold a candle to James.

Iain sent him a careless smile, including Mr. Lloyd in it. "Likewise."

He turned back to James. "It's been too long," he said. "A year? More?"

"Ten months," James said crisply and Iain couldn't help but smile at that, at his typical precision. It bothered him, though, that there was no answering smile.

The need to touch James was near overwhelming, an itch that grew in Iain till he could feel it prickling his fingertips. The effort he was expending to stop himself reaching out was enormous—and seemed suddenly ridiculous. He lunged at James drunkenly, slinging a companionable arm around his shoulders.

"Ah, but it's good to see you," he exclaimed, making his voice jovial—as though he was just a merry drunk. That was all anybody would think, wasn't it? And anyway, who cared what anyone else thought?

Beneath his arm, he felt James stiffen and shrink. The man gave an awkward laugh, bearing the weight of Iain's arm for a few seconds before he shrugged it off, glancing at his friends, then round the inn, nervously.

"Have you been drinking awhile, Sinclair?" James asked. His expression was only mildly enquiring but his voice was tight, and Iain felt a wave of sadness swamp him at the disapproval and the use of his surname. His arm dropped to his side, bereft.

"Awhile," Iain admitted.

"Are you here with friends, Captain?" That was the shorter, dark-haired man. The one who'd been pawing James earlier. Iain fancied he detected a faint challenge in the young man's gaze.

"I came alone," Iain said. "Though I was speaking with someone when you came in." He waved in the general direction of the table he'd been sitting at. "He was going to get some cards for a game." He looked up, catching James's eye. "Would you like to play with us? Two's a hopeless number for cards."

James glanced at his friends, half enquiringly, half apologetically. The dark-haired man opened his mouth—to protest, Iain suspected—but before he could speak, the sandy-haired one said smoothly, "What a good idea. Where's your table?"

Iain led them across the room. The table was still miraculously empty. Charlie, a fair-weather friend if ever there was one, must've forgotten about him. He never did come back with any playing cards, but Iain soon forgot about him anyway. The conversation with James and his friends flowed easily enough, and the sandy-haired fellow bought a jug of gin for them to share.

As drunk as he was, Iain still noticed that James was uncharacteristically quiet. He didn't look much at Iain either. It was funny—Iain hadn't realised how often James's gaze rested on him until, suddenly, he wasn't looking.

When the drink finally overwhelmed him, it took him unawares. He wasn't sure when his eyelids fell and his head lolled, only knew that, abruptly, James's lips were brushing his right ear, his breath warm as he spoke into it, his hand gently shaking Iain's shoulder.

"Come on," he urged. "Wake up, Iain. You're falling asleep—let's get you home."

"'M'fine," Iain muttered without opening his eyes. "Just resting my eyes."

"No," James's voice said in his ear, quiet and firm. "You need to go home. Come on, I'll take you. Philip says we can borrow his carriage."

Alone with James?

"All right," he said and lurched to his feet, reeling a little before steadying himself by gripping the edge of the table.

James's short Welsh friend looked distinctly put out at their leaving, but the sandy-haired one—Philip, whose carriage was being offered—seemed quite pleased. Perhaps he fancied his chances with Aled or whatever his name was once James was out of the way.

"Thank you," James was saying earnestly to Philip as Iain swayed on his feet. "I'll send your driver straight back after."

Philip waved him off carelessly. "In your own time, dear boy," he said. "I'm sure Alun and I can amuse ourselves here for a while."

James turned to Iain. "Come on, then," he said, placing his hand at the small of Iain's back and pushing lightly in the direction of the door.

Iain was so used to looking after himself always that it was a real novelty to let someone else do it. He found himself relaxing into James's care, allowing the man to guide him through the crowd of drinkers and out into the night, then down the street to where Philip's driver idled outside his carriage.

Iain stood there on the street, eyes closed, while James spoke to the driver, not even bothering to listen to what was being said. Then he let James coax him up the steps of the carriage and steady him as he climbed inside and sat down on the bench.

When James settled down next to him, Iain slumped against his side. He let his head fall onto James's shoulder, and in that moment, it was as though everything else just fell away. It felt so right to rest there, letting James be his bulwark. Letting James's warm strength absorb all of Iain's cares.

When had James grown this broad in the shoulders?

Iain sighed heavily, contentedly. He felt James's head turn, perhaps in surprise. Then the weight of James's head leaned against his own, as though he drew something in turn from Iain, as though they fed something in each other.

The motion of the carriage and the comfort between them must have rocked Iain to sleep. The next thing he knew, he was being shaken gently, wakening with a start.

"Iain—we're here. Come on."

With unquestioning obedience, he stumbled out of the carriage after James and then stood watching as it drove off into the darkness.

Only then did he realise where they were—at the Hart family townhouse.

"What're we doing here?" he said stupidly as James urged him towards the front door. "I thought you were taking me home?" He felt a bit less intoxicated now, though still thick-headed from his brief sleep in the carriage.

James glanced at him with surprise. "I kept asking you in the carriage where your rooms were. But you just kept telling me your old address in Manchester. I thought you could sleep the worst of the drink off here, and my driver could take you home in the morning."

Iain groaned softly and palmed the back of his neck. "Christ, sorry."

"It's all right," James said easily, rapping on the front door with his cane. "If you want to go home now, I can get Reilly up to take you."

"No, no, it's all right," Iain replied. "Don't wake your servant unnecessarily. If you really don't mind having me as a guest for a few hours, that is."

"Of course not," James said. He wasn't looking at Iain but

his voice was soft and sincere. "We mightn't have seen each other for a while but we're still friends." He paused. "I hope we'll always be friends."

Iain stared at James's averted profile, even though it hurt him a little to look. James had that uncertain look about him again, and Iain was the cause of it. He wanted to chase that expression away. He wanted to see James smile.

"Of course we're friends," he said. He lifted a hand, stroking his thumb across James's cheek. "Now and always." Reluctantly, he let his hand drop away, watching, fascinated, as James swallowed visibly. And then the door was opening.

The footman stood aside to admit them. He locked up again then handed a lit candle to James to take upstairs, enquiring softly whether his master needed anything else.

"No, thank you, Groves. That will be all."

The footman nodded and withdrew, leaving them to make their way upstairs.

James led the way, and Iain followed him, mesmerised by the lean length of James's legs as he climbed the stairs, the tight fit of his breeches, his taut, well-shaped arse. Christ, but he'd grown up comely, this lad of his.

Strange to think how right it felt to think of James like that. As *his*.

He followed James into a small sitting room. He'd been in here once before, only that time, James was the one who'd been drunk instead of Iain. Not that Iain felt so inebriated now. Now he was experiencing that strange, deceptive lucidity that sometimes came in the very depths of drunkenness.

"This is familiar," he said, smiling.

James was turned away from him, lighting a branch of candles from the single one he'd brought upstairs. He didn't look round at Iain's assertion, merely asked, "Is it?"

"Yes. Don't you remember the last time I was in here?"

James cleared his throat, still turned away. "I'm not sure I do," he said, and Iain knew he was lying.

"I took you out to see that boxing match at the White Hare Inn."

"Oh yes," James said faintly. "I remember now."

"Our positions are somewhat reversed tonight, though."

"In terms of…?"

Iain hiccoughed. "Being the worse for wear for drink." The words came out in a shambling slur, and he gave a self-mocking laugh.

"I've never seen you like this before," James said. "How long have you been drinking?"

Iain looked at the ceiling, considering the question. "Since around five, I think."

"Were you celebrating something?"

Iain laughed harshly, then shook his head. "No. Quite the opposite."

"Meaning?"

"Meaning I needed to get drunk."

"Why?"

Iain sighed, rubbing his hand over the back of his neck. "Because I'm bored rigid. I've been playing the courtier for a year now, and the truth is, I hate court politics. I'm good at it, but I hate it. The King is tedious and selfish, and everyone else at court is self-serving and manipulative. But my orders are to stay where I am—so I have no choice."

James's eyebrows rose at his vehement tone. "Couldn't you ask to be transferred? Let another officer take your place?"

Iain gave a bitter chuckle. "The only reason I'm there at all is because the King took a particular liking to me. And since my superior officers like having a window into the King's mind, I'm stuck. Though why they want to hear about the nonsense that goes on in there escapes me. The man might fancy himself as a head of state, but all of Europe knows who really holds the power in this country and it certainly isn't Georgie boy." Abruptly he yawned, then scrubbed his hands over his face. When he dropped his hands away, he saw that James gazed at him with a tender expression that made him feel the strangest pang of pure longing.

"You look exhausted," James said. "Come on, you can sleep in my bed. I'll take one of the guest cha—"

"No," Iain said. "Don't do that."

The words were out his mouth before he'd thought them through, and James was plainly startled.

"What?" he said, his tone suggesting he genuinely thought he'd misheard.

"Stay with me," Iain said.

James's shock was palpable. He stared at Iain open-mouthed for a few seconds before shaking his head. "You—you're not thinking straight. You don't want—"

"I do," Iain said. He stepped forward, taking a firm hold of James's slim hips and tugging him forwards so that his long lean frame slammed against Iain's broader one. They were practically the same height now, and Iain loved that. Loved that, standing, their chests and groins matched perfectly. Lips matched perfectly. He had a moment to see the sudden darkening of James's eyes before he pressed his mouth to the other man's.

James made a brief, weak sound of protest, his hands fastening round Iain's biceps with the apparent intention of pushing him away, except that when Iain licked his tongue over the seam of James's lips, the man's firm grip on Iain's upper arms loosened and he groaned in defeat, parting his lips to let Iain's tongue sweep inside his mouth.

It was so fucking sweet, that reluctant surrender. So sweet and so giving. So generous. He had always loved James's generous spirit. Had always loved this boy, this man. And now he wanted to show it.

Tearing his mouth away he stared into James's eyes—

those lovely grey eyes, turbulent now, with confusion and passion.

"Let me suck you," he whispered. He dropped to his knees without waiting for an answer, busying his fumbling fingers with unfastening the placket of James's breeches, ignoring his protests, and the hands that tried, halfheartedly, to push him away.

"Iain, I don't think—"

"I know what I'm about," Iain murmured, spreading the folds of fabric apart to reveal James's smallclothes. He breathed a hot gust of breath against the layer of thin linen that hid James's cock from his hungry gaze. "Let me do this. I want to—and you want me to. You know you do."

James groaned, and it was a groan Iain recognised. A groan that said, *This is a terrible idea, but I'm going to let it happen anyway.*

Iain smiled when he finally tugged the smallclothes down and revealed James's hard, elegant shaft. Like its owner, it was long and lean—and bent, curving toward James's right hip. Iain leaned forward and greedily engulfed the whole, warm length in his mouth.

Ah, fuck.

James's cock. So warm, so alive. *Pulsing* with life. Rude and blunt and entirely unsubtle. It reached for the back of Iain's throat selfishly, and in the oddest way, Iain relished the demanding cutting off of his air.

He gave himself up to the passion of service, of worship. He licked and laved and suckled and gorged. He dipped his head still lower to paint wetness all over the man's balls with his tongue, to mouth those tender orbs with his lips, to graze them with his teeth. And as he worked, the last vestiges of James's reluctance evaporated. His long fingers tunnelled into Iain's thick dark hair, and he began to cant his hips forward, begging for still more.

"Iain," he breathed. "God, Iain. You can't expect me to stop you now—"

Iain laughed at that, his chuckle muffled by all the hot, hard flesh in his mouth, and Christ but he loved that too—the sound of his own service, honest and unwavering, his very voice silenced by the male flesh hammering into him. He stroked his hands up the backs of James's thighs, and up further to grasp his arse, and he hoped James could read the language of those caresses. That the last thing Iain wanted was to stop this.

He felt like he was proving something—something important—to James. That James was desirable. That his body was delightful to Iain. That he was beautiful and, yes, wanted. And as hard as Iain's own cock was—and right now, it was very hard indeed—his own pleasure didn't really matter to him right now. He relished the bordering-on-painful press of the parquet floor beneath his knees as much as he did the pleasurable pulse of his shaft—because it was for James.

Jamie.

It wasn't long before the fingers stroking through his hair tightened, snagging, till the hips he held in hands began to stutter in his grasp. Above his head, James was moaning his name.

"Iain, God, *Iain*—"

And it was so bloody perfect, giving James this gift. Making this loving offering of his body. Usually sex was about taking for Iain. Or at least as much about taking as giving, but now, for the first time in his life, he just wanted to give and keep giving. Till he was all used up and there was nothing left of him at all.

His jaw began to ache, but he kept it open, kept his agile tongue caressing as James began to push harder, faster into his mouth. His hands were tight on James's hips but he made no attempt to temper the depth of James's thrusts into his throat. Right now, he'd happily choke if it would give James more pleasure. And he did choke, a little, on those last few thrusts of James's hips.

He heard James sobbing out an apology for his roughness, even as his hands held Iain's head still and his cock swelled that last impossible fraction. And then James was coming in salt-sweet, blood-warm pulses and Iain was swallowing his spend, loving this last part of the act perhaps most of all.

He rested his forehead against James's thigh after, dimly aware of James's hand stroking his head gently.

"I'm sorry," James whispered. He sounded appalled. "I was rough. You must think I—"

"I loved it," Iain interrupted.

"At least let me reciprocate," James murmured, drawing Iain to his feet.

Numbly, Iain let James lead him into the adjoining bedchamber and help him off with his clothes, working as tidily as any valet. James folded each garment neatly, piling everything up on the chair in the corner. Then he pulled off his own clothes, taking much less care with those, and led Iain over to the bed. Iain dutifully crawled in and stretched out. He was aware of his cock, hard and sensitive, even as his exhausted mind was trying to shut down.

A soft puff of James's breath extinguished the candles. Now it was dark, though Iain could see the faint, thin trail of smoke sent up by the deadened wick. He followed it with his eyes to the ceiling, then shuddered as James's hand circled his cock, taking hold of him.

"You're so hard," James murmured in his ear. "Like iron." He plastered himself against Iain's side, adjusting his body, and his grip, trying to get his hand as near to the position of Iain's own hand as he could. His grip was confident, knowing, and when he began to stroke it was with the expertise of a man who had done this many times before, to himself and to others, perhaps.

Iain opened his mouth to say something, but the words

caught in his throat, overtaken by a throaty groan of pleasure. He wasn't going to last more than seconds, he knew. And sure enough, a half-dozen more strokes of James's hand had his back arching off the bed and an unholy cry escaping him. He emptied his balls over his belly, over James's hand, and all the while, James praised him, whispering nonsense words of tenderness and affection in his ear, and it felt so damn good that all he could do was close his eyes and let all the good feelings surround him like a warm blanket as he drifted off.

He dreamed of Tom that night. It was a dream that had come to him on and off over the years.

He was in the river, just as he had been the day Tom drowned. He was circling his legs in the water to stay afloat when he heard Tom say his name. Except it wasn't that Tom was saying it to him, it was more that Iain heard it in his head, like an echo.

He began to look around for Tom, twisting and turning in the water in his desperation, whipping his head round as he searched. The frantic movements tired him out, and that made him feel panicky.

And then, finally, he saw Tom. Tom as he had been that day — completely vertical in the water but for his arms extended at his sides and unnaturally still. His mouth was open, chin lifting even as he began to slowly sink, and his eyes stared right at Iain with that glassy look that Iain would never be able to forget.

Iain tried to scream Tom's name, but he couldn't. His own mouth was filling with water, and he was sinking down, the river closing over his head. He opened his eyes under the water, and there was Tom opposite him, like Christ, legs crossed at the ankles and arms stretched out, palms towards Iain. Sinking down, down, while Iain struggled to breathe…

He woke in the greatest of distress, but without noise—

just one terrified, guttering exhalation that sawed out of his chest as his heart thundered in his ears.

He turned his head on the pillow, and there was James. Faintly smiling as he slept.

Happy.

Oh, Jesus in heaven. What had he *done*?

The effects of the drink made themselves known to him one by one—his mouth was dry as dust, his head thudding painfully. Nausea made his belly lurch. He felt wretched, and not just physically.

How could he have done this? Come back here with James and—oh Christ, but this was a mistake. Such a *mistake*. Regret swamped him, hot and smothering.

A year—ten months ago—he'd left Wylde Manor with the firm objective of making sure this didn't happen again. In the months that followed, James had written to him, begging him to consider the *true nature* of their friendship and to *examine his heart*. Iain's own infrequent return correspondence had ignored those outpourings entirely, merely reporting scantily on the day-to-day minutiae of his life, as though he was answering a different set of letters altogether, and eventually James had stopped mentioning it, his letters becoming more formal—and less frequent.

All these long months, Iain had been working at building a path back to where they had been before Wylde Manor—to the platonic companionship they'd once shared. They'd managed it once before, finding their way back to friendship after the mortification of James's first bumbling kiss in this very house. It hadn't seemed unreasonable to hope they could manage it again, given time.

Until now.

Until he'd ruined all his efforts in a single, drunken night. And now he was going to lose James, because it was happening all over again. And Iain knew, with leaden certainty, that when James woke up, he'd take one look at Iain and know exactly what Iain was thinking. He'd always been like a weather vane when it came to Iain's moods.

Lying there in the predawn, Iain realised he couldn't bear to go through it. To witness James's hurt and the inevitable unravelling.

He knew he was being a coward, but he did it anyway. Got out of bed and fetched his clothes from the chair, lifting the painstakingly folded pile of garments in his arms and carrying them into the sitting room. He dressed quietly, let himself out into the corridor and descended the stairs.

The doors of this house were well oiled, and the floorboards gave out no creaking. He was so silent that when he reached the bottom of the stairs, the night footman was still sleeping in his chair, and Iain had to waken him to be let out.

As the footman closed the front door behind him, the first pale fingers of dawn were probing the sky.

Iain huddled into his coat and began to walk.

17

20th April, 1822

Redford's Club, London

The man sitting opposite James was like no one he had ever seen before. He couldn't remember meeting any man he would've described as *pretty* before, especially not one who looked to be about forty years old. But yes, this man—Kit Redford—was pretty, with his fair hair and long lashes and sweetly shaped lips. He had an oddly innocent look to him—till you looked in his eyes.

The eyes were old. Very old. They were eyes that had seen everything and known more disappointment and sadness than most.

And yet the man hadn't stopped smiling since James had arrived on his doorstep, uninvited, an hour ago, for one last desperate attempt at tracking down Iain Sinclair.

"Won't you have a scone, Mr. Hart?" Redford asked. "My cook bakes them herself, and they're lighter than any you'll ever have had before, I promise you."

Scones—that was what he was being offered by Kit Redford, proprietor of one of the most debauched clubs in London.

"No, thank you," James said, trying to hide his frustration that Kit Redford did not appear to view his request with the same urgency that James felt. The man was reclining on a chaise longue across from him, sipping tea. Although it was two o'clock in the afternoon, he wore nothing but a satin dressing gown of peacock blue and pink and gold.

"Generally speaking," Redford said now, in his light, sibilant voice, "no one is allowed to step foot inside my club without two references from current members, but you only know Captain Sinclair." He paused, then continued, "And you say you don't want me to ask him for a reference."

"No," James said. "As I said, the only reason I want to come to your club is to make him see me." His face burned with mortification as he admitted it.

Redford's eyebrows rose. "You are...refreshingly frank."

"It's only fair to be honest with you," James replied. "He's refused to receive me when I've gone to his rooms, and he's not answered my letters."

"Why do you want to see him so badly?" Redford asked curiously.

"Because"—James swallowed hard, then made himself continue, despite the humiliation—"because I've loved him for years, you see, and he always said he didn't want more, only last week he did and then—" He broke off. He was rambling. Taking a deep breath, he tried again. "He came back to my house with me, stayed the night with me, but afterwards, he just left. Sneaked out while I was sleeping." He heard clearly the hurt and bewilderment in his own voice, and it made him feel raw and exposed. "And I just want to know why. Why he would do that."

"And what do you imagine his answer's going to be?" Redford asked. He smiled kindly. "The truth is, Mr. Hart, it's probably not what you're hoping to hear."

James sighed and nodded. "I know you're probably right. But as naïve as this sounds, I think he loves me in his way, and if I can just talk to him, maybe I can make him see it for himself."

Redford tilted his head to the side, considering that. "Tell me about him," he invited, settling back more comfortably into his sofa. "About both of you. From your first meeting."

So James did. He talked and talked—till the clock struck five and he glanced up at the mantelpiece, astonished that so much time had passed. It was easy, because Kit Redford stared out of the window the whole time he was speaking, almost as if he wasn't really listening.

When he was done, Redford didn't say anything right away, just looked out of the window. At last, though, he spoke. "You've been in love with Captain Sinclair for a long time."

"Yes," James admitted.

Redford looked at him then. Weary eyes in a startlingly lovely face. "From what you've told me, I suspect he does care for you in some way," he said. "But possibly not the way you care for him. And even if he does care for you in that way, he's probably not going to admit it. Probably can't even admit it to himself."

James waited, sensing there was more to come.

Redford sighed. "He comes in several times a month," he said. "No set day of the week. You may have to come along quite a few times before you see him." He sent James a surprisingly hard look. "I can't take you entirely on trust, of course. I'll be making some enquiries about you after this, and you'll have to sign an agreement. We'll call it…a temporary membership. One month." He paused. "And there will be a fee, of course."

"That's fine." James knew it was probably foolish to agree to such terms, but this was Kit Redford, a man Iain had decided to trust with his secrets, and trust was not something that Iain gave lightly.

Redford nodded. All at once, the hardness was gone, and

he looked sad again. "I'm afraid your captain is going to disappoint you, Mr. Hart. Few men are brave enough to take the risk of going against the world's ideas of what a man should be, and those of us who do sometimes pay a steep price for the privilege." He gave a twisted sort of smile. "But I can see you won't rest till you have this out with him. At least within these walls, no one will think the worse of you for it. And if your captain has a tenth of your courage, my dear, you may even have a chance at convincing him."

James spent four long evenings at Redford's without seeing Iain at all. He'd never been to such a place before, and he found the open flirtation that took place in the club room shocking enough, never mind the naked debauchery he witnessed in the back room.

Over those four evenings, he was flirted with, propositioned and pawed by a score of men, none of whom were Iain. It was all curiously unreal to him, seeing the masks of polite society fall away to reveal the true nature of each of Kit Redford's customers while they walked these halls. And then seeing the masks being donned again as they departed, upstanding men of society, every one of them.

This was where Iain came when he wanted release. Not to James, but here. Here, to find a warm, willing body he could share for a few hours before he went back to his usual life. To being Captain Iain Sinclair, war hero and King George's favourite. The perfect military man.

By Wednesday, the fifth evening in a row he'd come, he was beginning to question his purpose. Beginning to wonder whether he was entirely mistaken in thinking that Iain could want anything more than what Redford's offered. In the meantime, James had called again at Iain's rooms and been told that Captain Sinclair was not at home. Plainly, he did not want to see James. Did not even want to speak to him.

So why, he thought, as he rapped at the door of Redford's, *am I back again tonight?*

"This is the last time," he told himself under his breath as he waited for the door to open.

The footman who admitted him was used to James by now. He greeted him like the faithful customer he was turning into, murmuring pleasantries as he took James's greatcoat, hat and cane before ushering him inside. James went straight to the club room, where Kit Redford was already circulating amongst his patrons, resplendent in his perfectly tailored evening clothes. Midnight-blue coat and breeches and snowy white linen, a cerulean waistcoat lending a flamboyant touch.

Redford's expression brightened when he set eyes on James, and his urbane smile transformed into one that was a little more genuine, the sudden spark lighting up his attractive features in a way that enhanced his delicate beauty. He strolled towards James, holding out his hands. A huge sapphire-and-gold ring adorned his right index finger.

"My dear boy," he said, taking the single hand that James offered and wrapping it in both of his own. "I wondered if you might give up after four nights, but here you are again, as faithful as can be."

"As foolish as can be, you mean," James replied.

Redford smiled. "I know what I mean."

"Do I take it Iain's not here?"

"On the contrary, he was here in the club room just a few minutes ago." Redford cast his gaze around but apparently didn't see Iain. "Perhaps he's in the back room now?"

James stared at him, strangely shocked. He hadn't expected it to be so easy when it finally happened. Suddenly, his stomach was in knots, his pulse racing in his throat as his mouth dried.

"I'll—I'll go and check then," he said faintly.

Redford nodded. "All right," he said kindly. "I'll be watching out for you." He clapped James lightly on the shoulder before strolling away.

James steeled himself and set off, stomach churning with mingled dread and excitement, palms damp with nerves. The back room could only be accessed by a narrow servants' passageway, carefully tucked away so as to attract as little attention as possible. The club room and games room at the front of the building looked much like any other gentlemen's club, and beyond mild flirting, nothing much happened there. It was only when you ventured into the secret depths of the club that things changed. Behind the large wooden door of the back room was where the real business of Redford's happened. Where men could find a partner either to slip away with or to have right there, in front of anyone who wanted to watch. The casual nudity had astonished James the first time he'd come. The frankness of these men when they were away from the strictures of polite society was staggering.

He wondered how Iain behaved when he was here. Did he treat the men he went with as he'd treated James, with tenderness and care? Or did he just want a quick cocksucking, a convenient arse to fuck? James could understand if Iain saw it like that—Christ, he'd only been coming here a few nights, and even he, heartsick as he was, had been tempted. It was difficult to say no with all that naked flesh on display and the scent of desire and semen and male sweat in the air. Not to mention his own deprived body craving release.

Yet the thought of Iain doing that—wanting that—somehow crushed him. How could James ever compete with all this endless choice and novelty?

Taking a deep breath, he pushed the door open and stepped inside.

It was busy tonight, and something in the middle of the

room had captured the attention of the crowd. Men gathered around, necks craning to see the action. James wasn't much interested—he was more concerned with finding Iain, and he began to work his way through the melee, his gaze searching the sea of faces. He stopped, though, when a hard voice cracked out an order.

"Strip."

A murmur of excitement rose in the wake of that single word. James looked then, straining his neck to see past the men in front of him. He made out two men standing in the centre of the room. One was in military uniform—a junior officer, by the look of him, with coppery hair that glinted in the candlelight. The other man was of a similar height and build, but with dark hair and elegant evening clothes. Perhaps it was naïve of James to be surprised that it was the second man who was giving the orders.

Already the soldier was removing his uniform, his movements quick and efficient, the pile of clothes at his feet growing quickly, till he was fully naked, his pale skin glowing in the candlelight.

He had a beautiful body, as well formed as a young god, but his features were homely, even a little coarse. There was something arresting about him, though, as he stood there in front of all those avid eyes. He seemed almost to vibrate with desire—James found the naked expression on his face difficult to look at. The need there.

The second man unbuttoned the placket of his trousers and drew out his hard, flushed member.

"Suck it," he said in a sneering voice. "On your knees, if you please."

The soldier visibly shuddered, then folded himself onto his knees and shuffled forwards to do as he was bid.

"Hands behind your back."

Again, the soldier obeyed, taking hold of one wrist with his other hand. The dip of his head as he ducked to take the other man's cock into his mouth was submissive, the curving movement of his neck, graceful. And that young, godlike body, pale as marble, anatomically perfect.

God, but the intimacy of this went right to James's gut. Almost more so when he glanced around and saw how many of the other faces looked bored or not much more than mildly interested. Such a naked bit of real desire playing out before them, to be greeted with such apathy.

Unable to watch any more, James turned away to complete his circuit of the room. And just then, there he was. None other than Iain Sinclair himself, moving towards him.

James stopped in his tracks, stunned. Stunned, then hollow when he saw Iain glance over his shoulder at a man behind him, a big, brawny fellow who looked to be around the same age as Iain, with black hair and a compellingly attractive face. The man raised his eyebrows at Iain and smiled at him. And God, but he was a handsome fellow.

James realised then that Iain was about to walk past him without so much as noticing him. He stepped forward, right into Iain's path.

"Iain," he said, his stomach dropping as he noticed the expression of shock on the man's face. "Please—I have to talk to you—"

Iain reared back. "*James?* What the *hell*?" He sounded furious, truly angry. "You shouldn't be here!"

James drew away as though he'd been slapped. He shouldn't be surprised, but perhaps the stupidly naïve part of him had secretly thought to see that smile of pleasure that used to bloom on Iain's face just from seeing James.

James swallowed hard and straightened his shoulders. "I'm a member just like you. Mr. Redford let me join."

"Well, he shouldn't have!" Iain bit out. "I'd've blackballed you if I'd known!"

The big man had caught up with Iain now, and he stood at

his shoulder, a politely curious expression on his face as he shifted his gaze between them.

"Kit doesn't allow blackballing," Iain's companion said, and when Iain sent him a furious look, his lips twitched as though he were amused.

"Yes, but he needs references!" Iain snapped before turning, quick as lightning, back to James and demanding, "Who the fuck gave you a reference? Tell me their names!"

For several seconds, James just stared at him, struck dumb by the anger on his face. And then, just as he opened his mouth to respond, Iain grasped his forearm and began to drag him towards the door, muttering something at the other man as they passed him.

"What are you doing?" James protested, even as he allowed Iain to drag him forward.

Iain hauled the door of the back room open and pushed James outside, following him out into the dim corridor and slamming the heavy door shut behind them.

"What the *hell* are you thinking, coming here?" he yelled.

"I was looking for you!" James shouted back, angry and embarrassed in equal measure. "A few days ago, you were in my bed—by your own choice, I might add—though you ran away like a coward while I slept."

Iain's cheeks reddened. "What of it?"

What of it?

"I want to know why you left! Why you've been ignoring my letters—" James's voice broke with emotion, and he stopped abruptly, hating how betraying that was.

Iain just stared at him, his face a picture of misery.

"I've called at your rooms," James went on. "But I expect you know that already."

Iain closed his eyes as though he couldn't bear to look at James, and God but that was humiliating. This wasn't going anything like the way he'd hoped. He saw now that he'd made a mistake coming here. Imagining there was something between them that could be saved, that actually *needed* to be saved, when the truth was, Iain plainly wanted no more to do with him. And how could James even claim to be surprised by that? Iain had been proving it to him, over and over, since last summer.

Except for that one night, of course, a week ago—when he was in his cups.

I'm afraid your captain is going to disappoint you, Mr. Hart.

Kit Redford had been right.

All at once, standing there watching Iain squirm, James felt utterly defeated. Sick at heart and lost. After what had happened between them last week, he'd thought if he could just see Iain, speak to him, he'd be able to... What? Make him admit to feelings he simply didn't possess?

He realised he was staring dumbly at Iain. No doubt with an expression on his face that made his pain and disappointment all too humiliatingly obvious. His throat felt clogged and achy, and he knew with sudden certainty that if he didn't walk away now, Iain would witness the even greater humiliation of him weeping. Without another word, he turned on his heel and started striding away down the corridor.

"Oh bloody hell," Iain groaned behind him. "Where are you going now?"

The exasperation in Iain's voice flayed him. He wanted to howl, but instead he kept walking and forced himself to call over his shoulder, without turning round, "I'm leaving. You should be pleased about that."

He heard Iain's heels on the flagstones behind him, but he just kept going, afraid that if he paused for even a moment, he would disgrace himself beyond what he could bear. When he reached the door that led onto the club room, he yanked it open so hard, it shuddered on its hinges.

"James. For God's sake—"

That tone again. Apparently, he was nothing but an aggravation to Iain. A problem.

It was so very far from what he wanted to be.

He strode through the club room, Iain on his heels. Kit Redford looked over at his entrance, his attractive face creased with worry. He sent James a questioning glance, and James paused for an instant, giving a quick shake of his head in return that somehow expressed all the disappointment and heaviness in his heart.

The pause was unwise.

"James, wait."

Iain's hand landed on his shoulder, stopping him in his tracks.

He wanted to tug free. To run away, refusing to listen to whatever words Iain wanted to say now. But he couldn't quite bring himself to behave like that in front of the other patrons. Instead, he steeled himself and turned. And perhaps, as he did so, a tiny part of him still hoped.

The hope died as soon as he laid eyes on Iain. An unhappy expression marred his handsome face, and the firm set to his jaw spoke of settled determination. He seemed as resolved, as determined, as he'd been that day at Wylde Manor, ten months before, when he'd told James he couldn't consider anything beyond friendship.

"What is it?" James asked. And suddenly he was tired. Weary of it all.

"I just—I want you to understand."

"Understand what? That you don't want to see me?" He gave a weak laugh. "You've made it very clear these past few days. Admittedly, it's taken me a while to really take the hint, but I think I've finally got it."

Iain closed his eyes. When he opened them again, he said bleakly, "Of course I want to see you again—but as my friend. Not as anything more." His blue eyes searched James's face for a reaction, and whatever he saw there made him heave a sigh. After a pause, he added, "I admit I was shocked to see you just now. You don't belong here, Jamie. You're not like the men who come here. They're only looking for something quick and easy—"

"You're wrong," James interrupted flatly. "I'm no different from any other man here. If it wasn't for the fact that I've been hoping for something different—something only with you— I'd probably be the man standing in the middle of that room, being fucked in front of everyone."

Iain reared back a little, clearly shocked. "Don't say that!"

"Why shouldn't I say it? What does it matter it to you?" His voice had risen, but he didn't care anymore. "Fine, I accept that you don't want me. Am I to put myself away in a drawer because of it? Never come to a place like this, where I might at least get to fuck *someone* once in a while? Feel alive and not alone?"

Iain stared at him. He swallowed hard. "I assumed you came here to see me, but is that why you're here? To find someone to *fuck*?"

James laughed, though the awful wrenching noise that emerged from his throat didn't sound much like a laugh. "Christ, you're dense," he said. "I'm here because you've *broken my heart*, Iain. And because, despite that, like an idiot, I couldn't stop hoping that if I could only see you and speak to you, you might change your mind."

"Jamie—" Iain shook his head as though denying everything James had just said. "Don't do this. We're *friends*. We've said it a hundred times—we'll *always* be friends. I don't want that to change. *Please*."

"No," James said wretchedly. "I can't go along with this anymore. This isn't just friendship to me. I can't get by on whatever crumbs you choose to throw me."

"Crumbs?" Iain exclaimed. "My friendship is *crumbs* to you?" He stared at James for long moments, seeming genuinely hurt. "I don't understand you," he said at last, his voice edged with frustration. "I don't understand why you're insisting on making this so bloody difficult. Why can't we just be the way we've always been? Why do you have to ruin everything with this—this ridiculous, childish devotion! Don't you see that it's *absurd*? Christ, you're not a boy any longer—you need to accept that you can't always have what you want. None of us can. That's just how life is."

That stung. That *hurt*. It hurt so badly that James had to close his eyes for several seconds just to get hold of himself. And the worst thing was, when he opened his eyes, Iain still looked angry and frustrated, as though he hadn't the faintest clue what impact his words had had on James.

James didn't say anything more. Not one word. Instead, he turned on his heel and strode towards the front door.

"Where are you going?" Iain demanded behind him.

James didn't answer. He nodded at Kit Redford as he left, and Kit nodded back unhappily, his expression promising a further discussion to come. The footman stepped forward with James's coat, hat and cane. He took them automatically, murmuring the usual polite responses even as his heart crumbled to dust. And then the footman was opening the door and James was stepping out into the cold, clear April night.

Iain didn't come after him, and the truth was, James wasn't even surprised.

18

Now: 1824

28th May, 1824

Holmewell, Hampshire

Iain sat with his head in hands for a long time after James left the cottage, James's words ringing in his ears.

Will you not be satisfied until you have destroyed me?

The storm inside him raged ever harder, even as the one outside the cottage gradually passed, the lashing rain diminishing first to a downpour, then to a shower, then to nothing.

When he stepped outside, it was to see that the dark grey clouds had rolled away, and the bright, hot sun was already warming the earth. But it did not warm him. He felt cold inside, right to his core.

Don't ever follow me anywhere again.

Was James finished with him? The thought was unbearable.

He began the walk back to Holmewell, checking his watch and noting with disbelief that it wasn't yet one o'clock. He felt as though he'd lived an entire lifetime already this day but there was still the picnic to get through and then a long evening of entertainments. Dancing tonight, Kate had promised. The young ladies had been all atwitter about it the night before.

How would he do it? How would he play cricket and eat and dance after what had happened in the bluebell woods and in the cottage? How would he manage to politely converse when his mind was filled with thoughts of James and the very blood in his veins seemed to be beating out the tattoo of the question that had been echoing in his mind, over and over?

Was it possible?

Was it possible?

Was it possible to give up everything you were, everything you'd set out to be? Was it possible to turn your back on the world when you realised that the life you'd made for yourself was…empty?

Iain walked quickly, needing the distraction of physical activity. He could still feel James in his arms, the ghost of his lips touching Iain's. For two years, he'd been starved of any sight of James, haunted by the memory of the night they'd spent together two years before, that damned imperfect night. These two long years it had seemed like the only thing to do was to stay away, get *further* away. Free himself altogether.

He'd been stupid. He should've realised after all these years that, even though it was always Iain who walked away, he was always the one who came back too. Each time he'd gone, James had accepted his rejections, respecting Iain's stated wishes, but each time, Iain had been the one to return, tugged back by the invisible thread that connected them.

If he went to India, he wouldn't be able to return very easily. And, God, but the thought of that vast continental distance stretching between him and James made Iain feel hollow.

As he crested the brow of the hill, breathing a little harder from the swift pace he'd set himself, he glanced up and saw a kestrel high above him, hovering on the air, small and still and quivering. And then a second bird wheeled into a view. Its mate.

And in that moment, a profound truth hit him: he and James were a pair.

Iain would never be free of James, and he didn't want to be. His stated wish to make peace with James before he left England had been…a lie. One he'd told himself and allowed himself to believe. The truth was much simpler and much harder to live with—that he'd come here just to see James again, because he was miserable without him.

Because he missed him beyond anything.

The reason for his building unhappiness over the last few years, that unhappiness he'd been unable to articulate, even to himself, was suddenly as clear as day. And now the thought of leaving England struck him as madness. It was madness, wasn't it, to set out to make himself so unhappy? To make James so unhappy too?

And for what?

To please a father who was beyond all pleasing? Who was so deep in his cups most days he couldn't even remember what Iain said to him from one week to the next?

His father had told him over and over these last few years how disappointed he was in Iain's army career. Now he was disappointed in Iain's decision to leave the army. No doubt when Iain told him about the position in India, he'd be disappointed in that too, even though the only reason Iain had decided to take it was so he could continue to serve his country, and thus serve and honour his family. But regardless, it wouldn't be enough.

Nothing would ever be enough.

Iain had realised a long time ago that, given a choice, his father would have opted for a military career himself, that he yearned for adventure and glory. But that hadn't been his lot in life. His father was the only son, and by the time he was three-and-twenty, he had taken over the estate, with a wife selected by his own recently deceased father and the first of seven children in her belly: Tom. The boy whose death would break his father's heart.

Tom's death was the permanent shadow that loomed over their family. It hadn't just driven their father to drink. For a long time, it had leached all the happiness out of his mother too. But his mother had recovered, as much as she could, anyway. She still had two sons and four daughters to think of. She had their schooling to arrange, a household to run, and, given her husband's abdication of all responsibility, an estate to look after too. And she did it, took it all on, while Iain's father fell further and further into his cups and looked unlikely ever to crawl out.

In fairness, he had a few good memories of his father: his expression when he'd seen Iain in his brand-new uniform for the first time; the conversations they'd had about each new medal Iain had been decorated with; his rapt interest when Iain described his battle experiences. At these times, it had felt as though, perhaps, the man had been proud of Iain for a little while. But with peacetime had come less adventure. Less glory. Less pride and more criticism.

And for whom had Iain been living this life? For himself or his father?

For Tom?

What was it James had said earlier?

If I didn't choose to do the things that excited me, took the… comforts that I needed, then I would simply—never have those things. Would die without having lived."

Had Iain made *any* choices in his life that were really his?

He was halfway down the hill now, and Holmewell was in sight, but he slowed his pace, not ready to arrive, not ready to shamble on his old mask and join the other guests. Especially not now, as half a lifetime of memories flooded his mind. James moaning into that first, fumbling inexpert kiss. James riding by his side through the Derbyshire hills, then lying beside him at the swimming hole, his pale body kissed by the dappled sunshine. The two of them kissing and touching one another. Loving one another. James asleep as Iain stole out of his townhouse bedchamber. And just last night, James's mouth on his as they stood, cocooned together behind the curtains in the library.

The memories were as painful as they were sweet, each one proving to him, were proof needed, that James made him feel happy, made him feel *alive*, in a way that nothing and no one else in his life did. That James saw him, knew him, as no one else did, not even the friends who knew of his secret desires for other men, because James knew all of him, and somehow, remarkably, loved him anyway. Loved him still, Iain realised, thinking back to the man's devastated expression in the cottage earlier. Knowing that he still had that power over James, despite his many failings, made him feel ashamed and gratified at once.

It went both ways. James had power over him too, though he'd probably scoff at the very idea. All these years, James had been pulling Iain back to him, over and over, his desire to see James always ultimately stronger than the worry that things would get out of hand. As often as Iain had left, he'd returned, pulled back by that invisible thread.

That thread was love. He admitted it now to himself. It was love that had drawn Iain back, over and over. And each time he returned, his defences were further weakened, till this time, finally, he'd had to come into battle with no armour or weapons at all.

Nowhere to hide.

19

As Iain passed through the gates of Holmewell, greeting the gateman with a raised hand, he noticed distantly that it had turned out to be a lovely afternoon, warm and bright, not a cloud left in the sky. The storm might never have been.

The picnic would certainly be going ahead. Iain decided to head straight for the river rather than going back to the house. Turning off the main drive, he made for the gardens at the back of the house. He quickly crossed the formal pleasure grounds, neat and geometrical. Beyond that was the abundant utility of the kitchen gardens which provided the house with fruit, vegetables and herbs. Further still lay the ruthlessly maintained "wilderness" garden, complete with wide, flat paths suitable for even the most delicate of ladies' slippers to traverse. It was at the far end of the wilderness garden that one found the path that led to the broad, shady riverbank where the picnic was being held.

He heard the other guests before he saw them, the squeals and laughter of the children, the more muted sound of grown-up conversation. The tinkling of china and silverware.

By the time he came round the last bend in the path, he'd

managed to paste a smile on his face and was ready to greet his fellow guests with the usual sort of small talk.

Kate had outdone herself, setting up a muslin-draped canopy for the adults with proper tables and chairs and a more relaxed arrangement with blankets on the ground for the children—not that any of the children were sitting. They were all running around or swimming or playing what looked to be a brutal game of croquet.

Iain strolled up to the canopy. The first table he spied was a small one at which his parents sat. He noted the telling tension in his mother's jaw and the belligerent look his father wore as he defiantly lifted a wineglass and drained its contents.

"I'm just asking you to slow down, Arthur," he heard his mother mutter as he approached them. "This is a *family* occasion." The next instant, she caught sight of Iain, and her own mask, a familiar one, descended. She sent him a bright, if somewhat brittle, smile.

"My dear!" she exclaimed. "You're back. We wondered if you and James had been caught in the storm. Mr. Potts said you'd both insisted on carrying on despite the clouds."

"Isn't James here?" Iain asked, frowning. He cast his gaze around, but there was no sign of the man anywhere.

"No. Isn't he with you?" Iain's mother asked.

"Usually follows you round like a dog," his father muttered.

Iain glanced at him sharply, annoyed, disinclined, for once, to greet his behaviour with silence. "I beg your pardon?" he bit out.

His father looked up, surprised. "What?" he asked. His eyes were bleary, his mouth wet and slack. It was the middle of the day, and his father was drunk, shaming his mother. Shaming Iain, and Isabel too, who appeared to be staying as far away from their parents as she could.

For the first time in his life, it occurred to Iain to wonder if his father would have drunk like this even if Tom hadn't died.

"Did you have something to say about James?" Iain asked crisply.

His father smiled unpleasantly. That was one of the worst things about his drinking. The nastiness it brought out in him. When Iain thought back to the father of his early childhood, his memory was of a man who laughed frequently. But perhaps the truth was his father had always been like this. Perhaps it was just Iain's imperfect childhood memory that insisted that everything before Tom's death was perfect.

"He's always sniffing about you," the old man muttered nastily.

"Oh, *stop it*, Arthur!" his mother hissed, eyes flashing with sudden temper. "I don't know why you didn't just stay in your bedchamber if you're only going to drink yourself into another stupor today." She pressed her lips tightly together and looked away, blinking hard. His father sent her a sullen look, but he fell silent, staring balefully at his empty wineglass as though willing it to magically replenish itself.

"Well," Iain said at last, into the silence. "I think I'll go and ask Kate if James made it home all right."

"You do that, dear," his mother said, sending him a small, tight, apologetic smile. He found himself wishing that he could comfort her somehow. His answering smile felt horribly inadequate. There were times when he found his mother's dogged cheerfulness in the face of his father's ugly behaviour difficult to bear, but right now he'd have given a king's ransom to see it. For once, her deep unhappiness, though still veiled, was visible to him, and a wave of unexpected love flooded him for this brave, slightly distant woman who had raised him and his siblings. In that moment, it occurred to him that he had spent his whole life trying to please his father, a man who couldn't be pleased. And in all those years, not one word of criticism had ever passed his mother's lips.

Heart heavy, he wove through the tables under the canopy. Kate and Edward were sitting with Isabel and Bertie, who had little Margaret on his lap, playing with his pocket watch.

"Iain, there you are," Kate said, smiling up at him. "You look rather better than my brother did when he arrived home. He was soaked."

"Good, he made it back then." Iain cleared his throat. "I sheltered till the storm passed."

Kate nodded. "Yes, at the cottage. He told me."

"Why on earth didn't James stay with you?" Edward asked, frowning, and Iain felt warmth enter his cheeks. Kate looked amused, Isabel and Bertie curious.

"You can ask him yourself," Kate told her husband. "Here he comes."

Iain turned, and sure enough, there was James, walking towards the canopy, looking as fine as fivepence in a bottle-green coat and fawn trousers, his old-gold hair gleaming in the dappled sunshine.

But before he reached their table, he was hailed by one of the other guests.

"Mr. Hart," Mr. Potts called to him. "Do join us and tell us about your little expedition. I gather you got soaked, just as I said you would."

James smiled a little stiffly and made his way over to Potts's table, taking an empty seat next to one of the young unmarried ladies, a Miss Lloyd, Iain recalled.

Kate elbowed him. "Go and sit with James," she urged him. "You can't leave him to deal with Potts on his own. It's too cruel."

Edward chuckled. "You really ought," he agreed. "If you call yourself any sort of a friend. My brother-in-law could talk till the cows come home."

"All right," Iain said, though his stomach was already in knots at the very thought of approaching James again.

He began to walk towards Potts's table, wondering if James would stand up and walk off at his approach or if politeness would keep him rooted there. His nerves writhed like snakes in his gut as though he were going into battle rather than sitting down to tea and cake. It was absurd to feel so eaten up just to be approaching his oldest friend in the world.

"May I join you?" he asked when he reached the table, secretly astonished to hear his voice emerging just the way it always did, calm and clear.

There were four of them at the table already: Mr. and Mrs. Potts, Miss Lloyd and James. Everyone but James looked up when Iain spoke. When Iain saw Mr. Potts open his mouth, he just knew he was going to point out that there were no chairs. He forestalled the vicar's objection by turning away to ask the occupants of the neighbouring table if he might borrow one of their empty chairs. He took their easy assent as his permission to join Potts's table, ignoring the vicar's glare.

Once they'd all shuffled around to make room for Iain and he'd settled himself, Mr. Potts said, "So, Mr. Hart. Did you find your brimstone today?"

"Yes," James replied. Iain stared at him, willing him to look Iain's way, but he kept his gaze firmly on the vicar. "We were able to watch a number of them feed," he continued. "We also found some buckthorn bushes nearby which had eggs and some early pupae."

"Did you bring back any specimens, Mr. Hart?" This was Mrs. Potts, her expression polite.

"No, I wasn't looking for any. I have plenty of specimens already and am well acquainted with the minutiae of the anatomy of this species. Today, I wanted to observe the behaviour. I am interested in the way they feed and roost."

Potts laughed. "I'm not sure what you expect to discover," he said. "In my experience, all butterflies flit around in exactly the same way."

"Well, you see, that's where you're wrong," Iain put in. "Most butterflies settle with their wings open, but brimstones settle with their wings closed."

James turned to look at him, an almost comical expression of surprise on his face. "You noticed that?"

Iain's lips twitched at his obvious astonishment. "You weren't the only one watching, you know."

James's mouth hitched by the smallest degree on one side. The half smile transformed his slightly remote expression, making his grey eyes glint with sudden warmth. Potts soon intruded on the moment, though.

"You will forgive me, Mr. Sinclair," he said, his tone patronising, "if I venture a view, since I, unlike yourself, am a student of nature. The fact of the butterfly's wings being open or closed is neither here nor there—"

James interrupted him. "You're quite wrong, Mr. Potts. The whole point of the brimstone's appearance is to enable it to pass as a leaf. When it settles to feed or roosts at night, it is able to hide from predators, *provided* it closes its wings. By behaving as it does, it makes a place for itself in its world that is safe, right out in the open."

Potts frowned. "Careful, Mr. Hart," he replied, "one must not overlook the divine hand here. You speak as though this insect made its own place in the world, when the truth is, it was the good Lord who placed it there."

Iain waited to see how James would respond to this. The man's expression showed no reaction to Potts's statement, but Iain knew it would have irritated him.

After a brief silence, James said, "Do you know what the difference is between you and me, Mr. Potts?" His countenance was as pleasant as ever, but his grey gaze was hard.

"Pray, enlighten me, Mr. Hart," the vicar invited tightly.

"It is this. You are content with the lessons you've already learned, whereas I am endeavouring to learn more. That is why I am so passionate about nature, you see. Because if I look long enough and hard enough, I might just discover something new."

Potts's mouth twisted up, as if he'd just taken a swig of vinegar. "Like what?" he asked. "Heretical ideas about transmutation of species?"

James shrugged. "What are yesterday's heresies but tomorrow's orthodoxies? The history of science is of discovery upon discovery, each step leading to the next. It doesn't matter whether a theory is proved right in the long term, only that it takes us another step down the path of knowledge."

Mrs. Potts jumped in at that. "But doesn't the Bible warn us to beware the tree of knowledge, Mr. Hart?"

James turned his attention to the lady. "Let me tell you something, ma'am," he began. "Around one hundred and fifty years ago, a scientist called Francesco Redi carried out a series of experiments that proved that maggots did not spontaneously appear in rotting meat, but in fact emerged from eggs laid by flies."

Mrs. Potts pulled out her handkerchief and lifted it to her mouth. "Please, Mr. Hart. I hardly think this is suitable conversation for a picnic."

Iain bit his lip against a smile.

"My apologies," James continued gravely, "but the point is an important one. Until Redi discovered this, the belief was that maggots simply appeared out of nowhere, and this belief had been unquestioned since Aristotle's time. Redi proved it was wrong by scientific observation, and so an idea that would once have been rejected as heretical became an accepted orthodoxy." Smiling politely, he added, "It seems to me, ma'am, that a questioning mind, a desire to discover new things, can never be a bad thing. There is nothing to fear from more knowledge."

"I must disagree, Mr. Hart," Potts interjected. "Where would mankind end up if any idea could be entertained?

Where would one draw the line? Would you tolerate a debate over the very existence of God?"

"Of course," James replied mildly. "Why not?"

"Why not?" Potts snapped. "Because it is blasphemous, sir! Utterly offensive to any good Christian."

The vicar's raised voice attracted the attention of a few other guests, who glanced at their table, curious. Iain decided it might be time to change the subject, but before he could say anything, rescue came from the unlikeliest of places.

"Well, I've learned something today!" Miss Lloyd said. She had a high, breathy voice and a pronounced lisp, and Iain could've sworn that these were the first words she'd ever spoken in his hearing. "I had no idea maggots came from flies!"

Her expression was so astonished that Iain couldn't help himself—he laughed out loud, startling an offended look from the young lady and causing all of his table companions to turn to look at him.

"Forgive me, Miss Lloyd," he begged immediately. "I'm not laughing at you. It is merely that I am relieved to find there is another person at this table who knows as little about science as I do."

That was a lie, of course, but Miss Lloyd was mollified and sent him a grateful smile. In the past, he might have cocked an eyebrow at her and let his own smile linger, playing the part of the ladies' man, all part of his old disguise, but he found he didn't want to do anything that might make James feel unhappy. Instead, he glanced at the man who was prompting these thoughts to find that James was already watching him, his expression difficult to read. Watchful.

Iain held James's gaze briefly, trying somehow to communicate without words that he wanted to talk with him. Then he said to the table at large, "Excuse me, I think I'll take a stroll along the river."

He rose, returned his chair to its rightful place and ambled away, hoping James would take the hint and follow him.

He wandered down to the river's edge, enjoying the warmth of the sun. A pack of boys was swimming. They yelled and splashed loudly, clambering out in their wet shirts to run across a row of flat, broad stones on the opposite bank before jumping back in, every one of them apparently aiming to make the biggest splash possible.

There must be at least a half-dozen boys swimming. A similar number of girls—Iain's nieces among them—played some complicated game with ribbons on the opposite bank, complaining loudly every time one of the boys ran past and interrupted them. It was loud and noisy and joyful, and Iain smiled, remembering similar scenes from his own childhood.

Later, he wasn't sure what made him cast his gaze a little further to the right and see the single, half-submerged head that bobbed there. It was a boy, a little distant from his friends. He looked oddly peaceful, bobbing there in a still sort of way, mouth open, eyes glassy. Then he began to slide under.

Iain had seen a boy who looked just like that once before, and he knew what he was seeing. Knew the boy was drowning.

He shouted something—not words but a sort of wordless protest. It made the other children fall abruptly silent and turn to stare at him with shocked faces. Stare at the man who was now diving into the river, fully clothed.

A few swift strokes took him to the spot where the boy had been. He took a deep breath and dived under, blowing out air and opening his eyes to search as he swam further down with powerful strokes.

It felt like forever till he saw the pale gleam of the child's body, the white billow of his shirt. Iain grabbed at one thin, trailing arm and yanked hard. He began to swim upwards with one arm and both of his legs propelling him, his own lungs near bursting now.

The child's small body was strangely heavy, and Iain's sodden clothing was even heavier, but, fuelled by desperation, he kept going, kicking hard to drive himself upwards. And then, finally, he burst past the surface of the water, gasping air and surging towards the opposite bank, just a few merciful feet away.

He almost sobbed with relief when, a few seconds later, he gained his footing, stumbling onto the rocky riverbed on feet that were still kicking against water, tripping over himself as he turned to take a better hold of the boy, lodging his hands under the child's armpits and hauling his limp body out of the water and onto the grassy bank.

A man was running towards them. "Christopher!" he shouted hoarsely. "Christopher!"

It was Potts, his face wrecked with shock and worry. He reached the child just as Iain pulled himself out of the water. Potts threw himself to the ground, turning the child and leaning over him as he chanted the boy's name like a prayer. Iain could only be grateful, because he was fit for nothing, his heart pounding, blood roaring in his ears. It was all he could do to lie on his back, dragging air greedily into his lungs.

When the child began to cough, then retch, relief washed through him. The boy—that mischievous child from yesterday who broke china shepherdesses and pretended to put spiders down girls' dresses—was alive, thank God.

With his breath back, Iain slowly sat up, and Potts turned to look at him. Tears ran down his blotchy cheeks.

"God bless you, sir," he whispered. "I—you saved my son." A sudden, undignified sob escaped him, and he turned away. Another man arrived—Edward, his arms full of blankets. He handed a few to Potts, who began to bundle up the boy, then tossed one to Iain.

"Thank God you saw him, Iain," he said. "But how did

you know? The children said he wasn't splashing around or shouting for help."

Iain got to his feet, wrapping the blanket around himself. "I've seen it before," Iain replied shortly. "My brother drowned. That's exactly how he looked. Quiet and still, like that." He swallowed hard, surprised by the lump in his throat. It was ridiculous to feel so affected. The worst had not happened, and even if it had, it wouldn't have been an extraordinary event. It was the sort of thing one saw in the newspaper all the time, not important enough to be granted more than a small column of newsprint, near the bottom of page five, perhaps.

Boy, 10, drowns in Warton Bank.

But an everyday event like that could destroy a whole family, could set lives on entirely different courses than had ever been expected.

What if Tom had not died? Would it have been Tom, rather than himself, who fought at Waterloo? If so, would he have come back? Perhaps, if Tom had not drowned all those years ago, he'd he be dead now anyway, or perhaps Iain would be. Or Christopher Potts.

There were endless possibilities.

Life is not safe.

Well, James was right about that, wasn't he? But it was life. And the alternative was… Well, there was no alternative.

Iain looked over the stretch of water to the opposite river bank—James stood there, watching him.

Iain lifted his hand, giving a brief wave, and after a moment, James did the same, mirroring him.

Sudden happiness and certainty filled Iain. If he wanted to live—really live, rather than merely exist—then his path was obvious, wasn't it?

He needed James by his side.

Running away to India wouldn't change anything. It would just stretch that poor abused thread between him and

James to its breaking point. And what if that thread broke? Finally broke, once and for all?

He wouldn't be free. He'd be lost. Because he'd realised something true and vital today. The thread between them—the love between them—wasn't a chain, or a tether.

It was a lifeline.

2 0

By the time James became aware of what was happening, it was all over.

One of the children ran up to their table shouting, "Christopher's drowning!" and suddenly, Mr. Potts was running as though he'd sprouted wings, James on his heels. The plump vicar who'd climbed the hill so slowly this morning fairly flew over the wobbly stepping stones that stretched from one side of the river to the other and was the first to reach his son and the man who had rescued him.

While Potts fussed over the boy, Iain lay on his back, seeming exhausted. Only when Edward reached the opposite bank did he finally, slowly, stand up, accepting a blanket and wrapping it round himself.

That was when he caught sight of James watching him. He lifted a hand and James did the same, and their gazes caught and held. Iain was too far away for James to read his expression, but he felt Iain's attention on him, like sunlight concentrated through a magnifying glass, a single point so fierce and intense it was as if Iain was touching him. When Iain finally turned away, it was to jog the short distance along the bank to the stepping stones. He wobbled his way across, grinning and dripping river water, making the children sitting on the river-bank giggle at his ungainly steps. How Potts had done it so quickly, without even a stumble, James didn't know. The vicar wasn't usually the epitome of grace.

When Iain reached the opposite bank, he made straight for James, smiling at the other guests he passed who tried to speak to him, but not stopping for any of them. For some reason, probably foolishly, James found himself waiting for him, his heart hammering with the oddest sense of antic-ipation.

"Jamie," Iain said in a low, intense voice when he finally stood in front of him. "I have to speak to you. Now. Right now."

James's heart sped up, but he said warily, "Why? What more is there to say we haven't already said?"

Iain just shook his head, swift and impatient. "Not here," he said again. "Please."

"All right," James said, sighing. "Come on, let's go back to the house. You need dry clothes anyway."

As they approached the canopy, James saw that the other guests were all on their feet and milling around, abuzz with the excitement of Christopher Potts's near drowning. Iain's mother hurried towards them. She grabbed one of Iain's hands and chafed it between her own.

"Oh my dear!" she exclaimed tearfully. "You saved that little boy!"

James knew she must be thinking of Iain's drowned brother, and his heart ached for her.

"You need a hot bath," Mrs. Sinclair continued bossily, taking refuge in practical things. "Your skin's like ice."

Kate walked towards them as Mrs. Sinclair fussed. "A bath's being prepared for him just now," she said, patting the older woman's shoulder reassuringly. Then she turned to Iain and added, "I don't know how to thank you. If anything had happened to that child, I'd never have forgiven myself."

Iain waved off her thanks. "I don't need a bath, just some dry clothes," he said, casting a brief, impatient glance in James's direction that made a smile tug at James's lips, despite himself.

"You really should bathe," James told Iain wryly. "You don't want to catch a chill."

The ladies were voicing their agreement when Iain's father weaved over to join them. His face was flushed from the wine he'd already consumed, his high colour emphasising the broken veins on his once-handsome face and bloodshot eyes.

"Well, that was all very heroic, pulling that boy out of the river," he announced as he swaggered towards them. He clapped Iain on the shoulder and added, "It's a shame you couldn't have done as much for your own brother."

Iain's mother gasped at those cruel words, an awful wrenching sound of mingled shock and pain. Kate looked horrified.

Other than a minute flinch, however, Iain didn't react at all, just stared coldly at his father.

"Arthur, how could you—" Mrs. Sinclair began, her weak voice petering out.

"How could I what?" her husband slurred. "Point out what everyone's thinking?" He swayed on his feet.

"No one thinks that," Mrs. Sinclair whispered. "What could Iain have done? He was ten years old."

Iain's father glared at her. "You were always soft on him," he accused, his voice rough with some emotion. Anger, perhaps, and a sort of grief too. "You always babied him." He poked his thumb into his chest. "*I* was the one who had to discipline him. *I* was the one who had to teach him how to be a man."

Iain laughed at that, a harsh, disbelieving sound that drew Mr. Sinclair's attention away from his wife. He stared at his son, seeming surprised.

"You?" Iain exclaimed. "What did *you* ever teach me? How to drink myself into oblivion?"

"How dare you," his father spat. He pointed at James. "You and him. The pair of you are nothing but a—"

"Nothing but what?" Iain interrupted, eyes narrowing dangerously. He stepped right into his father's space, crowding the older man and shielding his mother at the same time. When his father took a step back, Iain followed him, not allowing him to escape.

"You can say what you want, you know," Iain went on, "but know this: I'm not a boy to be thrashed any longer. If anyone's getting a thrashing today, it'll be you—if you're thinking to insult me or my friend, that is. So, just be sure you're willing to take the consequences before you speak."

"I don't know what you mean," Mr. Sinclair mumbled. "I haven't insulted anyone."

Iain laughed humourlessly. "You've spent your whole life insulting me. Nothing I've ever done has pleased you. And nothing ever will, because *I'm not Tom.*"

"Oh, Iain—" Mrs. Sinclair said helplessly behind him, but Mr. Sinclair said nothing. Just stared unhappily at his son. James wasn't sure how to interpret his expression. There was anger there, certainly, a dull drink-induced belligerence, but there was grief and regret too. And bewilderment.

"Mama!" a voice called, interrupting the awkward scene. Isabel rushed towards them, Bertie a few steps behind her.

"Mama," she gasped again as she reached them. She walked past her father, ignoring him completely. "Are you all right? What's Papa done now?"

While Isabel and Kate fussed over Mrs. Sinclair, Bertie took charge of Mr. Sinclair, speaking to him in a low voice, then leading him, unresisting, towards the path that led back to the main house.

"Christ, Iain," James began when everyone was out of

earshot. "That was—hell, I don't know what to say." He paused. "Are you all right?"

Iain rubbed wearily at the back of his neck. "I'm fine," he said. "Better than you might think."

"I know how important your father's good opinion is to you."

Iain just shrugged. "It used to be. But just now, when I looked in his eyes, and I saw that I was right—that I can never make him happy—I just felt…relieved."

"Relieved how?"

"That there's nothing more I can do. Anyway, it's what you and I want that matters now. That's what I wanted to talk to you about." He glanced over at his mother and sighed. "I should just quickly check if Mama's all right first. Do you mind?"

James studied Iain. The man was beginning to shiver. "Of course," he said. "But given how chilled you look, I really do think you ought to have that bath too. We'll have plenty of time to talk after you get warmed through, if that's really what you want."

"It is," Iain confirmed through chattering teeth. "Listen, do you suppose we could go back to the c-cottage for our talk?"

James stared at Iain in surprise. "Why do you want to go there?"

"I want to us to be away from everyone else. Away from any possible distraction."

James found he didn't have it in him to say no, not when Iain gazed at him pleadingly, soaked to the skin and chilled to bone.

"All right," James said at last. "The cottage it is. I'll go ahead of you. Meet me there when you're ready."

James sought out Kate before he left, to tell her that he and Iain were going out to the cottage.

"We might be late for dinner," he added, trying to sound casual. It was already late afternoon, and they were supposed to be dining early this evening, before the local families arrived for the dancing party Kate had arranged.

Kate gave James a strange look that made his cheeks heat. Then she patted his arm and said, "You don't need to come back for dinner, Jamie. Or after." He opened his mouth to protest, but she put her finger over his lips and shook her head. "I'll make your excuses. Both of you. Just let me arrange some provisions for you before you go. I don't want you going hungry."

It was easier to agree than to argue with Kate, so James waited obediently in the hallway for her return from the kitchens, though he had to raise his eyebrows at the bulging knapsack she brought back.

"We're not going for a week, Kate! What on earth have you put in there?"

"There's not that much," Kate said. "Just some bread and cheese. And wine, of course. And some strawberries."

"Well, we won't star—"

"Oh, and some pigeon pie!" Kate interrupted. Then she coughed, adding more quietly, "And some cold ham."

James chuckled. "Is that all?"

"There might be some fruit cake in there too."

James laughed, then hefted the sack over his shoulder, grunting at the weight of it. "Well, I'd better go. It's going to take me three times as long to get there with this great load on my back." He grinned at her, and she grinned back a little sheepishly.

He'd gone only a few steps when she called after him.

"James?"

He looked over his shoulder.

Her fair brows were drawn together in a little pleat of concern.

"Just—I hope you and Iain can be friends again. He—" She broke off.

"He what?"

Kate gave a half smile. "Made you happy. I would like to see you so happy again, Jamie."

James didn't know what to say to that. He hadn't realised that Kate had noticed how much Iain meant to him, or how much James had missed him these last two years. His other sisters certainly wouldn't have done.

He cleared his throat. "I hope so too, Katie."

He reached the cottage an hour ahead of Iain. He used the time to fetch water from the nearby spring and light the fire. Despite the warmth of the day, it was cold and a little damp-smelling in the unoccupied, stone-built cottage. Iain had been chilled to the bone by his soaking in the river, and James didn't want him catching a cold.

He was pacing the floor, feeling oddly sick with nerves when Iain finally arrived. The man's soft knock at the door made James's heart leap wildly, and he had to take several deep breaths before he finally stepped forwards to open the door.

Iain stood on the stoop, tall and handsome and uncharacteristically nervous.

"These are for you," he said, thrusting out his hand.

Bluebells.

James stared at the flowers for a long moment, then looked up at Iain's flushed face. Iain was embarrassed, yet strangely defiant too. For some reason, his expression touched James's heart. Made him ache for the other man.

"Thank you," he said huskily, reaching for the flowers.

They managed an awkward transfer of the fragile blooms. "Come in," he added. "I'll put these in some water."

He heard the door close behind him as he searched for a receptacle for the bluebells. A little clay cup did the job—he slopped some water in from the ewer he'd filled earlier and dropped the flowers inside. They looked oddly charming, humble but lovely. He placed the cup in the middle of the scrubbed oak table, then turned to look at Iain.

"I spoke to Kate before I came away," Iain said. He smiled. It was a wobbly smile, James noticed. "I gather we're excused from this evening's entertainments."

"We are. Though she still insisted on providing dinner." James jerked his thumb at the knapsack that sat on the table. He cleared his throat. "I think she imagines we're going to be here longer than we are. I'm not sure what more there is to say between us that hasn't already been said."

Iain swallowed. "I have something new to say," he said. He looked nervous but determined too and James's heart skipped a little harder.

"What's that?"

Iain squared his shoulders, meeting James's gaze unflinchingly.

"I love you, Jamie."

James stared at him, stunned. Stunned even though Iain had said something similar earlier, during the storm.

I can't love you.

You don't *love me.*

But I do...and it's killing me...

Somehow, though, this was different. This was unequivocal. Unreserved.

Unmistakable.

James watched, dry-mouthed and unmoving, as Iain stepped toward him, closing the distance between them and taking hold of James's upper arms in his big hands.

"I'm not going to India," he said.

"What?" James said faintly.

"I'm staying in England," Iain said. "I want to be with you, if you'll have me."

"I—I don't understand," James stammered. Suddenly, there were too many feelings boiling inside him, fear and hope and joy, and he found himself searching Iain's eyes for some sign that he was misunderstanding his words, that disappointment was lurking somewhere close by.

"I know I always told you there could never be more than friendship between us," Iain continued. "But there was a time when you told me you *wanted* more from me, and I'm hoping that hasn't changed. I'm hoping that, despite everything, you're willing to trust me when I say I want that too now."

"Jesus, Iain—" James saw the man flinch at his pained tone. "You've walked away from me so many times..."

Iain winced, closing his eyes briefly. "I know," he said softly. "And I'm so sorry, Jamie."

"And now you want me to trust you?"

Iain opened his eyes at that, and his blue gaze seemed to bore into James. "Yes," he said at last. "Yes, I do want you to trust me. Whatever else I've done, I've never once made you a promise I haven't kept, have I? Until this moment, I never offered you anything but friendship."

Slowly James shook his head. "No," he admitted, a note of bitterness creeping into his voice. "You were always very clear about that."

Iain ran his hands up James's arms, curving his palms over James's shoulders, drawing him even closer, so that their faces were mere inches apart.

"Well, now I *am* promising more—if you still want me, Jamie. I admit I'm stupid and stubborn and damned slow on the uptake, but there's one virtue I do have—I keep my word. You know that much about me."

James's heart was galloping now, and he could barely

swallow against the lump in his throat. He stared at Iain mutely.

"*Do* you still want me, Jamie?" Iain asked softly. "Or am I too late?"

James couldn't look at Iain as he admitted the truth of his own feelings. He hung his head and whispered, "I do. I always have." He paused. "I think I always will."

James felt Iain's body sag in relief at that admission, but his own remained tense. Iain's hands on his shoulders were warm and steadying, but James couldn't bring himself to lean into that easy strength, and after a moment, Iain touched his chin, tipping James's face up again, to meet his grave gaze.

"You think this is a sudden turnabout," he said "And in a way it is, but the truth is, I've loved you for a very long time, Jamie. I've had no change of heart about *you*. My change of heart is about *me*."

James eyed him warily. "What do you mean?"

Iain sighed heavily. "You know I've always tried to be a certain kind of man for my family. My father wanted me to join the army, so I did. It was the only thing I ever did, after Tom died, that made him happy. I've spent my whole life—" His voice quivered and he broke off.

"You've spent your whole life trying to make up for Tom's death," James finished for him gently. "I know."

Iain closed his eyes and nodded. "It's hard to give up the idea they have of me. Or the one I thought they had, at least."

"Well, you've managed to leave the army, at least," James said, offering a half smile. "That's the worst bit done, isn't it?"

"I daresay," Iain said, smiling wryly. "And anyway, the most important thing to me now is that I don't lose any more time with you. I want to be with you, Jamie, starting now."

"You really want that?" James asked, still dubious.

Iain's gaze was serious. "More than anything."

James raised an eyebrow. "You, who never go with the same man twice?"

"I've been with *you* twice," Iain pointed out. "You're the only one, though."

Absurd to feel so pleased by that. "Am I?"

Iain nodded. "And I want you to be the only one from now on."

James swallowed and whispered, "Are you sure? Won't you miss having other men?"

Iain's blue gaze was very intent, his hands warm and heavy on James's shoulders. "Do you remember the night we argued at Kit Redford's?" When James nodded, he said, "After you left, I didn't know what to do with myself. I'd spent years doing my damnedest not to lose your friendship, yet I ended up bringing about my own worst fear with my actions. I won't make that mistake again. There isn't *anything* worse than being without you. I lived with the consequences of that mistake for two long years, and I was miserably unhappy. It took seeing you again to remember what happiness was. I can't go back now. I—I couldn't *breathe* without you, Jamie."

Iain was so close now that James could feel the warmth of his breath again his lips. He wanted to close the last fraction of an inch between them, but he was so damned scared. He closed his eyes against a sudden hot prickle of tears and whispered, "You can't let me down, Iain. My heart won't stand it. It's a bit bruised, you know."

"I know. And I won't."

"So, if you've got any doubts left, tell me now. I'd rather kn—"

"No doubts," Iain interrupted. "I promise."

"But just what are you promising me, Iain? What happens now?"

Iain swallowed. "Let me come back to Derbyshire with you. Remember I used to talk about setting up a stud farm? You could lease me some land at your estate, perhaps. Or not.

We'll work out some reason for me to stay to satisfy the world. Just let's be together."

"You'd do that?" James said incredulously. "Come to Derbyshire? Make a life there, just to be with me?"

Iain's smile was a bright, wonderful thing that made James feel lit up inside. "Yes, if you're agreeable."

James said carefully, "So, I would see you regularly. Every week?"

"Every day, if we can manage it," Iain said. "What do you say to offering me a bedchamber in that big, empty manor house of yours while I set up my new stud farm? I warn you, I might turn out to be one of those houseguests who never leaves."

James pretended to consider that, tapping his chin. "I could hardly refuse to let my oldest friend in the world stay with me in his hour of need. Or demand that he leave if he outstays his welcome."

Iain laughed, a soft intimate gust against James's lips that made him shiver. "That's settled, then."

"Good," James whispered. "And now that's out the way, do you think you might take me to bed?"

James led Iain into the bedchamber by the hand, stopping at the end of the big bed with its blue silk coverlet.

He reached for his cravat, and Iain whispered, "Can I undress you?"

"All right."

Iain removed James's clothing piece by piece, taking his time, lavishing care and attention on him. Standing behind him, he pressed small, delicate kisses to the back of James's neck as he unwound his cravat, stroked his thumbs over the firm points of James's nipples after drawing off his shirt.

"You're so beautiful," he murmured into James's ear as his

hands unbuttoned the placket of his breeches. "No one else has ever come close."

"Is that so?" James huffed out a laugh, part disbelieving, part absurdly flattered. "Did you think of me when you were with other men?" He meant it to sound lighthearted; the sting in his voice appalled him.

Behind him, Iain stilled, his lips hovering over the tender slope that connected neck and shoulder. Raising his hands from the buttons of James's trousers, he slid them about his naked waist and pulled him close. "On a few occasions, yes, I did," he admitted. "And I'm sorry, Jamie. When I think of you with someone else—"

"What?" James whispered. "What does that do to you?"

"It kills me. I hate it. That first time you told me about the others you'd been with, I wanted to hunt them down." He gave a soft, unamused laugh, then added, "Have there been many since the last time I saw you?"

James shrugged. "One," he admitted. "I don't get the same opportunities as you do in London. Jonathan and I have…an understanding."

Iain's arms tightened on him, and James gave a soft laugh of comprehension. "*Had* an understanding," he amended. He turned in Iain's arms and asked, seriously, "What about you? How many others since the last time we were together?"

Iain's gaze was steady. "Since that night? None."

James reeled at that. "What? *No one?* In two years."

Iain nodded, his expression curiously unreadable. "The last time was with you, after I saw you at the Black Boar Inn."

"I—why?"

Iain shrugged. "I couldn't bring myself to go back to Redford's after that last time. I wanted to forget that night had ever happened."

"It's not the only place you could have gone," James pointed out.

Iain just smiled at that. "True," he said.

Intriguing as that was, James decided not to push it further. "You must be desperate," he murmured instead, canting his hips forward to brush his groin against the other man's. "Two years with only your own hand?"

Iain groaned at the light touch, closing his eyes. His hands had been on James's waist, but now they moved lower, fingertips sliding inside his gaping breeches. James squirmed closer, encouraging him, and Iain's hands pushed down till he was cupping James's buttocks, cupping and stroking and pulling James closer with greedy hands.

"I want you in there," James whimpered against Iain's throat. "I want you to fuck me, hard and deep." He'd done that only once before and he hadn't even liked it, but Jonathan had loved it—as had James, when it had been his turn to do the fucking—and somehow the thought of inciting such pleasure in Iain was irresistible. He could have his turn another time.

Iain groaned against his ear. "Christ, are you sure?"

"Yes, very sure."

"Do you have oil?"

"Oil?"

Iain pulled back, giving him a careful look. "Have you done this before?"

James felt his face heat. "Once," he said.

"And you didn't use any oil? Or anything like that?"

James just knew his face was scarlet now. "No," he said in a small voice. He guessed that was a mistake.

Iain just smiled and kissed him, a small, sweet kiss, almost chaste. "Wait here," he said. "I'll check the larder."

James decided to remove the rest of his clothes while he waited, and by the time Iain returned, carrying a small earthenware dish, James was lying, naked, on the snowy sheets.

Iain's gaze travelled up and down James's body, his expression admiring.

"You found oil?" James asked.

"I did," Iain replied, setting his prize down on the small cabinet beside the bed before turning back to look at James.

"You're beautiful," he murmured, and his expression was so happy, his words so ready and sincere, that this time, James believed him. He let his own smile grow, and his gaze was steady on Iain while the man yanked off his cravat and shirt, then shucked his breeches and drawers and stockings till he was naked too.

He crawled up the bed, sliding his body over James's till he lay over him fully and they were face to face, chest to chest, groin to groin. It was almost too much all at once, after the years of longing. James wanted to explore every inch of skin, every nook and cranny of Iain's body. All that, and yet he couldn't drag his eyes away from Iain's bright gaze, found himself returning the man's steady regard as he waited, parched, for Iain's kiss.

Finally, slowly, Iain lowered his head, settling his mouth sweetly on James's, the soft bristle of his whiskers tickling the edges of James's lips. Teasing James's lips open with the tip of his tongue, he licked more deeply into James's mouth with a little moan that made James give a gasp of laughter, even as he kissed Iain back, opening up to Iain's seeking tongue and meeting it with his own, his hands coming up to cradle the man's head, fingers drifting into his silky hair.

Iain's hand stroked James's flank restlessly as they kissed, on and on. James wanted more, but he didn't want to stop the kiss to ask. Instead, he arched against Iain, pleading for more with his body, and finally, Iain gave him it, breaking their kiss to rake his teeth down James's neck, traversing the ridge of his collarbone with soft brushes of his lips before dropping lower, fastening his teeth gently on James's left nipple, making him gasp and writhe under the tormenting touch.

James was sure his cock was harder than it had ever been before in his life. It pushed up against Iain's stomach as Iain suckled lightly at his nipples, desperate for friction. And then Iain was going lower still, charting a course past ribs and belly and hipbones till he reached James's desperate shaft.

Iain greeted James's cock with a long, flat lick of his tongue up the whole length, pulling a gasp from James's chest. He enveloped the swollen head in his mouth and drove his mouth down, taking the whole throbbing length to the back of his throat, wresting a groan from James's chest, deep and wrenching, a shameless, unadulterated plea for more. Was Iain going to drag his climax out of him? Make him so dazed with pleasure that he wouldn't notice the pain of being sodomised?

Apparently not, because now Iain was pulling his mouth off James's cock and wriggling further down. Wantonly, James spread his thighs wider to accommodate Iain's broad shoulders, but when Iain pushed on the backs of his thighs, urging him to raise his legs and expose the entrance to his body, he resisted, swallowing hard.

Iain glanced up. "Come on," he said gently. "It'll help me make you ready for me."

"You don't have to do anything to make me ready," James said uncomfortably. "I can take you. I've done it before."

"I don't want you to just *take me*. I want you begging for me. Desperate for my cock." Holding James's gaze, Iain gently pressed his thighs towards his chest. "I want you to come with me inside your body, want to see you coming as I slide in and out of you."

"I don't see that happening," James said faintly, even as he let Iain move his body into the undignified position he seemed to want. "But you could make me come right now just by sucking my cock for one more minute."

Iain chuckled. "At least let me try."

"All right," James breathed, and then Iain was ducking down, his whiskers tickling the backs of James's thighs as he kissed an affectionate path to James's balls, pausing to lave his wrinkled sac with tender strokes of his tongue before moving down further.

His tongue—God, his *tongue*—dragged delicately, sinfully down the valley between James's buttocks, seeking out that most sensitive, private of all the parts of his body, and Christ but he felt exposed, visible to Iain in every particular. It was mortifying and exciting at once, and his face burned with fierce shame and fiercer lust as Iain took him apart, bit by bit.

Iain's tongue on him, *there*. Working at him, easing, pressing, softening. His fingers too. Pressing and pushing and wetness and—*Christ!*—moving *inside* him. And Iain was right. This felt so good that now the cries falling from his lips were pleas. Pleas for more, for Iain not to stop, *God, please don't stop*.

Iain rose to his knees, dipping his hand into the earthenware dish and bringing back fingers that dripped with golden oil. And then he was anointing James with the oil, his gaze moving between James's opening and his flushed, pleading face.

He leaned forward and kissed James hard.

"Are you all right?" he asked unsteadily.

"Yes," James gasped. "Just, do it now. Please, Iain. Fuck me."

Iain reached for the oil again, this time lifting his dripping hand back to his own thick shaft and slowly coating it with glistening oil. "Turn over, then," Iain murmured. "Much as I love looking at your face, I think you'll find it easier."

James rolled onto his stomach and got up onto his knees.

His nerves spiked again, but Iain's hand stroking the small of his back settled him. Iain's knees shifted closer, and he brought the fronts of his thighs into contact with the back of James's. The slow sweep of his big hands up James's sides soothed him briefly and then it was all too real as he felt the rude, blunt prod of that glistening cock against his hole…

He thought Iain was going to shove it straight in as

Jonathan had, but no, Iain was still playing with him. Now he slid his hard length along James's crease over and over, the end of his cock nudging and pressing, almost breaching James, only to pull teasingly away again. Iain kept adding more: more oil, more sensation, more pressing fingers. Only when James was near incoherent with desire did Iain finally, blessedly, push inside him. He moved achingly slowly, and it was long minutes before he was fully inside James's body, but once he was in, his iron control seemed to fracture a little, and he began punching his hips forward, his big hands gripping James's hips so hard, James knew he'd have bruises in the morning.

After the first few thrusts, something unspeakably pleasurable flashed inside James's body, and he cried out, astonished, almost appalled by the fierce sensation. Iain snarled out a satisfied curse at his reaction but didn't pause in his movements, just kept going. After that, though, almost every thrust delivered the same unbearable rasping delight.

All this time, James had been bracing himself on his hands, but when Iain grated into his ear, "Touch yourself," he reached for his cock and began to stroke in counterpoint to the devastating rhythm Iain set.

"I'm going to spend," he whimpered.

"I want you to," Iain assured him, licking his shoulder. "You've been so good, Jamie. Let me see you come for me."

He hadn't even finished talking when James's climax came. He howled as it gushed out of him, hot creamy pulses that just kept coming and coming, as though his balls wanted to empty themselves completely.

This wasn't anything like any orgasm he'd had before, the sort of orgasm that roared up his shaft from his balls. This came from deep inside him, from the very depths of his body, wrenched out of him by Iain's patient determination.

As the final throbs of pleasure died away, he realised that Iain must have climaxed with him. That he was slumped over

James's back, panting in James's ear, and that his softening cock was even now slipping out of James's body.

They collapsed, sticky and sex stained, onto the mattress.

After a few minutes, Iain lifted his weight from James's back. James was too tired to move, but he heard Iain leave the room, then return. He felt the coolness of a damp cloth against his buttocks, then the creak of the mattress as Iain climbed in beside him, the warmth and strength of his arms winding round James's waist.

"Thank you," Iain whispered in his ear. He kissed James's shoulder.

And within another minute, they were both asleep.

Iain dreamed of Tom.

Tom was, as always, vertical in the water, his arms extended to his sides. Very still. His mouth was open, chin lifting, eyes staring. But for once, his eyes didn't have that glassy, unseeing look. This time, he looked at Iain properly. He saw Iain.

And this time, Iain was standing. He was in the river with Tom, as he always was, but instead of treading water frantically, he stood on the riverbed, the stones hard and painful beneath his feet.

"Tom!" he called out. "Tom!"

Tom smiled at him. He smiled. *And then he drifted under the surface of the water, still smiling, and disappeared.*

Iain jerked awake on a gasp and James woke too, turning in his arms to say sleepily, "What's wrong? Nightmare?"

"Yes," he whispered. Then, honestly, "I'm fine."

"Do you want to tell me about it?"

"Not now. Another time, maybe," Iain murmured. He pressed a kiss to James's lips, lifting a hand to caress his cheek. It was a little rough now with new beard growth, and Iain stroked his thumb back and forth over the bristles, loving that contrast of rough and smooth.

James smiled at him. He looked so happy, it made Iain's heart hurt. Iain knew he needed to be sure not to do anything to diminish that happiness.

"Did I mention, earlier that I love you too?" James asked, his tone a little teasing.

"No," Iain murmured. "You've never actually said those words to me."

"I didn't actually need to," James said drily. "You already knew."

"It's always better to hear them from the horse's mouth," Iain replied. "As it were."

James laughed softly, then gave a soft, horsey-sounding whicker and added, "I love you, Iain."

Iain smiled happily, and probably foolishly. "I love you, too. I always will."

They came together in a soft, tender kiss, and any other assurances Iain had intended to give, any other vows he'd intended to make, were lost in the haze of building desire between them. Instead, he made his promises with his lips and his hands, with his worship of James's body and the pleasure they found together. He cast himself out of his tiny boat, diving joyfully into the ocean of James's love, and he let its waves lift him, let them carry him away and deposit him on new shores where the ground was firm and safe beneath his feet.

The End

AFTERWORD

I want to add a brief note about the descriptions of drowning and near-drowning in this book, as witnessed by Ian.

Drowning is often depicted on film as a dramatic event, with the victim shown to be violently and noisily struggling in the water. Whilst such behaviour may precede drowning, once the victim is in real trouble, they are reliant on an observant person recognising their plight. The instinctive, and uncontrollable, response of a drowning person is to extend the arms laterally, pressing down on the water, and lift the chin—both actions allowing the victim to continue breathing as long as possible. The victim goes very still and is unable to wave or shout out to signal their distress, usually quietly sinking below the water within a minute or so. Lifeguards are trained to recognise these instinctive responses.

Finally, thanks to Anyta Sunday for beta-reading this book and providing incredibly valuable feedback.

THANK YOU, DEAR READER

Thank you for reading this book!
Thank you for spending your valuable time with
Iain and James. I hope you enjoyed their company.

I love hearing from my readers. You can:

~ Email me at authorjoannachambers@gmail.com
~ Visit my website at www.joannachambers.com
~ Connect with me on social media through those
cute little icons below.
~ Sign up for my newsletter at my website for up to date
information about my books, freebies and special deals.

If you have time, I'd be very grateful if you'd consider leaving
a review on an online review site. Reviews are so helpful for
book visibility and I appreciate every one.

Joanna Chambers

ALSO BY JOANNA CHAMBERS

Unforgivable

GENTLEMAN WOLF, BOOK ONE IN THE CAPITAL WOLVES DUET

He must master the wolf within...

Edinburgh, 1820.

Thirty years after leaving Scotland, Drew Nicol is forced to return when the skeleton of a monster is found. The skeleton is evidence of werewolves—evidence that Marguerite de Carcassonne, the leader of Drew's pack, is determined to suppress.

Marguerite insists that Drew accompany her to Edinburgh. There they will try to acquire the skeleton while searching for wolf-hunters—wolf hunters who may be holding one of their pack prisoner.

But Drew has reason to be wary about returning to Edinburgh—Lindsay Somerville now lives there.

Lindsay who taught Drew about desire and obsession.

Lindsay who Drew has never been able to forgive for turning him.

Lindsay who vowed to stay away from Drew twelve years ago... and who has since taken drastic steps to sever the bond between them.

Marguerite's plan will throw Drew and Lindsay together again—and into a deadly confrontation with Lindsay's enemy, Duncan MacCormaic. They will be tested to their limits and forced to confront both their past mistakes and their true feelings.

But it may be too late for them to repair the damage of the past. The consequences of Lindsay's choices are catching up with him, and he's just about out of time...

———

Made in the USA
Middletown, DE
27 July 2021

44917058R00139